Crossings

Mel Odom

**An original novel based on the hit television series
by Joss Whedon**

SIMON PULSE

NEW YORK LONDON TORONTO SYDNEY SINGAPORE

Historian's note: This story takes place in the second half of the fifth season of *Buffy.*

This book is a work of fiction. Any references to historical events, real people, or real locales are used fictitiously. Other names, characters, places, and incidents are the product of the author's imagination, and any resemblance to actual events or locales or persons, living or dead, is entirely coincidental.

First Simon Pulse edition June 2002

™ and © 2002 Twentieth Century Fox Film Corporation. All rights reserved.

SIMON PULSE
An imprint of Simon & Schuster
Children's Publishing Division
1230 Avenue of the Americas
New York, NY 10020

The text of this book was set in Times.
Printed in the United States of America.
2 4 6 8 10 9 7 5 3 1
The Library of Congress Control Number: 2002104739
ISBN: 0-7434-2734-3

DEDICATION

For my children, Matt L., Matt D., Montana, Shiloh, and Chandler. And to Elizabeth Shiflett: Congrats again on the upcoming nuptials! May your life be everything you want.

Acknowledgments

Thanks go to the usual suspects: Lisa Clancy, Micol Ostow, and to Joss Whedon, without whom . . .

Chapter One

A dead man's finger lay on the month-old grave. If the grass had been a little taller, the mound of turned earth a little more smooth, Buffy Summers thought she probably would have missed seeing the amputated finger. The fact that the finger was the ring finger and there was a silver wedding band around it helped.

Buffy didn't stop walking, but she scanned the shadowed cemetery around her. Dead things and people ended up in the Sunnydale cemeteries—they just didn't always stay there. And that was assuming they didn't just up and climb off the metal tables and out of the vaults in the morgue before the funeral homes picked them up.

"Is that a finger?" Willow Rosenberg asked.

Buffy nodded. "Yep."

"Ewwww," Willow said.

Buffy kept walking.

"Are we just going to leave it there?" Willow asked.

"Did you bring a baggie? Because I'm not going to pick that up and put it in my pocket."

Willow rummaged through her purse. That was Willow: sensible even when taking a patrol tour. "I've got a hanky."

Buffy glanced at her friend. "Will, I'm not picking that finger up. The groundskeeper will find it tomorrow."

Willow put her hanky away. "Do you think the groundskeeper will return the finger to the family?"

"Yes. Sunnydale cemeteries have very good, very dedicated groundskeepers." That was mostly true. Buffy believed having good cemetery staff was kind of a karma-induced benefit in a town that existed so close to a Hellmouth. Seeing as how the town's final resting places were plagued nearly every night with some kind of demonic thing, groundskeeping needed dedicated individuals so visitors wouldn't know the graves got left or robbed on a regular basis.

"Leaving the finger lying there still makes me feel creepy," Willow said.

"Trust me on this," Buffy replied. "Finishing up patrol with some dead guy's finger in your pocket is even creepier."

Willow thought for a moment, then nodded and looked away from the amputated digit. "You're probably right. I mean, suppose I had the finger wrapped in my handkerchief and I forgot."

"Your purse would stink."

Willow frowned. "I mean before that. Suppose I forgot, and then somebody needed to borrow a handkerchief. So here I go, reaching into the purse, trying to be a good friend or a concerned fellow human being or whatever, and I give them my handkerchief. Then this finger rolls out."

Buffy looked at her friend. "I really think you'd

notice you had a dead guy's finger in your handkerchief before you handed it over to a friend or even a passing acquaintance."

"Yeah. You're probably right. That would be hard to miss." Willow pulled her long plaid coat tighter around her. "I guess the Craulathar demon went this way."

"Unless there's another creature out scouring Sunnydale for corpse parts to create a demonic ritual," Buffy agreed.

Giles had identified their quarry as a Craulathar demon from a race of necromancers that built mystic energy from the dead. Or, in this case, dead parts. Starting almost three weeks ago, someone had started robbing graves in the local cemeteries. The Sunnydale police department had increased their patrols—luckily without losing any officers—and seemed to have achieved some success. The grave robberies had slowed, then finally stopped. Then six days ago someone started robbing funeral homes. Giles had identified the Craulathar demon from the tool marks left on the corpses after the various organs and appendages had been taken.

In all her years as the Slayer, Buffy hadn't realized a book existed that covered the subject of demonic surgery tools. As it turned out, the book on the Craulathar demon tools was only part of a huge series. The illustrations were particularly vile and disgusting.

Buffy paused by a tall gravestone with a cherub standing on it. Moonlight turned the alabaster almost silver, but shadows lay in the cracks of the stone. "Will?"

"What?" Willow looked at Buffy with those big innocent eyes.

After seeing everything we've seen, Buffy couldn't help thinking, *only Willow's eyes could still look so innocent. Please, God, always let her retain that innocence. Don't take it away.*

So many other things had been lost lately, and Buffy knew she'd never get them back. She didn't want her friends changing. Even as much as all of them had gone through, they were still the most consistent world she had.

"Not the slaying," Buffy said. "That hasn't gotten any harder. I'm talking about Dawn. You know, raising Dawn by myself now that Mom is gone."

Dawn was her little sister, which was a complicated story all in its own right. Their mother, Joyce Summers, had died only weeks ago. During that time, part of Buffy had gone numb and dead inside, and Angel's visit from Los Angeles had only further served to remind her of everything that had been lost.

"Oh," Willow said, suddenly sad.

Throat constricting, Buffy said, "Don't go getting misty on me."

"Okay," Willow said staunchly. "I won't. And if I do, why, I'll just look away." She made a show of turning her head away. "I'll just look away and—and—*Look out!*"

Startled by Willow's voice, Buffy shoved her thoughts about Dawn and her mom away and went into full Slayer mode. Her peripheral vision caught their attackers first, spotting three lean and hungry shapes vaulting toward them across the cemetery grounds to Willow's right.

Moving quickly, Buffy stepped in front of her friend. Willow could fight as well, she'd learned over the years, but Buffy hadn't brought her friend along to fight. Willow was there for company and as a sounding board.

The three vampires were all young and probably newly turned, judging by the cocky way they acted. They wore street leather and Party Gravy concert T-shirts. Their hair was razored to the scalp, and they all had French ticklers on their chins and wraparound metallic yellow sunglasses. Buffy recognized them as vampires from the way they moved and the tingle her Slayer senses made.

"Hey, babes," the vampire in the middle said. He smirked, obviously thinking he was ultracool. "You two just got so lucky."

"How do you figure?" Buffy asked, hiding a stake behind her thigh.

The vampire smiled again. "You could have gone all night and never met us." He slapped his hands together, one of them racing ahead of the other like a racecar leaving a competitor in the dirt. "Another few seconds, and we'd have been two ships passing in the night."

The other two vampires laughed and high-fived each other. "That's telling her, Felton," one of the vampires said.

"Look," Buffy said, "I'm searching for a Craulathar demon."

The vampires swapped looks, then glanced back at Buffy. "Don't know no Craulathar demon," Felton said.

"You couldn't miss him," Buffy said hopefully. "Big guy. Probably seven, eight feet tall. Two curved horns jutting out of his forehead. Purple skin. Probably had his pockets full of hands, feet, eyeballs . . . that kind of thing."

The tall, skinny vampire shook his head. "We haven't seen anything like that."

"Enough talk," Felton grumbled. "Let's get back to you and me." He eyed Buffy and cocked an eyebrow. "How do you feel about vampires?" He morphed, changing his face from human to demonic.

"Most of them lack staying power," Buffy said.

"Oh, yeah?"

"Oh, yeah," Buffy said. "And they have this tendency to go to pieces." Bringing the stake out from behind her leg, she took a step forward, throwing her body in line behind the wood.

The sudden move caught Felton flat-footed. He stared down in disbelief as Buffy thrust the wooden stake through his heart. An instant later, the vampire turned to dust.

The tall, thin vampire cursed and brought out a baseball bat. He swung at the Slayer without any wasted motion.

Buffy threw herself backward, letting the metal baseball bat rocket over her head. Moving smoothly, using her strength and speed and skill, she executed a back flip and landed on her feet, meeting the tall vampire as he charged her with the bat above his head.

Throwing her left arm up, Buffy slapped the vampire's wrists, pushing the blow out and away from her body. Then she stepped in, holding the stake with the sharp end jutting down from the bottom of her hand like a knife fighter. The vampire's crossed arms holding the baseball bat prevented her from sinking the stake into his chest and penetrating his heart. Instead she settled for raking the sharp end of the stake across the vampire's face, cutting him from his left ear, across his nose, and all the way to his right cheek.

The vampire howled in pain as dark blood wept down his ruined face. He drew the baseball bat back for another swing.

Buffy swiveled into a roundhouse kick, getting all of her weight into it, pushing off her foot on the ground and following her hips through. The vampire sailed back and struck a gravestone, shattering a ceramic pot filled with plastic flowers. The flowers tumbled down into the stunned vampire's lap. Before he could get up, Buffy staked him through the heart, reducing him to dust.

The short vampire didn't waste time bemoaning the loss of his friends, or in making tracks away from the Slayer.

Buffy tracked the fleeing vampire, flipped the stake

into a throwing grip, and drew her arm backward. Then she stepped forward and rifled her arm like a major league pitcher. The wooden stake flipped end over end, then struck the vampire in the back, disappearing in the resulting cloud of dust.

After checking her perimeter, making certain that no other vampires were in the vicinity, Buffy rejoined Willow. The action had taken place so fast that Willow hadn't had time to react.

Willow held up her own stake. "It was in my purse. Kind of got stuck."

"It's okay," Buffy said. "There were only three nasties."

Willow nodded and kept the stake in her hand. The weapon wouldn't do much good against the Craulathar demon when they found it, but she had magick spells, too. "Anyway, getting back to what you were saying about Dawn. About having to be her mom now."

Buffy started walking again, getting back into the groove and the feel of being on patrol. The sad part was, patrol was what she felt best at. Somehow she found a quiet inner peace while facing death every night.

"I'm struggling with how I'm supposed to take care of Dawn," Buffy admitted.

"You look like you're doing a good job with her. She's doing okay. I mean, as okay as she can be after losing her mom."

You can't be okay after something like that, Will, Buffy thought. She was scared Dawn could never be okay again. But she got up out of bed every day and made an effort to go to school, and she patrolled every night. Maybe the routine didn't allow for much of a life, but no extra time also meant staying away from some of the brain-numbing pain she'd been going through after her mother's death.

"I want her to feel secure," Buffy said. "That's my main concern. She's just lost her mom."

"So have you," Willow pointed out quietly.

"I know." Buffy let out a tense, tight breath, pushing the harsh pain from the front of her mind to the back. *Why couldn't there have been more vampires? I didn't even break a sweat.* More vampires would have meant a little more time without thinking about missing her mom and what she was supposed to do about Dawn. "But I'm her big sister. I'm supposed to know what to do for her, what to tell her."

"Do you?"

"No."

"Buffy," Willow said, "when your mom died, and I don't want to sound too hard or distant, but did you expect someone to map out what you were supposed to do or feel or need?"

Buffy shook her head, unable to speak. *Maybe not, but it would have been nice.* Everything right now was just so confusing.

"Are you doing everything you can for Dawn?" Willow asked.

"Yes." Buffy thought about the question. "No. I mean, I don't know, Will."

"Does Dawn think you're lacking in parental qualities?"

"No." Buffy sighed. "But it's because she's getting to do what she wants to do."

"What does she want to do?"

"Stay up later." Buffy looked at her friend and felt a little defensive. "I mean, I'm out on patrol every night again." For a while after her mother's death, Anya, Xander, Tara, Willow, and Giles had helped out with patrol while Buffy tried to deal with her own loss and help Dawn out.

Willow shrugged. "Dawn's a lot like you. She probably doesn't need a whole lot of sleep. And the rest of us have proven you can get by on a lot less than the recommended eight hours."

Buffy rounded the corner of the cemetery, following a psychic trail left by the Craulathar demon. She scanned the grounds constantly, looking for shifting shadows. "Dawn used to go to bed by ten. Then she started stretching that by an hour or two. Now she's up till two or three o'clock in the morning."

"That's bad."

"I got a call from the principal," Buffy said. "Me. It's strange, you know, because my mom used to get calls about me. Now I'm getting the calls. Principals just never go away."

"What did the principal say?"

"Dawn's sleeping through some of her classes. And she's not getting to school on time. After a night of patrol, I don't even feel like getting myself up, much less forcing Dawn out the door. It's a losing battle."

"Have you talked to her?"

"Yeah." Buffy stepped wide of a mausoleum. Anything could be lurking in there. "I make with the early-bedtime speeches. She gives me angry and belligerent."

"Is there anything you can do to cut down the time on getting her off to school?"

"Such as?"

"I don't know. Do you make her lunch? If you can make the lunch at night instead of in the morning, it might help."

Guilt flooded Buffy. "I don't pack her a lunch. I just give her money. The arrangement works out better for both of us."

"Lunch money. You kinda miss out on wondering what's in the brown bag if you do it that way."

Buffy thought about that. "Maybe I could brown bag Dawn's lunch money. Make it more momlike. What do you think?"

"I think that Dawn getting to school late and sleeping through classes is not good," Willow answered. "And I think you're adding more stress to your own life. Something needs to give."

Buffy nodded. "I know. I just don't know how I'm going to handle it. I was supposed to be Dawn's sister, not her mother. She was supposed to have a mother. And she did have a mother, a really good one, and this whole situation is just wrong and unfair."

"I know," Willow said calmly. Then something caught her attention. She pointed. "Hey. Is that an ear?"

Buffy looked at the bloody, wrinkled lump of flesh on the ground in front of them. No question, Will was right. The ear meant they were getting closer to finding the Craulathar demon.

"Wow," Willow whispered. "This demon is either really sloppy, or he's got extra parts. If this is any indication, he'd lose his head if it wasn't screwed on."

"Or someone else's head," Buffy commented. She continued leading the way through the cemetery.

Chapter Two

"That guy is a red-shirt security person, right? That means he's going to get killed soon," Anya said.

In disbelief Xander Harris turned his attention from the movie screen and the bucket of extra-buttered popcorn in his lap. He looked at Anya. She was the love of his life, but she was also an ex-demon that had lived more than a thousand years before becoming human. Neither of those things had prepared her for the experience of going to a classic science-fiction movie.

"Anya," Xander protested in a hoarse whisper. "You can't just blurt that out in a movie theater."

Wide-eyed, a mix between only marginally embarrassed and truly miffed, Anya gazed at the crowd. "Now you're going to tell me that these people didn't know that the red-shirted guys get killed in every show? You told me everybody knew that. And this is an old movie, and the theater is full of people who've seen this movie before."

She was a honey blonde with a killer figure sheathed in white pants and a red cable turtleneck sweater. Her widely spaced eyes held Xander's in a way no woman's ever had before. *Of course,* he thought, *part of it might be that whole ex-demon thing.* But she'd given that up.

Xander looked around the audience self-consciously. The theater was dark and comfortable, almost an extension of the star-filled space on the big screen. Maybe the Lamplighter didn't offer first-run movies or surround-sound ambience, but it was one of the places Xander had grown up in. He'd believed in vampires for the first time in the Lamplighter—before he got to high school and realized there really *were* vampires.

"Whisper, okay?" he begged softly. "We're on a covert op here."

Anya looked around as well. "You didn't tell me we were on a covert op. Are there vampires in the theater?" She reached for her purse to dig out a stake.

"Anya," Xander said patiently, "love of my life, I love you in spite of the fact that you're socially inept."

Anya looked at him with a sullen expression. "No vampires?"

Xander shook his head. "No vampires."

The man sitting on the other side of Anya leaned in. "Shhh," the man said. His ears were strangely shaped, with pointed tops.

"His ears," Anya gasped, opening her purse.

Xander grabbed Anya's hands before she got the stake out. The popcorn barrel exploded from between his knees and rained down over the people around them.

"The ears are fake," Xander said hurriedly.

The man waved at them in disgust. "Man, you two are crazy. I came here for the *Star Trek* marathon," the man groused. "Now I'm getting the *Heckle and Jeckle Show.* Maybe you want to refund my ticket."

"This is only the first movie," Xander objected. "Things don't even get started good until the next one. Everybody knows that."

"Look," the man said, "you're killing my buzz here. The original film's success is what made the rest of the franchise possible. I don't like trying to watch a movie while I'm getting stressed."

Anya looked at the man more closely. "Maybe you have your ears on too tight," she suggested.

"Hey, watch it," the man warned. He touched them gently. "I paid good money for these ears. They're custom made."

"Does the guy in the red shirt die?" Anya demanded, pointing at the screen.

Xander melted into his seat in disgusted defeat. *I knew I should have caught the matinee while Anya was still at the Magick Shop with Giles.* But doing that would have meant calling in sick to the construction job, which wasn't exactly a cool thing to do when that job was what paid the rent and put food on the table.

"Of course he dies," the man with the alien ears said. "He's a red shirt."

Anya glanced at Xander. "See? I told you so."

In the next moment, the theater doors crashed open and a young man stepped through. His rude arrival was bad enough, but he also had the gall to hold the doors open and allow light from outside the theater to pour in, disrupting the pleasant darkness and casting shadows over the movie screen.

"Close the doors," someone shouted.

"Man, who is the moron?" someone else asked.

"Why can I never find a Disruptor when I really need one?"

The guy ignored them.

Xander's eyes adjusted to the light, and he recognized the intruder as Robby Healdton. Xander knew

Robby from the video game arcades in Sunnydale. The moment a new game hit a mall, Robby usually showed up—his pockets filled with game tokens—and started playing the game. Crowds gathered to watch Robby work, and he was the stuff of legend. The guy had reflexes in a space fighter that would have put a Slayer to shame. He was a year or two older than Xander and hadn't ever made it through high school.

"This won't do," the man with the pointed ears said authoritatively. "This won't do at all."

Xander stared at Robby, knowing the guy was acting weird. And any time weird stuff started showing up in Sunnydale, Xander Harris paid attention.

"Close the doors," someone yelled again.

Robby swung the doors back and forth, like a kid acting out of spite. "Make me," he challenged.

"Security!" the man with the pointed ears commanded.

"Sir," two men dressed like the red-shirted security officers on the screen responded. Both of them were big and looked like they knew their way around a gym.

"Escort that man out of here," the man with the pointed ears said. "Clear the bridge and have the management notified."

"Yes, sir." Without hesitation, the two wannabe security officers made their way to the aisle and back toward Robby Healdton.

Anya grabbed Xander's hand. "Maybe we should go help them. They're red shirts. They're going to get killed."

Xander sat, feeling confused and tired and jealous all at the same time. He'd only wanted a simple evening: the marathon of movies and maybe a pizza on the way home.

"They'll be fine," Xander said, consoling himself with the remnants of popcorn in his bucket, now gone cold and congealed.

The two "security officers" hooked Robby by the arms and escorted him from the theater. He fought them, digging his heels in and cursing.

Xander looked at the guy in disbelief. Why would Robby crash a theater like that? Especially a science-fiction moviefest that he probably would have been more inclined to be part of than to interrupt? It didn't make sense. For a moment Xander thought about stepping outside and checking on Robby, then dismissed the idea. He had enough problems and responsibilities of his own without borrowing from others.

The double theater doors exploded open again without warning. A red-shirted "security officer" flew through the air for a moment, then landed, bouncing a couple of times with bone-jarring thuds on the stained carpet. He didn't get up again.

Shouts, frightened and indignant, raced through the crowd. A few people stood up but appeared uncertain about what to do.

Then Robby reappeared, holding the other "security officer" in one hand. The security guard's toes dragged across the carpet as Robby carried him. Blood dripped from a wound on the security guy's head, and he only looked half-conscious.

Xander was on his feet before he knew it. *This is* so *not good,* he thought. He frantically tried to remember the last time he'd seen Robby, wondering if he'd noticed anything wrong with him.

"Oh, man!" somebody yelled. "Call the cops! This guy is freaking out!"

Xander didn't hold out any hopes for assistance from the Sunnydale police. As soon as they heard something about a guy able to throw grown people around like party favors, law enforcement personnel would be slow to react and might not come at all until the danger had passed.

"What do you think you're doing?" Anya asked.

"Going to help," Xander replied, brushing her hands from his arm. Playing the hero went against all his natural instincts, but years of spending time at Buffy's side fighting the worst the Hellmouth had to offer up had changed him. Maybe he didn't have the speed and strength of the Slayer, but he'd learned a thing or two about surprise and treachery.

"You're missing the movie," Anya protested.

"I've seen it," Xander said, and then he was rushing through the crowd.

Another moviegoer charged Robby. The guy was actually reaching for Robby when Robby backhanded him and sent him flying back down the aisle. If he wasn't dead, the guy was definitely going to be vacationing in the hospital at least overnight.

Wow, Xander thought, *those aren't video game geek moves.* The group nearest Robby abandoned their seats and rushed toward Xander like a human tidal wave, all of them aiming for the second exit on the other side of the theater.

"Foolish mortals," Robby roared. "You can't escape me." Then he turned around and ran back out the exit.

Foolish mortals? Xander thought. A chill of foreboding whispered through him. *Okay, now we're getting way off the map of everyday life. Normal people just don't run around spouting lines like "foolish mortals."*

"What's going on?" Anya stood at his side.

"Beats me." Xander stared at the closed exit door that Robby had disappeared through. Other moviegoers in costumes as well as those in street clothes poured through the door. "Robby called us all foolish mortals—"

Anya sighed wistfully and nodded. "Yes. I can remember those days. You're all full of immortality, knowing you're going to live forever, and these people with flickering lives just want to get in your way and insist on shoving some kind of responsibility down your throat. Those times were terrible."

Xander looked at her as people around them screamed for help and the police. "Nostalgia Lane isn't a place I want to go right now." He gazed at the door. "If Robby is telling them they can't escape him, why did he run out the door?"

"Because he's planning on coming back," Anya said. "He probably went to get something."

Before Xander could ask her what that might be, Robby ran through the doors again.

"I'm back!" Robby roared, and he brandished a fire ax above his head.

Xander remembered noticing the fire ax in a protective glass case in the theater's entryway. The weapon had a full wedge-shaped head on one side and a curved pick on the other.

Without hesitation Robby brought the fire ax smashing down against the nearest seat, aiming at the head of the "alien" moviegoer seated there. Luckily Robby's blow missed its intended target and sliced into the back of the seat.

Taking advantage of the momentary respite, Xander charged across the aisle, thinking the whole time that he ought to be looking out for his own neck the way most of the rest of the people in the theater were doing. But he couldn't. He'd been hanging with the Slayer too long for that. And Robby was a friend. Somewhere inside his heart Xander couldn't believe his friend would launch an unprovoked attack.

Doubled down low, listening to the screech of wood as the theater seat released its hold on the fire ax, Xander slammed a shoulder into Robby's side. While he wasn't as large as an NFL linebacker, Xander expected that Robby might at least be rocked on his feet.

Instead Robby backhanded Xander with his free hand, knocking him away as if he were a small pest. Fiery black comets spun in Xander's vision, and noises suddenly sounded cottony as if he were submerged underwater.

Xander fell backward, taking down a whole group of fans who screamed and pushed at him as if he'd attacked them. For a moment Xander's world was reduced to flailing arms and legs. Groggy, his legs feeling like rubber beneath him, he forced himself up.

Robby succeeded in tearing the ax free and raced after the fleeing movie audience. "You're gonna die!" he shouted in mad glee. "You're gonna die, humans! I'm gonna kill you all!"

Xander glanced at Anya, relieved that she was okay.

In full berserker mode, Robby screamed, his voice going hoarse with the effort. He swung the ax again, narrowly missed an "alien" in full retreat, and buried the ax blade in the wall near the exit.

Crossing the distance at a dead run, Xander slammed into Robby again, this time from behind. With surprise on his side, Xander succeeded in knocking Robby against the wall. Squealing in pain, Robby turned and snapped his teeth at Xander's face.

Xander pulled his head in, as if he was trying to turn into a turtle. "Robby, man," Xander yelped. "Get a grip!"

Robby's teeth gnashed on empty air, but his chin was pressed against the side of Xander's head.

Xander wrapped his arms around the guy, but knew immediately that he wasn't strong enough to hold Robby prisoner. At about the same time that thought raced through Xander's mind, Robby shrugged him off and slapped him away again. This time Xander felt his lips split from the impact.

Even as Xander crumpled to the floor, seven or eight

moviegoers—adults as well as guys in high-school letter
jackets—slammed into Robby. For a moment, the group's
sheer weight and power overwhelmed Robby.

"Step on up," Robby crowed in that insane voice he
was using. "Step on up, foolish mortals, and die." He
laughed and tugged at the ax embedded in the theater
wall. Abruptly the ax handle snapped off, leaving the ax
head trapped. In obvious anger, irritated at the crowd continuing to pummel him with fists, Robby threw the ax
handle down and plucked the ax head from the wall. He
set himself, then raised the ax head again, even though a
couple of men held on to it.

"Look out!" someone yelled. "I can't hold the ax!"

Yelling warnings and curses, the group of men
moved back from Robby. He pursued them with an evil
grin, chopping and swinging at them, chasing them back
to the movie screen. There was no way out.

Xander crossed the room, took the broken ax handle
from the floor, and launched himself after the demon.
Xander trotted down the aisle, coming up behind Robby,
then stepped up like Ken Griffey Jr. taking his position in
the batter's box. Targeting the back of Robby's head,
Xander swung for the fences.

The wooden ax handle connected with a resounding
THWOP!

Robby turned around, his face frozen in a hideous
snarl.

Okay, Xander thought, *that obviously didn't go as
well as I'd hoped.* He choked up on the ax handle, trying
not to pay attention to the fact that his hands had gone
numb from the blow. Anything human, he knew, would
have dropped. Ergo, Robby wasn't human. At least,
Robby wasn't human anymore.

Robby's mouth moved. Xander thought maybe he
was trying to say "foolish mortal" once more for effect,

but no one would know. As Xander watched, Robby smiled, his eyes crossed, then he fell face first to the carpeted theater floor.

Breathing hard, Xander looked down at his vanquished foe in bewilderment. Something was definitely wrong.

Chapter Three

"If we'd stopped to pick up all the parts of human corpses we found along the way," Willow whispered, "I bet we could have built our own person."

Buffy glanced down at the sock-covered foot. It was lying on the grass next to the mausoleum that appeared to be the Craulathar demon's destination.

"Don't remind me," Buffy said. "I've been having thoughts of Frankenstein's monster in a box."

"It reminds me of the Visible Man," Willow replied.

Buffy looked around the corner of the mausoleum. Only shadows covered the ground, long and lean from the moon to their backs. The shadows of trees bent and twisted as the wind threaded through the branches, creating a kaleidoscope of shifting shadows.

Through the years Buffy had learned not to trust shadows. They hid and harbored dark and bloodthirsty things.

"Don't you mean the Invisible Man?" Buffy asked as she took a fresh grip on the stake she held.

"No," Willow answered. "I mean the Visible Man. You know, the toy model guy that comes encased in see-through plastic so you can look at all his organs and bones and things. Xander had one. Back when his parents were hoping he'd be a doctor or something. Or maybe his dad bought it to gross him out. Back then, you could never tell with his dad. Anyway, you could see the brain, the liver, the lungs, the eyes—"

Buffy stared at her. "This is so not a good time for describing that."

Willow stopped, shifting from bright interest to embarrassment. "Ooops."

Moving flat against the wall, Buffy followed the line of the mausoleum to the entryway. A stone door closed the mausoleum off, but it was slightly ajar. Even in the dim moonlight, Buffy saw bright metal where the black hinges had been ripped loose.

"There's something about this place," Willow whispered.

"What?" Buffy asked.

"Power." Willow studied the mausoleum and put out a hand to touch the cut stone. "You can feel the power in this place." She was a witch of considerable and growing talent, and the skills she'd mastered in the last year were nothing short of amazing.

"Maybe *you* can," Buffy said. "But all *I'm* getting is a definitely creepy vibe." Reaching up, she touched the broken hinges. "Someone forced his or her way inside. Recently."

Willow nodded. "Guess we have to go inside."

"Yep," Buffy said. She put her hand on the door, gripped tightly, and shoved. The heavy stone door slid to the side with a thud that echoed over the cemetery. Buffy waited for something to pounce out of the shadows. Even though nothing did, she still didn't breathe a sigh of relief. She peered into the darkness.

"The Craulathar demon must be really busy if he didn't come to see what *that* was all about," Willow said. "Fitting all those pieces together can't be easy. Maybe he's just kind of involved in what he's doing."

Buffy shot her another look.

"Maybe I'll stop talking about all the pieces now," Willow said.

"Good idea," Buffy said. "Do you have a flashlight?" She hadn't anticipated prowling through a mausoleum. Usually the monsters she hunted down came for her in more open areas.

"Nope," Willow replied, digging in her purse. "No flashlight. But I have this." She held up a thick, tapered candle. "When you're a witch, you never know when you're going to need a candle."

Buffy took the candle and waited. "Matches?" she prompted.

Willow finished a quick search of her purse and looked stricken. "I forgot."

"The candle was a nice idea, Will," Buffy said, not wanting her friend to feel too bad.

"Tara would have remembered," Willow said. Tara Maclay was Willow's girlfriend and fellow witch.

Buffy handed the candle back. "For next time." She returned her attention to the darkened mausoleum. Light flared behind her. When she glanced over her shoulder, she saw Willow touching a flaming finger to the candle-wick. The wick drew the flame and lighted even as Willow's finger went out. Her skin was unblemished, protected by the magick she used.

"Witchy stuff," Willow explained. "Sometimes better than matches."

"Thanks." Buffy took the lighted candle.

"The candle," Willow said, "is going to make it easier for the Craulathar demon to see us coming."

"Yeah," Buffy replied as she started into the large building, "but at least I can see that he's seen us coming." She had to move slowly so the flickering candlelight would survive.

The pale candlelight caused shadows to shift and flow over the stone walls inside the mausoleum. The smell of dank earth filled Buffy's nose and made her sneeze. She lifted the candle higher and glanced around.

"You know," Buffy said, "no matter how many times I've been inside a crypt or a mausoleum, I still can't escape that whole jittery thing."

"Me neither," Willow replied. "Some creepy things are just—you know, *creepy*. Even when you know they're creepy and that should take away some of the basic creepiness."

The mausoleum was one of the oldest in Sunnydale, built back before the city was even an official township. Vaults lined the inner walls, and the hallways leading down to them looked like holes punched into a cavern. Instead of stone, the mausoleum floor was hard-packed earth that showed patches of grass and moss.

"I guess not many people come here anymore," Buffy said.

"Maybe the family moved away," Willow suggested.

"Or were all killed," Buffy said. "This is Sunnydale, after all."

Only a little farther on, a low buzz filled the air. Buffy stopped, pressing up against the cold limestone wall at the corner of the next hallway. She felt the droning buzz echo through the cold, sweat-slick stone. Looking back the way they came, she could barely make out the doorway.

"Will, how far would you say we've come?" Buffy asked.

"About a hundred feet."

"That's funny, because from the outside, this mausoleum didn't look a hundred feet long. More like thirty."

Comprehension dawned on Willow's face. "The mausoleum isn't a hundred feet long. The demon must have worked a spatial alteration spell inside the mausoleum."

"Give it to me in plain English," Buffy suggested.

"Okay," Willow said. "Evidently the demon made the inside of the building bigger than the outside."

"You can do that?"

"Not me. But I've read about it. And it's kind of what happened at that frat house's Halloween party last year. The one where Gachnar the Fear Demon showed up. Only this is, like, more real. More magickal."

"You gotta love that," Buffy said dryly.

"It also means we have to be more careful," Willow said. "Any time you do spatial alteration spells—well, you screw up the real world, bring a piece of it over into a demon world. Or bring a piece of a demon world into the real world." She paused, smoothing her fingers along the limestone. Tiny violet sparks shot from her fingertips.

"Meaning?" Buffy asked.

Willow glanced at her. "That we might not be alone here."

A rustle—like a knife being drawn from a leather sheath, or maybe scales shifting along stone—reached Buffy's ears. She glanced up and spotted two lizard-looking creatures clinging to the mausoleum's ceiling.

Both creatures were basically humanoid, but there was no mistaking their reptilian natures. Smooth dark-green scales covered wedge-shaped heads that held lidless, green-yellow eyes the size of personal pan pizzas.

The arms and legs ended in hands with thumbs and three fingers, flared out at the ends into thick pads. Long and skinny, the creatures looked as thin as runway models. A stump of tail marked their hindquarters. Lipless mouths framed emotionless features with blunt noses.

But Buffy saw hunger in their eyes. She recognized the desire on a primitive level that transcended even the abilities she'd gained by becoming the Slayer.

The first one yawned suddenly, as if bored. Moving with whiplike intensity, an ochre forked tongue shot out and tested the air. Before the tongue returned to the curved mouth, the creature released its grip on the ceiling and dropped. Whipping around, the creature lunged at Buffy. As the fingers darted out, claws jutted into view.

"They're Sampres," Willow shouted, diving back from the second creature.

Buffy moved by instinct, bending and sweeping into a roundhouse kick toward the attacking creature. When her foot connected with her opponent's face, she felt like she had kicked a wall. Although the creature's path changed, Buffy also knocked herself from her feet. She fell backward, losing the candle as she hit the hard-packed earthen ground.

Miraculously, or maybe aided by Willow's spell, the candle didn't extinguish when it also hit the ground. The flame clung precariously to the wick as the candle rolled across the floor and stopped against the wall. Weak light continued to flood the hallway.

Placing her hands against the ground above her head, Buffy flipped to her feet in time to face the Sampres that came at her. She remembered the creature then from Giles and Willow's research. Craulathar demons created servants to attend to and protect them during long magick rituals.

"Human, die!" the Sampres said in a raspy voice. He snapped a hand at Buffy's face, and the candlelight sparked from the razor-sharp claws.

Buffy ducked, dropping to one knee, then bounced back up as soon as the Sampres's hand passed over her head. Putting her shoulder and her weight behind the blow, she drove her hand into the lizard-creature's face hard enough to turn his head.

Driven backward by the blow, the Sampres still unleashed his other clawed hand, driving the claws toward Buffy's neck. Moving quickly, Buffy raised her left hand, caught the blow across her forearm, and used the force to her advantage as she spun and delivered a backhand blow to the lesser demon's temple. Off-balance and falling fast, the Sampres executed a back flip and raked one of its back hands at Buffy's head.

Caught unaware by the surprise move, Buffy barely managed to avert her head and keep the demon from ripping out her left eye. One of the claws grazed her cheek just below her eye. Fear thudded through her when she realized how close the blow had come, but she didn't hold back, chasing after the creature.

The Sampres landed on his forepaws. The ochre tongue flicked out again as he cocked his head to one side, transfixing Buffy with one green-yellow eye. Balanced on his forehands, the Sampres slashed at Buffy with both back hands.

Throwing herself down, aware that Willow had managed to evade her own opponent so far, Buffy slid beneath the Sampres demon's attack. On her side, she kicked the demon's hands from beneath him, causing him to topple. Before the thin creature could get to his feet, Buffy threw herself onto his back, wrapping her legs around his midsection as she reached for the wedge-shaped head. She caught the Sampres's rounded chin in one hand, barely maintaining her grip, and placed her other hand at the back of her opponent's head.

Knowing he was in trouble, the Sampres went ballistic, bending and twisting like a rodeo bull. Claws raked against the hard-packed earth, then against the stone walls as he strove to dislodge Buffy. Clinging to her prey, the Slayer tightened her grip—then twisted. Bone snapped, and the demon went limp.

Buffy scrambled up, thinking instantly of Willow, knowing the Sampres had probably outclassed her friend in sheer fighting skills—especially with all the natural equipment the demons had. Buffy gazed back down the hallway the way they had come.

The candlelight barely illuminated the two figures.

Buffy ran toward them, watching Willow duck out of the way again. Willow's red hair flew as razor-sharp claws cut the space where her head had just been. As close as the blow had come, Buffy was certain Willow had lost a lock or two of hair.

Willow came up, her face visible in the weak candlelight. Her mouth moved and she gestured toward the Sampres demon. An invisible wind picked the creature up and tossed him through the air, blasting him through the hallway. Buffy ducked and watched as the demon smashed against the wall on the other side of the intersection where the present passageway dead-ended.

The meaty splat echoed through the passageway. Slowly, as if his flesh had been driven into the grooves between the mortared stones, the demon slid down the wall and crumpled into a lifeless heap.

Buffy bent down and picked up the candle. The flame flickered but held.

"You're hurt," Willow said when she reached Buffy.

Only then did Buffy notice that her cheek below her left eye burned. She touched her fingers to the area. Her fingers came away stained crimson.

"It's not too bad." As the Slayer, her powers of recuperation were superhuman. Healing fast was one of the perks of fighting demons and vampires to extinction on a daily basis.

"Actually," Willow said, grimacing a little, "it's pretty awful." She took a pack of tissues from her purse and mopped at Buffy's face.

"Ow," Buffy said.

"Sorry," Willow apologized. "You know, this could be really bad."

"I don't scar, Will," Buffy replied. "You've seen that. I'm the most healingest person we've ever seen."

"I know that. I meant it could be really bad that the smell of all this fresh blood might attract—you know, demony things."

"Oh. Not a good thought." Buffy took her friend's hands away from her face. "We'll fix me later. For now, let's see if we can finish this thing." Willow took one final swipe at her face, but Buffy ducked her and continued on.

The hallway around the corner continued another eighty or so yards. A cavern filled with light glowed at the end of it.

"Good thing there aren't any other paths to take," Buffy said. "I didn't think to bring any bread crumbs."

Sonorous chants filled the passageway, growing stronger as they neared the lighted cavern ahead. Buffy was pretty certain the original mausoleum builders hadn't constructed the building to lead down into a cave— especially one under the graveyard—and she took the presence of the cave before them as one more indicator that maybe they weren't exactly in the Sunnydale they knew anymore. Flattening herself against the limestone wall, Buffy peered into the cavern.

Primarily, the cavern was a natural formation, a pocket deep in the earth—in *some* earth, anyway—created by rain and the local water table. Stalactites hung from the dome-shaped ceiling, and stalagmites jutted up from the cavern floor.

But someone, or some*thing*, had altered the cavern. Stone steps were carved along the right side of the cave, following the round shaft in a tight spiral that grew closer and closer together.

Stepping out onto the spiral stone stairs, Buffy peeked over the edge. At the bottom of the dark tunnel fifty feet below, the Craulathar demon rocked on his knees and held his hands out at his sides. He howled now, and only some of the sounds were words. The rest was raw anger and pain.

Buffy glanced back at Willow.

"I don't know," Willow whispered back.

Buffy looked down at the demon again. Things were better when they knew something about what and who they were up against. Despite the severity of the moment, Buffy wondered about Dawn, wondered what her little sister was doing and whether they'd have an argument in the morning again because Dawn didn't feel like going to school. Facing that was almost harder than facing the Craulathar demon.

The Craulathar demon was eight feet tall. From Buffy's perspective, she couldn't get a good sense of his size, but the books about Craulathar demons had been specific. The creature was broad chested with a tall neck that made him look somewhat bovine. His eyes occupied either side of his wide face, giving him great peripheral vision but virtually no binocular vision. A chestnut hide covered him in short hair that glistened in the light of the campfire in front of him. Curled horns jutted out a good eighteen inches on either side of his head, sweeping forward, then curling backward like a goat's horns. Broad and angular—centered around a huge, flat, bat's nose—the demon's face looked homely and vacant. He wore a

UCLA warm-up suit and sneakers.

A gunnysack sat on the ground next to the Craulathar demon. As he continued to sing, the creature occasionally reached into the sack, seized a body part, and took it out. He'd say a few words over the part, then heave it into the campfire. The flames reached up almost like a living thing, then rapidly consumed each offering.

The sweet smell of burning human flesh—and Buffy was disturbed greatly that she could recognize that smell—filled the cavern. Without warning, the Craulathar demon screamed out in renewed fury. Then the fire blasted up in front of him.

Unable to stare into the harsh glare, Buffy turned her head away and closed her eyes. When the brightness dimmed against her eyelids, she opened them again and stared at the demon through a maze of twisting spots, watching as he stood and walked into a circle of light that was half again as tall as he was. He disappeared, but the circle of light remained.

"That's not good," Willow said.

"What is it?" Buffy asked.

"An interdimensional bridge." Willow ran her fingers through her hair thoughtfully. "As in, a bridge that goes from one world to another."

"Then, he stole all those body parts to make a bridge so he could go back home?" Buffy asked. Actually, that kind of made things simple.

"Or bring someone else back into this world," Willow said. "The bridge didn't close down after he went through."

Knew there had to be a catch, Buffy thought, groaning inwardly. "This is not really a problem, right? I mean, all we have to do is close down that interdimensional bridge and trap him over there."

"Yeah," Willow said uncertainly. "But that sounds suspiciously easy."

"Maybe it will be." Buffy started down the steps, hurrying. Willow had a hard time keeping up with her.

The interdimensional bridge looked like a spiderweb. The bridge had height and width, but unless the onlooker entered the light area, there was no depth. Violet and blue light pulsed inside the bridge opening, making it look like the other world was lit in black light.

Buffy raised the candle she still held, her hand caked with cooled wax, but the light didn't penetrate far. The only thing that she could see clearly was a bone bridge arching over a red and orange glowing chasm. A stone building seemed to sit at the other end of the bridge, but she wasn't able to make out the details.

Curious, Buffy lifted her arm to the interdimensional bridge, poking her fingers toward the shimmering surface.

"Don't," Willow warned.

By the time Buffy realized what Willow had said, her fingers were already in contact with the opening to the bridge. Lightning flashed inside the cavern, and an incredible force smashed into Buffy, knocking her from her feet and up against the wall behind her.

"I tried to warn you," Willow said as she helped Buffy to her feet. "The interdimensional bridge is protected. They always are."

"It's okay," Buffy said, taking a deep, shaky breath. "We'll just do this a little differently. Can you get me through the barrier to close the gate?"

Willow looked at the shimmering doorway leading to the bridge area. "Breaking through magickal barriers can be tricky. I need to know more about how the spell is put together."

Aching, her face burning where the Sampres demon had raked her with a claw, Buffy said, "Then we need an expert on things darkly magickal."

"I can anchor the gate," Willow suggested. "Make sure it stays open till we get back. Unless, of course, the demon finishes up while we're gone."

"Do that," Buffy agreed. "Do you know where Giles is?"

"Giles is at the *Othersyde* taping with Tara," Willow reminded her. "I don't think he really wanted to go, but when he found out I was going on patrol with you, he decided to keep her company."

"I think we'd get noticed stealing through a studio audience in a live taping to find our friends," Buffy said. "And if Derek Traynor really is as psychic as the *Othersyde's* producers would have you believe, I don't want him announcing that we're there to help close an interdimensional bridge to keep a demon out of Sunnydale."

"Right," Willow said. "So who are we going to get?"

"Spike," Buffy answered. She picked up the candle, lit it from the magickal fire, and headed back up the stone steps.

"What if the Craulathar demon has finished whatever he's doing by the time we get back?" Willow asked, following her.

"Then we'll track him down," Buffy said.

Chapter Four

Spike sat alone at the end of the long bar in the Alibi. He drank whiskey and was working on getting intoxicated. Staring at the bottom of the empty shot glass in front of him, he worked on pushing himself into a positive mental attitude. *Bein' drunk would be nice,* he told himself. *Have a nice buzz on, be the life of the party. Maybe a quick scuffle. That wouldn't be so much to ask, now would it?*

There was no answer.

Smoke drifted through the shadowed interior of the bar. Sweat-stink collided with the stench of beer, liquor, and drinks of choice that had been brewed from things never born into the human world—and then there was the strong odor of demons. The Alibi was a rundown place in Sunnydale, hardly suitable for more than establishing just what its name promised. Sunnydale police officers feared going there.

For Spike, though, the bar was a home away from

crypt and a necessary refuge from dark thoughts. His brushed black denim jeans, motorcycle boots, black turtleneck, and thigh-length black leather jacket matched his mood.

Willy, the night bartender at the Alibi, sidled up to Spike. Willy was thin and sallow with stringy brown hair. He was dressed in a white shirt that looked too big for him.

"Get you another drink?" Willy asked.

Spike looked at the man, smelling the blood in him, craving it so badly and knowing there wasn't anything he could do to get it. "You're takin' too long comin' back around. I'm workin' on a powerful thirst here."

Willy shrugged but didn't look concerned. "It's a busy night."

Rage boiled over inside Spike. He barely resisted morphing into his vampire face and tearing Willy's throat out. The only thing that kept him from doing that was the bloody chip that the Initiative had installed into his head last year.

The Initiative, a government-funded covert operation, hunted down demons and tagged several of them with electronic chips to monitor their behavior and movements. A few, like Spike, had been implanted with experimental chips that kept them from killing humans and allowed the research scientists to record them in their natural environments.

That had been a bloody awful year, and even as fast as the time passed for Spike since being bitten by Drusilla all those years ago in England, that time had seemed to drag interminably. When he'd first found out the computer chip prevented him from attacking humans, Spike had turned suicidal. If he couldn't kill, there was nothing to live his undead life for. Strangely enough, Buffy and her little pack of Slayerettes had become Spike's reluctant companions. At their side, he'd learned he could still kill things—as long as they weren't human. That was something.

Moving with all the unnatural speed accorded to vampires, Spike reached across the bar and grabbed Willy by the shirt. Even that small, non-lethal action sparked a cavalcade of pain that marched through his head. It was like his brain was caught in a mosh pit from hell. Actually, that was a welcome idea. He forced the pain away, knowing he didn't dare harm the bartender. But then, the bartender didn't know he wasn't going to harm him.

"Don't," Spike said, voice filled with menace, "ever presume to talk to me that way again."

Willy's face blanched, and he tried to get away.

Spike reached out and took the whiskey bottle from him. "Now go away."

Willy left.

Quietly Spike poured the shot glass full of amber liquid. He left the whiskey bottle uncapped and nearby. Tonight might be another long night on his calendar, but he didn't intend to spend it sober. Slamming the drink down his throat, he felt the liquid burn the whole way down, ripping like a napalm explosion in his gut.

"Hey. That's Spike, isn't it?"

"No. That's the excuse for a demon that used to be Spike."

The whispered conversation caught Spike's attention. He glanced up from pouring himself another drink and stared into the mirror on the other side of the bar, which provided him with a clear view of the men talking about him behind his back.

Four Walphurg demons sat at one of the back tables. They were all broad and fat, and their features were unmistakably porcine. Hogs' jowls framed blunt piggy noses, and uneven yellow tusks jutted from their lower jaws. A spoonful of brains would have been a tight fit in back of their almost nonexistent foreheads. Clad in black biker's leathers with "Spurs" written across the back in chrome, they watched Spike from behind mirrored sunglasses.

"Spike hasn't been the same," a demon biker said, "since the Slayer started to spank him regularly."

Unable to control the anger that fired him, Spike's hand crushed the glass he held. Razor-edged fragments dug deep into his hand. He fed on the pain, licking the blood from his hand and fueling the rage inside him. His smile felt tight against his face even though he couldn't see the expression in the mirror.

Spike brushed the glass fragments from his injured hand. Since he was a vampire, the wounds would heal quickly, but that would require time spent digging the tiny shards out of his flesh. Not a pleasant task, but since there was pain involved, the work at least promised interest.

A man stepped away from the crowd that had filled the Alibi and came straight for Spike. The vampire picked up the man's reflection in the mirror at once. A deep unease twisted through Spike's stomach, and he didn't like the way the feeling took the edge off his anger.

The man was tall and slim, in his early twenties if that. His skin was so black, the weak light in the bar showed blue undertones. A snap-brim fedora darkened his features, and he still looked young despite the short-cropped goatee he wore. Red streaked his eyes, and road grit clung to his jeans, chambray shirt, and long leather jacket. His boots were worn down at the heel, and he looked like a man who had gone for weeks without a proper bed to sleep in. He carried a guitar case slung over his back.

"Something I can do for you?" Spike asked.

"I'm looking for a man, calls himself Spike," the man said. His voice carried the smooth resonance of the Mississippi Delta.

"Never heard of him," Spike said.

A smile flickered across the guitar man's face. "That's funny, because the last person I talked to in a waterin' hole up the street told me that Spike was a white-haired vampire with a real attitude. Told me I could probably find him here." No rancor sounded in the man's easygoing tone. He had a singer's voice, husky and dry, one that rumbled like a car engine starting on a cold morning.

"People who come here," Spike said, "usually don't want to be found, you see."

The man put his thumb to his hat brim and pushed it back a little. "I can see that. I just got a little business to take care of. Ain't nothin' gonna hurt ol' Spike. Ain't nothin' to be worried about none."

The Walphurg demons burst out laughing.

"Now, you see," Spike said in a low voice, "that's where you're wrong. The guy you're looking for, he doesn't worry about anything. He's fearless. A real vampire's vampire. And what the bloody hell would you be needing a vampire for?"

The man's gaze remained level and his speech stayed easy. "I'm lookin' for the Chosen One."

Spike turned and looked more directly at the man. Trouble clung to him, to the faded jeans and the worn leather jacket. He was a man used to hard and long roads, to days spent with slim hopes and fragile dreams. But there was an inner fire to him as well that bordered on fanaticism.

The guy was, Spike realized in a rush and from his own experience, the kind of man that could get others killed if they chose to believe in him.

"You're looking for the Slayer?" Spike turned his

back to the bar, remaining on his stool and hooking his elbows over the edge. He grinned expansively.

Several nearby demons cursed and spat at the mention of the Slayer.

"Yeah," the man said.

"And what would you want to see the Slayer about?"

"Business of my own," the guitar man said. "Can't see that it's any business of yours."

Spike checked the impulse to smash the guy's face in. The vampire smiled. "Me neither. So why don't you get out of my face before you get hurt."

The man's jaw tightened. "Tell the Slayer I'm lookin' for her. She'll want to know. My name's Bobby Lee Tooker. I'll be in town."

Ignoring the guitar man, Spike reached under his jacket and took his cigarettes from his shirt pocket. He flicked his lighter to life and lit a cigarette, taking a drag deep into his lungs then blowing it out. He squinted through the smoke at the guitar man. "Go away, Bobby Lee Tooker."

A momentary angry flicker passed through Bobby Lee's eyes. Then he touched his hat brim and walked to the nearest table and started asking questions. No one wanted to talk to him.

"Spike's lost his nerve," one of the Walphurg demon bikers said. "Man, that's a sad thing to see." He looked at the other demons, then they all guffawed with laughter.

Spike pushed off the stool and walked toward the Walphurg demons. Most of the men and demons seated in front of him pushed their chairs out of the way as he neared.

The Walphurg demons glanced up at Spike's approach.

Spike took another hit off the cigarette, then blew smoke out. "You blokes sure have been running your mouths tonight."

Conversations around the table quieted.

"At least," the biggest of the Walphurg demons said, "he's still got his hearing."

The other demons joined his raucous laughter and high-fived each other.

The big biker demon glanced up. "You still standing there?"

"Yeah," Spike said. "I just wanted to wait a bit."

The demon frowned. "Wait for what?"

"To get your full attention before I killed you," Spike replied in a dry voice, then smiled. "Kind of what I like to think of as 'the perfect moment.'" He lifted his boot, then rammed it into the table's edge, watching the two demons on either side of him leap into action. Spike morphed then, letting the demon take his face, sloughing away most of his humanity and leaving the naked hate and hunger for anyone to see.

The table slammed the big demon back against the wall and Spike's foot kept him trapped there. Spike reached for one of the metal and plastic chairs vacated by the bar patrons fleeing the vicinity. The vampire swung the chair toward the demon on the left. Flesh ripped and bone broke when the chair connected, but the chair didn't survive the impact either.

The demon biker on the right reached under his leather jacket and brought out a chopped-down, double-barreled shotgun. Screams and curses filled the Alibi as the patrons saw the Walphurg demon lift his shotgun and point it at Spike.

Still keeping one foot on the table to pin the big biker demon against the wall, Spike fisted the metal tubes from the broken chair and reversed them, leaning into the blow. He caught the shotgun barrels in one hand while he used the other to drive the metal tubes through the Walphurg demon's heart.

One of the shotgun barrels fired, filling the room with a thunderous boom and a brief cloud of muzzle flame.

Releasing the metal tubes thrust through his opponent's heart, Spike slapped the dying demon away and yanked the shotgun from his grip. One full barrel remained. The last biker demon brought both hands down and smashed the table to splinters.

"Impressive," Spike said laconically.

The big demon reached under his jacket and whipped out a huge chrome pistol. "You're gonna die, bloodsucker."

"Wow," Spike said. "You even come with clever repartee. Who knew?"

Chapter Five

After taking a last drag on his cigarette, Spike took the cigarette from his mouth and flipped it into the demon's face just as its finger tightened on the trigger. The glowing coal caught the demon in the eye, causing it to roar in pain and its shots to go wild.

"Nighty-night," Spike said, and he squeezed the shotgun's trigger.

The load caught the demon biker full in the face and reduced his features to bloody ruin, driving his head back against the wall. The dead demon dropped to the ground.

Spike threw the empty shotgun on top of the biker's corpse, then reached under his jacket and dragged out his cigarettes. He shook one out of the pack and lit up. A quick search through the demon's clothing netted him four sets of keys. Then he turned and grinned at the crowd.

"Looks like I own some motorcycles," Spike told them. "I'll sell them all at once or to individual bidders. What's it going to be?"

The bar crowd stood in stunned silence.

"Come on, come on," Spike snarled. "I ain't gonna be bloody greedy about this."

The door opened unexpectedly, drawing the attention of everyone inside the bar.

Buffy Summers stood framed in the doorway. "Spike," she said. "I need help."

Spike glanced at her, noting her disheveled appearance and the wound near her left eye. Whatever she had tangled with tonight had been quick.

"I'm kind of in the middle of something here," Spike said.

Buffy glanced at the bikers' bodies. "Looks like you're all done."

"We're just getting into the post-homicide auction," Spike disagreed. "The selling of the worldly goods of those vanquished in savage but honorable combat."

Buffy shot him a look. "This is important."

"So is this. The economy's going to hell in a hand-cart. I'm doing my bit to increase trade. You know, selling and buying?"

"Fine," Buffy said. Then she was gone, and the door slammed behind her.

Fine?

Spike seethed. Things weren't fine. She hadn't even mentioned what she needed him for. And whatever she'd encountered was obviously dangerous, or she wouldn't have come into the Alibi looking like that.

"Bloody hell," Spike muttered. He spat the cigarette out, morphed back into human features, then dug through the dead biker's jacket for extra shotgun rounds. Pocketing the ammunition, he kept two out and reloaded the shotgun. He'd learned a long time ago that fighting wasn't all about fangs and martial arts. For good measure, he took the whiskey bottle from the counter. He was on his way to the door when the stranger approached him.

"Was that the Slayer?" Bobby Lee asked.

On his way to the door, knowing that he might not find Buffy until it was too late, Spike lowered the shotgun's muzzle to point at the man's face. "Bloody back off, banjo boy."

Bobby Lee stopped and raised his hands. His face showed no fear. "I need to speak to the Slayer."

"No way," Spike replied. "Whatever trouble you're pushing, mate, she doesn't need none of it. Understand?"

"You're making a mistake."

In spite of the tension he felt and the situation he'd just stepped away from, Spike laughed. "Bloody hell. Don't go off thinkin' this is my first mistake." He gestured with the shotgun. "Just don't you make your last one."

Tires screeched out on the street.

Spike turned from the stranger and hustled through the door. Out on the street he spotted the demon bikers' motorcycles illegally parked at the corner under a darkened lamppost. All of them were Harleys—big, rough powerhouses. That was encouraging.

Buffy's station wagon, the one that Joyce Summers had owned and left to her daughter, disappeared around the corner at the intersection. Willow was at the wheel, and Spike was grateful for that. For all her vaunted talent and skill as the Slayer, Buffy couldn't drive.

Spike didn't bother yelling after them. They wouldn't have stopped anyway, and it was bad enough that he'd left the Alibi like some little bloody lap dog after Buffy had come calling. All the reputation building he'd done by killing the demon bikers had been shattered in the instant Buffy had stepped through that door and called out to him.

Throwing a leg over one of the Harleys, Spike motored into the light traffic cruising through the street, cutting off a burgundy Corvette and startling the driver of an SUV full of teenage girls. Horns blared as he past them, but he ignored them, concentrating on Buffy.

Willow glanced up into the rearview mirror of Buffy's mom's car. They had taken it for the evening because the Craulathar demon's trail had led them all over Sunnydale for the last few days and they'd always been one step behind. Headlights reflected in the rearview mirror.

Buffy sat in the passenger seat and stared through the back windshield.

"Maybe we should have waited," Willow suggested.

"No," Buffy said.

"Well, I mean, Spike's not really one of us," Willow went on.

"He'll come."

"He might not," Willow insisted. "You weren't in the Alibi long enough to tell him what was going on."

"I told him I needed him," Buffy said.

"Oh," Willow said. She nodded in support though she didn't completely feel it. "Telling him you needed him, that was probably all he needed to know."

"That's what I thought," Buffy said. "He's either in or he's out."

"You know, with this thing the Craulathar demon is doing, it might have been better if we made sure Spike was in."

"He will be."

Willow sailed through another intersection. "Did you tell him we were going back out to the graveyard?"

"Nope."

"That might have been an idea."

Buffy turned to face her. "A really good idea, Will. But there wasn't time."

Willow hesitated a moment. It was okay that Buffy was in charge; she usually was. But Willow needed to know that they had some sort of a plan going on. "How's he going to find us?"

"I don't know."

"But we're going back out to the graveyard?"

"Yes. Willow, don't wig on me. If Spike doesn't make it to the graveyard, there's no one else we can go to. Stopping the Craulathar demon will be up to us."

"If he's not already finished doing what he was going to do."

"If he has," Buffy said confidently, "then we can still deal." She paused. "I'm in a quandary."

"About the demon? Because I can understand that. I mean, we've never taken on a Craulathar demon before."

"Not the demon," Buffy said.

"Then what?"

"Dawn."

"What about Dawn?"

"Whether I should call her and find out if she's in bed or if she's blowing off the talk we had today and is staying up watching television."

"You mean, check up on her?" Willow asked.

"Yeah."

"Checking up on her isn't so good. She might get upset."

"I know. I thought about just going by the house when we finish with the Craulathar demon. Just kind of peek in through the windows."

"That's kind of creepy, don't you think?"

"I'm not happy about it." Buffy folded her arms and looked annoyed. "The situation wouldn't be any better if I stayed there to yell at her."

Willow nodded. "Probably not."

"There's no way to handle this without some kind of confrontation, Will."

"There should be another way."

"Maybe you could use your witchy powers and check on Dawn through a crystal ball or something."

Willow looked at Buffy. "You know I can't do that. I mean, for one, I don't know the spell. And for another, I wouldn't feel comfortable doing that. That's spying, you know."

Buffy sighed. "I know." She was silent for a moment. "Will, Dawn and I survived my mom's death, but I don't know if we're going to survive this whole relationship change. I wasn't even a very good sister, and now I'm having to be her mom. I'm in way over my head."

"You are a good sister, Buffy." Willow smiled. "You've been like a sister to me, and I don't think I could have had a better one."

"Thanks. But how many sisters would have led you into battles with vampires, demons, and the odd mummy girl?"

"Not many," Willow agreed. "But that's only one of the things that makes you special."

"I wasn't there for Dawn much as a sister," Buffy said. "We didn't do sister things. Except for fighting. We were pretty good at that a few times. But I had this whole other life I couldn't share with her."

"You can't share this life with many people," Willow said. "And what choice do you have with Dawn?"

Buffy glanced at the back window again. "None. That's what I hate about what's going on with us now."

"Not having a choice?"

"There's a lot of things I don't have a choice about," Buffy replied. "This whole Slayer gig, for one. But I hate not being able to give Dawn a choice."

"Oh." Willow fell silent, not knowing what to say.

A single headlight charged through the traffic behind them, rolling out into the oncoming lane briefly, then sweeping back in front of the car behind the station wagon. Car horns blared, sounding dim and far away because they were moving.

"What's that?" Willow asked, feeling a little nervous.

"That's Spike," Buffy said. "I told you he'd find a way."

Then Willow saw Spike's platinum blond hair blowing in the wind above the motorcycle's handlebars. Surprisingly, Willow only felt a little better about the coming confrontation with the Craulathar demon. Memories of Spike from before the Initiative installed the no-violence-to-humans chip still haunted her. Was he coming to help, or to cheer the demon on?

Xander stood in front of the Lamplighter with the other survivors of Robby Healdton's attack on the theater crowd. Flashing lights lit up the neighborhood and drew spectators from the nearby restaurants and a gym down the street. Police cars, an ambulance, and two fire engines staked out the front of the Lamplighter.

Standing there, though he'd been through events and situations like this one dozens of times, Xander still felt a little surreal. Anya stood next to him, pressed in close for warmth, holding one of his hands tightly in both of hers.

The theater doors burst open as EMTs shoved their way through. Two of the white-shirted emergency rescue personnel guided the clattering gurney from the lobby while another one pushed from behind. Popcorn and soft-drink spills littered the lobby floor, and employees wearing black slacks and red vests worked to clean the carpet, trying to get everything back to normal. There was still enough time for one more showing in the other theaters, and there was talk that the moviefest would continue.

Xander stared at Robby Healdton on the gurney. Someone had tied him to it, using a backboard to further immobilize him. Still, he jerked and jumped within the constraints. White foam flecked his mouth.

"You can't keep me here!" Robby yelled. "You're all idiots! I'm free! I'm free! I'm just here on a temporary visa, mortals!"

The crowd parted in front of the gurney even before the uniformed police officers cleared the way. No one wanted to be near Robby.

"Man," said a guy standing next to Xander, "he's so totally cracked."

Anger surged through Xander. Guilt spurred the emotion on as he remembered how the ax handle had felt crunching into the back of Robby's head.

Xander stepped forward, pushing Anya's hands away as she tried to stop him.

"Xander," Anya protested.

"Hey," Xander said, drawing the guy's attention.

The guy looked at Xander curiously.

"That's my friend there," Xander said. "He's got a few problems right now, but there's no reason to say that. You don't even know him."

"Bwaaa-hahahahaha," Robby bellowed from the gurney as they passed only a few feet away. "By the Dark One, this is the most fun I've had in decades! It's been well worth the price of admission, Dredfahl!"

Xander watched Robby straining against his bonds. Then he looked back at the man he'd addressed. "Okay, maybe my friend is having more than a few problems, but he's a good guy. You shouldn't be talking about him like that."

"Yeah," the guy said, turning and walking away. "Right. The whole town is full of nuts. Like really I'm supposed to notice one more."

Xander started to go after the guy, but then he realized that wasn't his way. He was just angry, that's all.

There had been too many hurtful and confusing things going on lately, and a lot of them were still going on. He forced himself to breathe out and felt Anya take his hand again.

"Xander," she said. "I'm here."

"I know," Xander said, and he loved her for that. Maybe Anya said the wrong thing a lot, but she knew how to be with someone. "I know. Thank you." He turned and watched as the EMTs loaded Robby into the back of the ambulance.

A uniformed police officer with sergeant's stripes on his sleeves and a clipboard talked to the officers by the gurney. One of them pointed at Xander.

That can't be good, Xander thought.

Chapter Six

The police sergeant walked through the crowd and stopped in front of Xander. "Mr. Harris," the sergeant said in a flat monotone.

Dad? Xander quickly glanced over his shoulder, fearing the worst. If his father was there, things were definitely going from bad to worse.

Anya nudged him. "Xander, he means you."

Xander glanced back at the policeman. "Oh. Me. You mean *me*, Mr. Harris. I thought you were . . . you were looking for someone else."

"According to the on-site officer, you struck Mr. Healdton," the police sergeant said, referring to the clipboard.

"Actually," Xander said, "there were a lot of people that hit Robby."

"You hit him with the ax handle and temporarily stunned him."

Xander hesitated, wondering how much trouble he was going to be in.

"Yes, he did," Anya said. "And it was a pretty good swing."

Xander wished the earth would open him up and swallow him down. "I just didn't think there was any other—"

"Good job," the sergeant said. "From the way some of the other witnesses tell the story, you probably saved some lives in there." He shook Xander's hand and walked away.

"Let me loose!" Robby screamed from the back of the ambulance. "Let me loose, and I'll kill you all! I'll pickle your brains! I'll pop your eyeballs! I'll cause your women to be barren and your cows to go dry!"

"Boy," Anya said in surprised appreciation, "now *that's* an old threat you don't hear anymore."

Xander guided Anya through the crowd, deliberately avoiding the gazes of the people watching him. More than anything, he wanted to understand the craziness of the evening. It wasn't like he was unprepared for craziness. Sunnydale had always been crazy in one way or another; getting to know Buffy and Giles had only put a fine point on it.

"Hey, Xander," a tense, nervous voice called.

Looking up, Xander spotted a tall, athletic platinum blond dressed in green leather pants, a cream colored blouse, and a Sunnydale High windbreaker.

Xander stopped. "Hey, Stephie."

The girl halted in front of Xander. She reached up and smoothed a stray lock of hair from her tear-streaked face. "I heard about Robby. I came as soon as I could, as soon as I could. I still can't believe Robby could do such a thing."

"He did, though," Anya said. "He was terrible. Fierce."

Stephie stared at Anya.

Xander worked damage control immediately. "Stephie, this is my girlfriend, Anya. Anya, this is Stephie McConnell. Robby's girlfriend."

"Oh," Anya said, "I'm very sorry about your loss."

Growing pale and panicked, Stephie glanced at Xander. "Nobody told me Robby was—"

"Robby's not," Xander said quickly. "He's alive."

"Good." Tears streamed down Stephie's face, and she wrapped her arms around herself. "Because I don't know what I'd do if he was dead."

"You thought I meant that he was dead?" Anya asked. "No, I just figure that after what he did tonight he probably won't be out of jail for a long time."

Apprehension filled Stephie's face. "Xander, you know Robby. He wouldn't hurt anybody. He *wouldn't*. He couldn't, you know. He wasn't into violence."

Xander thought about all the arcade games he'd played with Robby Healdton. Many of those had been nearly as gruesome, frightening, and bloodthirsty as a nightly patrol with Buffy. Maybe police investigators looking into Robby's life wouldn't feel so certain that he wasn't into violence.

"Stephie," Xander said calmly, "it was Robby. I saw him myself." *I even cold-cocked him when he wasn't looking.* It was amazing how quickly Xander felt drained of the remaining dregs of heroism the police sergeant had given him.

Stephie grabbed Xander's arm. "You don't understand," she said. "That wasn't Robby. Not the Robby you and I know."

Xander remembered how Robby had talked, and the strange braying laughter. That hadn't sounded like Robby. "He did seem more than a little off," he said.

Desperate hope crumpled the girl's face. "Robby hasn't been himself, Xander. He's been involved in something." She glanced over Xander's shoulder.

Xander followed her gaze, watching as the ambulance pulled out between the rescue vehicles and police cars. "What are you talking about?" he asked.

"It's a secret," Stephie said.

"What's a secret?" Xander asked.

"The video-game project Robby was working on."

Xander thought about Robby, trying to remember past conversations they'd had lately. They'd talked games and gaming, comics and movies and *Trek,* and maybe Robby had mentioned that he wanted to design video games. "Robby designed a video game?"

"He's designed lots of them," Stephie said impatiently. "But he couldn't get hooked up with a development team. He'd ship game design documents out and hope for the best, you know. But it just wasn't happening. Then he got this notice."

"What notice?"

"About him helping test some new beta software for a VR game."

"Total immersion virtual reality?" Xander shook his head. "No gaming company has hardware or software that can do that."

"This place did. Robby told me about it."

Xander looked around, seeing that the ambulance had reached the end of the block. "Stephie, how did you get here?"

"I took a cab." The girl looked guilty. "I boosted a few bucks from my mom's mad-money stash."

"You going to the hospital?"

"Yeah. My parents will probably kill me, but I don't want Robby waking up there alone. Knowing his parents, they aren't going to come out for this, and his roommate will probably put out a notice looking for Robby's replacement tomorrow. They had a big argument last week over Alfred."

"Alfred?" Anya asked. "Aha. A suspect. Maybe he put something in Robby's drink, or even his food. Who's Alfred?"

Xander and Stephie looked at Anya. "Alfred's Robby's cat," Xander said.

"Have Robby and the cat always gotten along?" Anya asked. "Are you sure the cat is really a cat?"

"Alfred's a cat," Xander said, glancing at Stephie and knowing the girl was thinking Anya's questions were just too weird, but also knowing that Anya was completely serious. "Scratch the cat as a suspect. Stephie, let Anya and me give you a ride to the hospital."

"Sure, Xander. I'd appreciate that."

Xander took both girls by the elbows and herded them back to the parking lot where he'd left his car. "And I want to know more about this video-game project."

As Buffy opened the car door and stepped out, Spike rolled up on the Harley, locking his tires and shredding grass and earth as he came to a stop outside the cemetery's front gate. She looked at him, noting the exasperated expression.

"Glad you could make it," Buffy said, heading to the back of the station wagon.

"That's the thanks I get for coming?" Spike growled, leaning across the handlebars.

Willow already had the back of the station wagon open. Lifting the spare tire cover to reveal the weapons hidden underneath, she said, "Spike looks upset."

"So?" Buffy replied. "Spike always looks that way." Still, maybe the vampire appeared more angry than normal.

Spike dismounted the motorcycle and stared at Buffy. He took out a cigarette, cupped his hands, and lit it. The breeze pulled the smoke away instantly. "You going to tell me what's going on, Slayer?"

"Craulathar demon," Buffy replied, returning her attention to the selection of weapons in the back of the station wagon. "Familiar with them?"

"I've tangoed with a Craulathar demon or two," Spike answered. "Big guys. Early interaction between them and humans resulted in some of the Minotaur myths."

"Yeah." Buffy chose a short-hafted, double-bitted battle-ax with a strap that fitted around her wrist.

"You ever taken one on before?" Spike asked.

"Nope."

"You asked me along hoping to get some pointers?" Spike's tone became insulting.

Willow took a crossbow and a quiver of bolts. She slid the quiver strap over her shoulder and loaded a bolt into the crossbow.

"Slow weapon," Buffy said, addressing her friend's choice.

"I know," Willow said, "but I thought it would give us a little distance. And the bolts have silver tips. The books said the Craulathar demons are susceptible to silver."

Buffy nodded. A lot of evil things she fought had a weakness to silver, light, and other things that were primarily pure in nature.

"Sure," Spike said derisively. "Craulathar demons are susceptible to silver, all right. It gives them an incredibly bad rash for a few days. Generally makes them mad enough to track down whoever exposed them and kill them."

Willow looked uncertain.

"The crossbow's a good idea, Will," Buffy said protectively without sparing a glance for Spike. "Take it." She closed the back of the station wagon and headed for the cemetery.

"What are you going to do?" Spike demanded.

"Surely you're not interested," Buffy said.

"I'm here, aren't I?"

"There's a Craulathar demon in a mausoleum inside the graveyard," Buffy said. "I've been trailing him for a few days."

"He's been taking body parts?" Spike asked.

"Yeah. Most of them from cadavers at the university morgue and others from funeral homes."

Interest showed in Spike's dark eyes. He took another drag on his cigarette, and the coal glowed orange for a moment. "How many parts did this guy need?"

"Don't know," Buffy said. "But it's enough that he's cast a spell over the mausoleum and opened a gateway to another world."

"You've seen it?"

"Yeah. I didn't know Craulathar demons even did stuff like that until I saw it."

"He's trying to bring his mate through," Spike said.

"Mate?" Willow asked.

"Sure," Spike said. "You know, 'single white demon seeks same . . .' That sort of thing."

"The books that we looked through didn't mention that," Willow said doubtfully.

Spike stepped over to the station wagon and crushed out his cigarette underfoot. He tried the rear door, but it was locked. He looked up at Buffy. "If I'm going to help you, I'm going to need something with a little heft."

Buffy tossed Spike the station wagon's keys.

The vampire caught the keys effortlessly, opened the door, and scanned the collection, eventually selecting a seventeenth-century mace. The weapon had a spherical head with spikes sticking out, capable of puncturing flesh as well as shredding through it. Spike rested the mace over his shoulder and looked at Buffy.

"Why would the Craulathar demon bring a mate through?" Willow asked.

"You know," Spike said, shrugging. "The usual reasons. He wants to bring up a lot of little Craulathar demons that look like him. Where is this guy?"

Buffy led the way. Despite Spike's arrogance and earlier reluctance to come with them, she was glad he was there.

Nothing living or undead roamed the cemetery grounds as Buffy passed through. Willow followed her, and Spike brought up the rear. Buffy hesitated at the mausoleum entrance.

"What are you waiting on?" Spike asked.

"When we came through the last time, there were two demons guarding the way," Buffy replied.

"Did you kill them?"

"Yeah."

Spike shook his head wearily. "Then they're gone."

"There could be more," Willow pointed out.

"I don't think there's a demon-henchman fire sale going on," Spike said. "If this guy had two guards and you killed them both, he's all out of guards."

"Unless he pulled some through this dimensional rift thing," Buffy said.

Spike rolled his eyes. "Come on, Slayer. The Craulathar demon has gone to all this trouble to secure a mate. The spell that opens the gateway is expensive in terms of magick, and this guy isn't going to settle for demon guards as a consolation prize."

Buffy looked at Willow.

"Spike's probably right," Willow admitted.

Taking a firm grip on the battle-ax, Buffy stepped into the mausoleum. The dank smell of earth swirled around her again. She stared into the impenetrable darkness.

"Will, do you have your candle?" Buffy asked.
Should have stopped and got a flashlight.

"You knew it was dark and didn't get a lamp?" Spike asked.

"Hey," Buffy objected. "The plan was to go back and get you. It's not dark down there where the gateway is."

"Fantastic." Spike reached into his jacket pocket and brought out a Zippo. He offered the lighter to Buffy.

Buffy took the lighter, popped the top, and flicked the wick to life. The yellow-and-blue flame split the darkness and chased it back a few feet. Encased in a fragile and wavering bubble of light, Buffy started forward. She traveled the passageway quickly, following the familiar turns to the cavern.

Chapter Seven

"Impressive special effects," Spike said in quiet appreciation as they went deeper into the mausoleum where the Craulathar demon had holed up.

"The demon's channeling some powerful dark magicks," Willow said. "He's tied the portal to himself, which is why I can't shut it down from this end."

"You guys must have come across an ancient Craulathar demon," Spike agreed. "This is definitely not a fly-by-night operation here."

"I didn't invite you here to be part of a mutual admiration society," Buffy grumbled.

Only a short distance farther on, Buffy entered the cavern and followed the steps down. She stared through the circular area in the center of the spiral stairs.

The violet-and-blue glow remained at the bottom of the steps. The stink of cooking flesh hung heavy in the still air. On the other side of the two-dimensional circle of light that made up the gateway, the bone bridge extended across the chasm that glowed red and orange. The stone building could be seen in the distance.

"A way station," Spike said.

"What?" Buffy asked.

"That building," Spike went on. "Kind of like a dimensional way station. Where two dimensions overlap to form a brief nexus. It takes magick on both ends to get to the nexus point."

"So?" Buffy asked. She went down the steps and felt the static electricity that filled the air. The smell of ozone filtered through the stink of burning flesh.

"So whomever your Craulathar demon is summoning," Spike said, "is probably pretty powerful too."

"Doesn't matter," Buffy said. "If we shut the bridge down from this end, the Craulathar demon and his little friend can't get back to our world."

"And you have a plan for that?" Spike asked.

"Destroy the bridge," Buffy said. "I like to keep things simple. How do I do that?"

"The Craulathar demon's magick maintains the gateway," Spike said. "Kill the demon, destroy the gateway."

"See?" Buffy said. "Easy."

"Not entirely."

"Why not entirely?" Buffy asked. "If the demon comes through, we kill him. End of gateway."

Spike pointed toward the glistening flat surface of the gateway. His finger stopped. Shoving his hand palm forward, he pressed again, harder this time. His hand stopped as well, flat against the power that held the gateway open.

"Your demon's got a shield in place," Spike said. He rolled his hand into a fist and slammed it against the shield. A flat, hollow *bong* rung in response.

"I knew about the shield," Buffy replied. "At least it didn't knock you across the room."

Spike gave her a wry grin. "I guess you forgot to warn me."

Buffy crossed her arms. "I thought maybe you'd know more than I do about the shield."

"I do." Spike dropped his mace to the stone floor and pressed both hands against the shield. "I know that your demon is definitely drawing his strength from the darker powers. This shield is fortified against good. Probably why it zapped you so hard, you bein' the Slayer an' all." He paused. "Willow, if you use your powers, I think you can open the way for Buffy and me. Get us into the way station and let us do a bit of slaying so I can get on with my evening. It's not like I was hanging about at the Alibi waiting for the two of you to roll up."

With some effort, Buffy resisted making a comment.

"What do I do?" Willow asked. "I haven't learned anything about breaking into alternate dimensions."

Spike glanced around the room, then picked up the spiked mace. He held his shirt and jacket open, then drew the weapon across his chest, opening a furrow in his flesh that wept blood.

"Ewwww," Willow said.

Spike grinned at her. "Getting squeamish, are we, witch?"

"I'm just . . . just not into bloody things, you know."

"An' you, in the trade you're in," Spike taunted. "Witchcraft has a darker side to it too, you know. It's not all floating spells and turning stuff into flowers." He dragged his fingertips through the blood seeping on his chest. Kneeling, he drew his painted fingertips across the stone floor, inscribing symbols with fluid ease, stopping now and again to get more blood. When he was finished, he buttoned his shirt over the wound.

"Do you recognize these symbols?" Spike asked Willow.

Willow leaned closer to the blood painted on the floor. Seeing her friend's obvious struggle to examine the symbols, Buffy leaned in closer with the candle. Willow turned her head sideways, raking her fingers through her hair to pull strands from her face.

"Yeah," Willow said. "Some of them. They're really old. Portal spells."

Spike looked at the symbols and nodded. "Yeah. They're supposed to be. I ain't up on witchcraft much, but I know of a few spells. 'Course, I don't have the magick in me to make it work. But it needs blood of the undead. The question is, can you use this?"

"I think so." Willow knelt and took the candle stub from Buffy. She looked at the candle's length doubtfully. "Should have gotten another candle."

"We'll make do with what we have, Will," Buffy said.

Willow knelt before the bloody symbols Spike had drawn on the stone floor. Turning the candle on its side, she allowed melted wax to drip onto the floor. When she had the wax pool large enough, she pressed the candle stub against the floor. The cooling wax held it fast. The yellow candle flame danced at the tip of the wick.

> *"Spirits of moonlight,*
> *Guardians of the flame and the stone,*
> *Allow me egress*
> *And make this doorway my own."*

Although Willow had been practicing witchcraft for a few years now, watching her perform the craft still creeped Buffy out a little from time to time. Maybe the creepy feeling had something to do with the surroundings, because some of Willow's more potent spells were never cast in the safety of a familiar kitchen or living room. Working on magick in a mausoleum with a

Craulathar demon waiting on the other side of a magick shield kind of inspired creepiness.

Willow pushed her hands out, passing her palms only inches above the fluttering candle flame. For a moment Buffy thought even that slight movement might extinguish the delicate flame. Instead, flame leaped from the wick and coiled like fiery twin serpents against Willow's hands.

> *"Path of darkness,*
> *Become a path of light.*
> *Keep the balance, restore the balance.*
> *All things must serve the day and the night."*

The fiery serpents shot from Willow's palms and slapped into the stone floor where Spike had drawn the symbols. The vampire blood caught fire at once and flames shot up nearly three feet tall.

"Okay," Buffy said. "I'm sure *that* won't be noticed." She glanced toward the dimensional portal and saw the Craulathar demon kneeling in front of a burning pyre on a floating island at the end of the bone bridge.

Either the Craulathar demon hadn't noticed the flames or he didn't care.

The wavering glare of the burning symbols reflected in the violet-and-blue glow of the portal. The surface shimmered, taking on a virulent, greenish hue.

"Buffy," Willow whispered.

Buffy looked at her friend in concern.

"It's ready," Willow said. Strain marked her features. "But you might want to hurry."

"I'm on the case," Buffy said, hefting the ax. "Hold it as long as you can. I'll be right back." She crossed the floor to the portal and shoved her free hand out. Up close, she saw her reflection—dulled and shifting like an image trapped in a soap bubble about to burst. *That is so not a good thought.*

Instead of being repelled as before, though, her hand slid into the portal. The world on the other side of the violet-and-blue two-dimensional gateway was even colder than the mausoleum.

Buffy glanced at Spike. "Coming?"

"If you can do it, I can do it."

Taking a short, quick breath, Buffy stepped toward the portal and entered. A heavy, dewy sensation enveloped her, pressed against her, but didn't hold her back. In the next moment, she stepped onto the bone bridge.

A quiver ran through the bridge. Glancing down, Buffy saw only a long fall that ended up in the swirling depths of a fierce lava pit. The liquid rock and super-heated magma rolled in thick waves like cake batter. Only occasional heated breezes lifted from the lava pit to stave off the chill that leeched into Buffy.

How can lava be so close and still feel so far away? Buffy wondered.

Gargling, growling cries captured her attention. She gazed at the other end of the bone bridge where the Craulathar demon continued to kneel in front of the burning pyre, feeding corpse fuel to the flames.

On the other side of the portal now, Buffy saw the twisting smoke gathering depth and texture above the greedy flames. Something formed there, something, she felt certain, that was not good at all.

The bridge shivered again, but this time the source was behind her. She glanced back and watched Spike step through the portal.

Whatever magick held the bone bridge together didn't like Spike's presence. The bridge continued to shake and shiver, and the waves grew stronger.

"Doesn't like me very much, does it?" Spike asked.

"Go back," Buffy said, turning her attention to the leaping waves of lava below. "We can't cross the bridge like this." She lifted her gaze and glanced back at Willow on the other side of the portal.

Without warning, the candle in front of Willow guttered. The flame quivered like a live thing caught in a trap, then went out.

The portal disappeared.

Xander paced in the hospital waiting room. God, he hated waiting rooms. There was so much *nothing* to do, so much of an absence of *something* to do.

How is it, Xander wondered, *that you can hang with your buddies in places you're not supposed to, even when those places are covered with No Loitering signs, and be perfectly content with nothing to do? And yet, when you're in a place designated as a waiting area and even called a waiting room, that waiting is so uncomfortable?*

He didn't have any answers. In fact, the questions seemed to be growing by the minute. Despite his friendship with Robby, the real thing that had drawn him to the hospital had been the total weirdness of the incident that had landed the guy in the emergency room. "Foolish mortals" definitely carried demonic overtones. Being in the waiting room was kind of like baby-sitting a time bomb. There was no question about him being in the wrong place to avoid Sunnydale's dark side, but whether it was the wrong time, too, remained to be seen.

Other people occupied the waiting room. All of them hung in small groups huddled in worry and fear. Some of them looked like they'd gotten out of bed to come down to the hospital room, while others looked like they hadn't been to bed in days.

Anya reappeared with Stephie McConnell from the hallway. Anya held the other girl's arm with obvious trepidation that Stephie probably would have noticed if she hadn't been worried out of her mind.

"Any word?" Stephie asked.

Xander shook his head. "Not a peep."

"What's taking so long?" Stephie asked.

Xander guided her to a chair in the corner where they had relative privacy. "Maybe they're doing a thorough physical. Something made Robby go all crazy at the theater. He definitely wasn't his normal self, and I think you got them to believe that."

"I feel like I should be doing something more," Stephie said.

"Like what?" Xander asked.

"Helping. Somehow. I don't know how. Robby's going to be in a lot of trouble."

Xander didn't say anything.

Stephie focused on him and squeezed his hand tighter. "Robby is going to be in trouble, isn't he?"

Xander searched for a tactful way to respond.

"Yes," Anya said. "Robby's going to be in a lot of trouble."

Emotion overcame Stephie again. She released her hold on Xander and held her face in her hands. Anya gazed at Xander in triumph, but the look quickly faded when Stephie started sobbing.

"Oh, hey," Anya said, tentatively patting Stephie on the shoulder. "It's going to be all right." She shot Xander a look: *Help me!*

Xander frowned in frustration, showing open-jawed amazement that Anya would even ask. *You're the one who started this!*

Anya glared at him like everything going on was his fault.

"Instead of worrying about what's going to happen," Xander said, "maybe it would be better to do something else. Something possibly productive."

"What?" Stephie looked up at him. Tears streaked her face. "Robby hasn't been himself since he started working on that stupid video game."

"Let's talk about the video-game project again," Xander suggested. "You said Robby found out about the computer game beta testing through E-mail."

Stephie nodded.

"But he didn't know who had sent the E-mail?"

"Right. Robby checked the E-mail address but couldn't trace it back anywhere. He's good at that kind of thing."

"I know," Xander agreed. Other than Willow, Robby was the best Internet hacker that Xander knew. "But the people testing the game picked him up here in Sunnydale."

"Yes."

"And he never knew where they took him?"

"No. Robby always rode in the back of a cargo van. I mean, there were seats and everything. Just no windows."

"Did he ever say how long he rode in the van?"

"No."

"Did he say whether he thought the people that picked him up drove him out of Sunnydale?"

Stephie shrugged, then shook her head. Fresh tears started from her eyes. "I don't know. If he said, I don't remember. Do you think it's important?"

"Probably not," Xander said. Sunnydale experience had taught him that a lot of things were important that most people would miss. Whether or not the computer game testing facility was in Sunnydale seemed like an important thing. Especially when there was so much weirdness attached to Robby, and Sunnydale was situated over the Hellmouth. "Where did they take Robby?"

"They let him out of the van inside some warehouse," Stephie said.

"Didn't Robby think that was weird?" Xander asked.

"The whole video-game scene is weird," Stephie argued. "And there's so much money involved in everything. That's what Robby said when I told him the testing center sounded strange. The guy he talked to said they had to be careful because if information got out before they released the game, someone else could beat them to it and they could lose all that research and development money. Does that make sense?"

Xander didn't hesitate. "Yeah, actually it does. Info on the Net about upcoming games is getting scarcer and scarcer. Game developers are really controlling everything now."

"Everything about this game was so secretive," Stephie said. "I could understand some of it, but I think they went really overboard. I mean, you'd think Robby had joined the CIA or something. Robby really got into the whole double-oh-seven thing."

"That does sound intense," Xander said. He immediately thought of the secret research that the Initiative had been doing beneath Sunnydale. And that was only one of the secret things going on that the Slayer's crew had uncovered. "I know some guys who have done beta-ware testing for different game companies. But nothing that involved this much secrecy."

"This game was supposed to have innovative virtual-reality effects," Stephie said. "Maybe that's why they were being so secretive. Robby told me that when he was playing the game, he had the feeling he really was on another world."

"Something that cutting-edge," Xander said, "you'd think someone would be talking about it, priming the market for ultimate saturation."

"What kind of game was Robby testing?" Anya prompted.

"Some kind of fantasy thing. Robby said the game was an AI-sensitive role-playing game."

"An RPG with artificial intelligence?" Anya asked.

Xander looked at Anya in surprise. Okay, so those talks he sometimes had with her about games and science fiction and comics hadn't all been in vain. She knew that red shirts got killed and role-playing games were called RPGs by dyed-in-the-wool gamers.

"Yes," Stephie said. "I did some RPG gaming with him. My parents totally wigged when they found out I was playing 'Diablo'. Too demonic, you know. Robby said they'd feel the same way about this game if they ever caught me playing it."

"There were demons in the game?" Xander asked. *Okay, that gave my Spidey senses a little jolt.*

Stephie wiped her face and nodded. "Robby got to play as a demon. He thought it was so totally cool."

"What kind of demon?" Anya asked.

"There are different kinds?" Stephie asked.

Anya rolled her eyes. "Of course there are different kinds. Just like there are different kinds of people. Only demons are generally easier to tell apart. You take humans, and they tend to come with two arms, two legs, one head. Now demons on the other hand—"

"*Some* games," Xander said, interrupting because Anya was warming to the subject and he didn't want to go there, "really get into demons. They have all kinds of demons. Did Robby ever tell you what kind of demon he was?"

"If he did, I don't remember."

"If you don't remember what kind of demon Robby played," Anya said, "how are we supposed to help you?"

Stephie looked stricken.

"It's okay," Xander said.

While Stephie was lost in thought, Anya leaned in close to Xander and whispered, "The fact that Robby and his friends were playing demons could be important."

"Got that," Xander assured her.

"Some of the demons in the games you've shown me were modeled on real demons."

"I know." He and Anya had discussed that similarity before. A lot of demons in video games these days were lifted directly from real demons, only the game designers didn't know they were actually seeing the things they thought they only imagined. Most people didn't want to believe in demons, which gave the demon races a kind of strength and invisibility in the real world.

"Maybe you can remember what the demon looked like." Xander hoped that might help. Several games had trademark characters and mythical races. If he could narrow the field down, maybe he could figure out what software design company had recruited Robby for the beta testing. There was still no proof that the computer game was the source of Robby's strange behavior, but checking it out couldn't hurt, and things were certainly looking up in that direction.

"Big," Stephie said confidently. "I remember Robby said he was really big in the game. As the demon, I mean. He had horns."

"How many?" Anya asked.

"How many horns?" Stephie looked like she couldn't believe the question had been asked.

"Yes," Anya replied.

"I don't know. I can't remember, or maybe he never told me. The number of horns is important?"

"Very," Anya replied.

"He had wings," Stephie said. "I remember that. He was learning how to fly in the game."

"Learning to fly?" Xander asked. The fact that wings were involved was good. That anatomical revelation eliminated a lot of demons. "He didn't know how to fly?" He figured that should have been built into the game's AI.

Stephie shook her head. "No. Robby said one of the really cool features in the game was that he actually had to learn so many things. Or relearn them."

"Relearn?" Xander asked.

"Yeah. It was like he already knew how to fly once but had forgotten. Like riding a bicycle again after being away from one for years."

"What did Robby do in the game?"

Stephie shrugged. "The usual stuff. Killed other things, other people, other players."

"With what?" Xander asked. Weapons were important. Sometimes games could be identified by their arsenals of choice.

"Medieval things. Swords. Axes. Spears." Stephie's brow furrowed. "Oh, yeah, Robby said the kind of demon he was could throw fireballs."

"Fireballs?" Anya asked. "You mean fireballs like they just whipped out of thin air?"

"No. Robby said something about having this really cool power to set boulders on fire and throw them at enemies."

"What enemies?" Xander asked. Despite the need to get to the bottom of the mystery of what was going on with Robby, he was intrigued by the game's premise as well.

Stephie shook her head tiredly. She wrapped her arms around herself. "I don't know, Xander. Robby didn't say much more than I've told you. And if he did, I can't remember." She wiped her nose with a sleeve, brushing away fresh tears. "I'm sorry."

"Hey," Xander said, realizing he'd gotten too much into the chase and had forgotten about being a friend. "It's okay. I'm not the best at remembering things either."

"He's not," Anya piped up helpfully. "I could make you a list of all the things he's forgotten."

Xander put an arm around Stephie, feeling her shake. He felt bad for her, and he felt scared for Robby. If Robby's behavior wasn't in some way demon-related—and Xander was willing to bet that it was, virtual reality or no virtual reality—then Robby was in trouble like no other.

"Miss McConnell?"

Xander looked up and saw a middle-aged man with a golfer's tan on the backs of his hands in green scrubs standing in the doorway.

"Yes," Stephie answered, wiping at her face.

"I'm Dr. Haskell," the man said. "We need to talk about Robby."

Xander stared at Dr. Haskell. From the expression on the man's face, the news wasn't good.

Chapter Eight

"**N**one of us knows when we're going to leave this life," Derek Traynor said. He stood in front of his studio audience clad in a somber off-the-rack dark gray suit and a black turtleneck. Handsome and relaxed, he held the attention of the hundred guests at the taping of *Othersyde* with the effortless ease of a natural-born showman. The overhead lighting glinted off his blond curls, the steel hooped earrings in his ears, and the silver ankh necklace. He was in his early twenties, and his smile betrayed a bit of the mischievous rogue. He'd have looked perfectly at home in a highwayman's garb or a sea captain's rolled boots.

The hair color, Tara thought, *is probably the only fake thing about him.* Of course, she hadn't seen him do his show in person yet. She sat in the third row back, in one of the slightly cushioned seats that only barely made sitting comfortable.

Rupert Giles, arms crossed over his chest and posture

erect and very British, sat beside Tara. Giles wore dark slacks and a sports jacket with leather-patched elbows. He took his glasses off and absently cleaned them with his handkerchief.

Tara was glad Giles was there. She'd been excited about seeing Derek Traynor and had hoped that Willow could go with her. But Buffy had asked Willow to accompany her on patrol before Tara had sprung the surprise studio tickets on her. Willow, kind and thoughtful as ever, had suggested Giles as her stand-in. As surprised as she was at getting the studio passes over an Internet site contest, Tara had been positively astonished when Giles had agreed to accompany her.

Othersyde, with all the pop appeal the show carried and the pleasant tour through things spooky and goosebumpy, simply didn't seem like something that would have been Giles's cup of tea. The Watcher certainly stood out in a crowd that was comprised mostly of college students, elderly couples, and middle-aged men and women obviously there for the more arcane interest in the show.

"None of us gets to choose the time of our passing," Derek continued. The concealed microphone picked his voice up easily and amplified it throughout the building. "Therefore, we don't always get to say the things we need to before we leave this world. Sometimes there's a lot to be said by those who have left, and those who have been left. That's why a medium such as myself is so necessary."

Several people in the audience nodded.

Evidently, Tara decided, they were fans of the show. Willow didn't share the same interest that she had in *Othersyde,* but was willing to watch the show with her when they weren't doing homework, working on a new spell, or helping Buffy cope with the loss of her mom or with staking the latest rash of vampires newly risen from their graves.

Derek grinned and held up both hands. "And here I am in Sunnydale, California. I'm sure a lot of people around here have things that need to be said."

The statement drew polite but nervous laughter from the crowd.

"According to the things I've read about and seen on the Internet," Derek said, "Sunnydale deserves its own section in the book of urban legends." He grinned again. "Hopefully tonight we won't be writing any new legends."

Giles sat quietly and listened.

Tara didn't know if the Watcher was bored or lost in his own thoughts. Nervous, wishing she could just mind her own business but groaning inwardly because she felt so responsible for trapping Giles there, she leaned over and whispered, "I'm sorry."

Giles looked at her. "Whatever for?"

"For Willow asking you to come along in her place tonight," Tara said. "If you want, you can probably slip out during one of the intermissions."

Giles waved the offer away. "Truthfully, the idea of gathering for a brief evening of sleight-of-hand or mentalist tricks is attractive. Relaxing, you might say."

"*Othersyde* isn't all trickery," Tara said. "In fact, there's a good possibility that none of the show is faked."

Giles raised his eyebrows and nodded, but his doubt was evident to anyone that knew him. The Watcher might still look like the stodgy British librarian he'd once been at Sunnydale High, but those who knew him recognized his moods easily.

"Have you heard of Derek Traynor before?" Tara asked.

"No," Giles said. "As you know, I prefer a dusty tome to the idiot box."

Derek approached the crowd. "I've been a medium

all my life. When I was little and my mom used to leave me at home in the apartment we had in Brooklyn while she worked, my grandmother used to come watch me." He shrugged. "Probably not a weird story when you hear it like that. The thing was, Nana Burke had passed three years before I was born."

The story was an old one to anyone that watched the show, but Tara saw a few surprised looks on the faces of some of the people in the audience. Evidently not everyone there was a fan of the show. One of the cameramen panned over the crowd, getting their reactions. Television monitors mounted on either side of the stage area showed the camera views. One camera stayed focused on Derek while the other panned the crowd.

"He says he was raised by his grandmother's ghost?" Giles asked.

"Yeah," Tara said. Having grown up with magick herself, she could appreciate his paranormal childhood.

"Imagine my mother's surprise," Derek went on, smiling broadly, "when I started telling her some of the stories my grandmother told me about my mom's childhood. It sure preempted the parental speeches in my house, I tell you."

Polite laughter rumbled through the studio.

"My mom would say, 'How many times have I told you not to do that, young man?' I'd tell her, 'Not as many times as Nana Burke told *you* about it, Ma.' Needless to say, my mom wasn't very happy about the situation. Nana Burke had come to me because I had what she called the gift. I'm Irish. Gaelic, actually. Nana Burke was *very* precise about that."

More laughter followed.

"Nana Burke had a smidgen of the gift, herself." Derek held his thumb and forefinger a fraction of an inch apart. "She used to tell fortunes, make charms, stuff like that. But she told me she'd never met anyone with as much of the gift as I had."

The second camera focused on an elderly man in the audience who showed doubt on his craggy features.

"You know," Giles whispered to Tara, "if this man really does have the kind of power that he says he has, this is probably the worst place for him to use it."

"I know," Tara said. "That was part of what excited me about coming here." *And the fact that Derek often comes and sits with his audience.* She hoped to meet him, get an idea of how his power worked so that maybe she could add to her own knowledge.

"Do you know how he does this?" Giles asked.

"You mean, has he had any training?" Tara replied.

"Yes."

"No. I've read both his books about his experiences. He says he's kind of like a tuning fork. When he gets ready to receive messages, they kind of come to him. Some of those who have passed over have haunted him. Bugged him until he found whomever he was supposed to get in touch with and gave them the message."

"Fascinating."

"That's how he got the television show," Tara went on. "He was working as a waiter in a Manhattan restaurant and met Susan Kane, the show's producer, and gave her a message from her dead father."

"And Ms. Kane believed the message was really from her father?" Giles asked.

"Not at first. But her father wouldn't leave Derek alone. Six months later, Derek followed Susan Kane to Hollywood, got past her security guards and her agent and staff by proving himself, and convinced her the message really was from her father."

"How did he prove himself?"

"The father did it," Tara replied. "He recruited other

individuals that had passed over and put them in touch with Derek. As he met each person, he already had a story to tell them about a family member that had passed."

Giles looked mildly cynical. "Derek could have researched those people."

Tara nodded. "He could have. But they bought into it."

Giles returned his attention to the young host.

"Derek Traynor has a lot of fans," Tara said, "but there are a lot of detractors, too. People that think he's a fake. That's why security is so tight on the set and guests are screened."

Giles started to say something, then didn't.

"I know," Tara said, letting him know she wasn't as starstruck as he might be thinking. "Invitation-only guest lists provide a lot of opportunity to do background checks."

"That did cross my mind," Giles said.

Tara glanced back at Derek. "I think he's for real. For what that's worth."

"I see."

Derek Traynor spoke to the crowd, still charming and polite. "Doing the show in Sunnydale is a surprise," he said. "You can ask Susan Kane, my producer." He gestured to the studio control room.

On the other side of the darkened glass amid a myriad of equipment lights that resembled fireflies, a woman with frosted hair raised her hand and waved.

"We were supposed to be in Boulder, Colorado," Derek said. "Boy, are the people in Boulder probably mad this week." He mugged for the camera. "But don't worry, Boulder, I'll be there soon."

The crowd laughed, and Tara couldn't help joining in. His showmanship and winning attitude were infectious.

Derek folded his hands before him and spoke directly into the camera. "Strange as it may sound, I got up one morning about a week ago and felt as though I had to be here." He pointed at the stage he stood on. "In Sunnydale. Doing this show." He shrugged. "Don't ask me why. I don't know. Yet." He grinned daringly. "But I will."

The crowd applauded.

"He's certainly convinced of his own worth," Giles said.

Derek pressed his palms together, closed his eyes, and launched into a reading. When he opened his eyes again, he turned to the right and faced the people in the gallery there. "I'm over here somewhere."

The people seated there looked at Derek, then at each other.

"He doesn't know who he's searching for?" Giles whispered.

"No," Tara answered, saddened a little that Derek hadn't come to her. She'd been hoping that her mother might contact the medium for her. There were so many questions she would have liked to ask her mother about her family if she got the chance. "Derek gets a general idea, but he has to figure out who has contacted him and what they want."

"Interesting," Giles said.

Derek walked toward the section of the audience that he'd picked out. "I'm seeing initials. An *M* and a *J*. First name Marta, Martha. Something like that. Can someone help me out?"

An elderly woman with thick glasses and gray hair lifted a hand. "My aunt's name was Margo."

Derek thought for a moment, then nodded. "Maybe. Your aunt has passed?"

"Yes. She—"

"Wait." Derek held a hand out. "Let me do this without help. To make sure we're both talking about the same person."

The woman nodded.

A small buzz passed through Tara and she took a short, quick breath. Part of the buzz was the adrenaline from watching Derek actually do the show, but part of the effect seemed to come from whatever power he used to connect to the other side.

Giles looked at her. "Is something wrong?"

"I don't know," Tara answered. "I felt . . . something."

Renewed interest filled the Watcher's face. He sat a little straighter.

"Your aunt is showing me something about her chest, and I get the feeling that there was some kind of medical problem. Cancer or a heart attack. Does that sound right?"

The woman knotted her fists and pressed them to her mouth. Tears filled her eyes.

Tara's eyes felt a little misty too. She could only guess at how the woman must be feeling. Sitting in her dorm or down in the community room at college watching the show had conveyed some of the emotions, but being in the middle of them was even stronger.

"Asthma," the woman gasped. "Aunt Margo died of an asthma attack."

"You were close to your aunt," Derek said. "She's showing me that."

"Yes," the woman croaked.

Derek looked a little troubled. "She's trying to tell me about some kind of pet you had. But it wasn't an ordinary pet."

The woman shook her head and smiled through her tears.

"Pepe?" Derek asked. "Some kind of dog?" He interrupted himself. "No, that's not right. The pet wasn't a dog. At least, it wasn't a living dog." A surprised look filled his face. "The dog was a *sock*? Is that right?"

The woman nodded and laughed. "Pepe was a sock

puppy. My aunt raised me after my mother died. We lived in an apartment when I was a little girl. I wanted a puppy, but we couldn't have one in the apartment. So Aunt Margo sewed me a sock puppy that I named Pepe. I loved that puppet, but I was embarrassed, too. I never told anybody about it. That always bothered my aunt, and she used to tease me about it."

"Well," Derek said, "your aunt's getting her revenge today, because you just told a national audience."

The crowd laughed, but it was all good-natured. The woman looked embarrassed but thankful at the same time.

"Your aunt wants you to know that she loves you," Derek said, "and that she thinks about you all the time."

"Thank you," the woman said.

Derek placed his hands together again and concentrated. An almost uncomfortably long period passed, longer than Tara had ever seen on an *Othersyde* television show before. Then an electric jolt shot through her just as Derek Traynor was hammered to the ground by an invisible blow.

Six men dressed in black security T-shirts rushed onto the stage from behind the cameras. They formed a circle around Derek and gazed at the crowd suspiciously.

Men and women seated in the crowd rose to their feet. Excited voices filled the air.

"Derek!" Susan Kane stood in the doorway to the stage control room. "Derek!"

The security men helped Derek to his feet. Instead of the confidence he usually exuded, the show's host looked shocked and in agony. He pushed the security people away from him.

"I'm okay," Derek said. "Give me a minute."

"Go to commercial," Susan Kane said.

"No," Derek said loudly. "No commercial. Stay on me. This is important." He looked wildly around the crowd.

"Is this normal for his shows?" Giles asked.

"No," Tara said, feeling something hovering around her. "I've never seen this before."

Giles looked at her with concern. "Are you all right?"

"I just . . . just feel really weird all of a sudden," Tara answered.

The security people grudgingly gave way around Derek Traynor, but they still continued to stare at the crowd with suspicion, as if someone there had been responsible for what had happened to him.

"Someone here," Derek said, "knows Donny Williford." He scanned the crowd, spinning quickly and almost losing his balance. "Who is it?"

No one said anything.

"Donny Williford," Derek repeated. "Someone here knows him. His girlfriend is here." He squeezed his eyes shut, then opened them again. "Amy. Amy, you're here. Donny says that you're here."

"NO!" a young woman shouted. She wore red capri pants and bright yellow midriff shirt that showed her navel ring. Her blond hair was cut in a short shag.

Derek turned to the woman. "You're Amy?"

"You're not talking to Donny!" Amy said. She pressed her hands against her face and shivered hysterically. "Donny's not dead! He's at home! He's *not* dead! Tell them you're not talking to my Donny!"

"Hey," Xander said, putting as much encouragement in his voice as he could while he spoke to Stephie. "Everything's going to be all right. You just heard the doc say so."

Stephie sat in one of the chairs in the waiting room. Her hands were closed into fists and crossed over her lap. She was leaning forward and rocking slightly, as if she might be sick at any moment.

"Actually," Anya said, "the doctor didn't say everything was going to be all right. He said he didn't know what made Robby fall into a coma."

Xander shot Anya a warning glance. *Tact. Really got to work on tact.*

Stephie looked up at Xander. "What if Robby doesn't wake up?"

Xander patted her on the shoulder, knowing the gesture wouldn't do any good but not knowing what else he was supposed to do. "He will. Robby's a fighter."

"What will they do with him?" Anya asked. "The police, I mean. If Robby doesn't wake up, will they just put him in jail anyway for attacking those people?"

Xander knew Anya was honestly curious about the situation, but the timing was so incredibly bad he couldn't believe she'd asked.

"They won't do that to Robby, will they?" Stephie asked.

"No," Xander said, trying to sound confident. "We'll get Robby a good attorney. Everything will be okay."

"But if he doesn't wake up, he's not going to be able to tell anybody why he attacked those people in the theater," Stephie said. "There has to be a reason. Robby wouldn't just do something like that."

"I'm sure there's a reason," Xander responded.

"What?" Anya asked.

Holding his frustration in check with effort that would have taxed a Vulcan, Xander said, "Why don't you get us some coffee? Looks like we're going to be here for a while." He reached into his pocket for money.

"No," Anya said. "I'll stay here with Stephie. She might need someone to talk to."

"Anya—"

"Girl stuff," Anya said, like she was a master of girl conversational skills.

"I'd love coffee, Xander," Stephie said. "There's a vending machine down by the nurses' station. I've been here before."

Xander still hesitated, hating the thoughts that ran through his head about Anya staying with Stephie.

"Go," Anya directed. "I want coffee too."

"Right," Xander said. Getting out of the waiting room for a few minutes suddenly sounded great. He was basically useless there playing Support Guy, which wasn't his best role. His head was full of worries about Robby as well. While Xander had been attending Sunnydale High he'd lost a number of acquaintances, and he still lived a life that guaranteed more such losses. "You're sure you'll be okay here?"

"We'll be fine," Anya replied.

Stephie nodded.

Xander turned and left, making his way through the waiting room's double doors and into the hallway beyond. The nurses' station was only a short distance down the hall on the right and on the rear of a four-way intersection. A young nurse in maroon scrubs talked on the phone. Across the hallway from the nurses' station, a sign on the wall announced the presence of a vending machine area.

Digging in his pockets for change, Xander started for the vending-machine room. He caught sight of a man dressed in an electric-blue suit approaching the nurses' station.

Tall and thin, his cheeks sunken and his ebony skin slightly ash-colored, the man would have drawn attention anywhere. He had a flowing mane of white-as-cotton hair that touched his shoulders, but baldness had chased his hair back in a horseshoe pattern from his forehead.

The nurse looked up at the man, cradling the phone receiver on her shoulder. "Can I help you?"

"Robert Healdton," the man said in a papery, dry voice.

"Is he a patient here?" the nurse asked.

"Yes."

Xander paused at the doorway, wedging himself in the corner. The guy didn't look like anyone Robby would know.

The nurse checked the charts on the computer. "I'm sorry. Robert Healdton has been admitted to the ICU. Only family members can see him."

The man lifted his right hand and traced a pattern in the air. Brief flames seemed to trail his fingers for just a heartbeat. "Where can I find Robert Healdton?"

The nurse pointed. "The Intensive Care Unit. It's that way. Just follow the orange stripe on the floor out in the intersection."

"Of course." The man traced another symbol. "Forget that I was here. Return to your work."

The nurse obediently looked away and resumed her phone conversation.

Moving with smooth grace, the tall man in the electric-blue suit walked away from the nurse's station. He crossed the intersection and pushed through the double doors leading to ICU.

Weirdo, Xander thought. *He just used a Jedi mind trick on the nurse, and that can't be of the good.* He hesitated only a moment, then followed. The nurse appeared to still be under the effects of whatever the man in the electric-blue suit had done to her, because she never noticed Xander. A sinking feeling grew inside Xander's stomach.

Chapter Nine

Panic dug icy claws into Willow's skin and tried to yank it from her flesh. She knelt on the stone floor in front of the dimensional portal that Buffy and Spike had walked through only a moment ago. The burning pyre to her right blazed and threw orange embers into the air that died before they reached the stone ceiling hidden in the shadows above.

The cavern turned colder.

At first Willow thought the change in temperature was only her imagination, but the flickering fire reflected from icy patches on the walls around her. The cavern *was* getting colder. Maybe the chill was the result of the power being used, but there was also the possibility that the chill was part of a protective spell that was only now starting to act.

Anxiously, Willow concentrated on the dimensional portal. She could feel that her connection to the portal was slipping. Glancing down, she saw that frost had started to cover the mystic symbols Spike had drawn on the cavern floor in his blood.

Something was trying to cut her link to the portal. As she realized that, another layer of frost added to the ones already there and obscured the symbols a little more.

Carefully Willow chanted, turning part of her attention away from the portal, even though she knew it was dangerous. If she lost her connection to the portal, she was going to lose Buffy and Spike as well.

The milky translucence covering the portal shifted. For a moment she spotted Buffy and Spike on the bone bridge leading to the island where the Craulathar demon was. The bridge trembled like a dog shaking off water.

"Buffy!" Willow called. She couldn't tell if Buffy or Spike heard her because another chill flooded the cavern, turning it even colder, and fog blurred her view. When she breathed out, Willow saw her breath in a long, gray vapor trail. She looked down at the mystic symbols. A new layer of frost crept over them, reducing them to dim images she could barely see by the light of the candle. "No!"

If the symbols completely covered over, she knew she would lose Buffy and Spike. Only the protection she offered through her spell kept them safe in the demon dimension.

Willow cupped a hand and made a pulling motion toward the burning pyre. Human bones burned atop the fire, glowing red and orange like coals. As she watched, some of the bones disintegrated, leaving less fuel for the fire.

Time was running out.

She spoke in a trembling voice, her teeth chattering from the cold.

"Spirits of fire, hear my call.
You have the power to destroy and to mend.
In you is birth, and in you is death.
I welcome you as my friend."

Power surged through Willow as she felt her heart beating fiercely in her chest from the use of her craft as well as from her fear about her friend.

Obediently a fiery serpent no more than a foot long leaped free of the burning pyre. Comprised solely of flame, the serpent fought her control. If she'd summoned it from a friendly fire, she would have had more control over the tiny elemental force, but if she'd drawn flame from the candle she was certain the candle would have extinguished.

The fiery serpent twisted and coiled in rebellion, rising up like a hooded cobra.

"No," Willow said. "You're mine. I made you. You will do what I say." She concentrated on the tiny elemental. The creature was inanimate, possessing no life of its own, but it fought her because it had been dragged from the pyre that had been crafted from evil, while Willow's intentions were good.

Hissing, the fiery serpent spat flaming raindrops toward Willow. Thankfully the fire fell to the ground inches short of her.

"Move," Willow ordered. She felt the heat of the fiery serpent on her face and hands. The heat was much hotter than she'd believed possible. "Those are my friends that we're going to save."

Reluctant, the fiery snake elemental lowered its hooded head to the stone floor and writhed over to the frost-covered symbols. The frost hissed and burned, lifting from the stone surface in a whirling miasma of blue-gray smoke.

However, the heat also dried out the symbols. Horrified, Willow watched as the blood of one of the symbols blackened and started to flake.

"No!" Willow shouted. If the symbols were destroyed, her link to Buffy and Spike would be destroyed. "Stop!"

But the fiery snake continued on a path of destruction, moving faster now, as though the elemental knew its actions caused Willow distress. The serpent seemed to almost preen.

Part of one of the symbols flaked away, the dried bits of blood rising in glowing embers in the smoke that coiled toward the stone ceiling high above.

"No!" Willow shouted. She reached for the elemental.

Coiling instantly, the fiery serpent struck at her.

Heat burned across the backs of Willow's fingers and brought blazing pain. She drew her hand back, seeing the tiny blisters that had already formed on her fingers.

The serpent turned from her and continued the assault on the frost and the symbols.

Willow gestured again, telling herself that she knew evil things couldn't be used in a spell. Even if the spell was intended for good things, the smallest act of evil or selfishness could taint the spell. She'd had no business trying to use the flames from the pyre.

She gestured again, using a simpler spell that she and Tara had been working on.

A two-foot-tall tornado formed in the air above the fiery serpent. The tornado's eye danced across the stone floor, drawing in the smoke left by the evaporating frost and the burning blood. In the next moment, the tornado attacked the fiery serpent, drawing the elemental into the funnel. The fiery serpent whirled like it had been trapped in a blender. If the situation hadn't been so serious, the scene might have been funny.

Whipped around inside the tornado, the fire elemental didn't last long. The flames burned brightly for an instant, then winked out. Only a thick puff of black smoke belched from the top of the tornado.

As the wind force died away, Willow glanced back at the floor. One of the symbols had been nearly eradicated by the fire. Only a few flecks of blackened blood stained the floor. Even if Willow had more vampire blood to work with, she doubted she could reconstruct the symbol.

Then the frost started to pebble up on the floor again, growing thicker, blotting out more of the symbols Spike had drawn.

"No," Willow said fiercely, leaning forward and scraping at the creeping frost with her hands. Blisters on her burned fingers burst, but she ignored the pain. The candle guttered, dimming for a moment. Coldness numbed her fingers, taking away some of the pain. For a moment she felt good about that. Then she noticed that the frost had started sticking to her flesh.

Hypnotized and terrified, Willow watched helplessly as the frost crept up her fingers and started coating her hands. "Buffy?" She glanced at the portal but couldn't see through the fog. Coldness crept up her arms, followed by the thin layer of frost.

Something scraped the stone floor behind Willow, and she had the distinct impression she wasn't alone anymore.

"Donny's not dead!"

Tara watched as the young woman, Amy, tried to step from the audience toward Derek Traynor.

"Donny's not dead!" Amy shouted again. "He's over at his friend's house!"

Derek reeled on his feet, obviously in a lot of distress. "Donny's not there, Amy." His voice no longer held jocularity or the calm sincerity. Now he sounded disturbed and amazed. He stared at the young woman as she approached him, but Tara felt certain the television medium wasn't seeing her.

Two of the security guards stepped in front of Amy, blocking her path to Derek. "Sorry," one of the guards said, holding his hands up. "You gotta stay back."

"Make him stop," Amy demanded. She dug in her purse frantically. "Make him stop saying that about Donny now. This isn't funny."

"Donny's somewhere else," Derek said. "He's trapped. He wants to get back to you, Amy, but he can't. Something—*someone*—is stopping him."

"Liar!" Amy screamed. She took a cell phone from her shoulder bag. Hands shaking, she punched in a number.

"Derek," Susan Kane, the show's producer, called from the open door of the studio control room. "Are you all right?"

"I'm fine, Susan," Derek replied. "But I've never . . . I've never seen anything like this."

Welcome to the Hellmouth, Tara thought.

"What is it?" Susan Kane asked. "What do you see?"

Amy held the cell phone to her ear. She crossed her other arm over her body defiantly, but the effect was lost by the tears and the trembling.

Tara could almost hear the phone ringing as the call went unanswered at the other end. She was certain everyone in the studio audience could.

"Donny's with someone," Derek said hoarsely. "He's with a friend. They're not . . . they're not themselves. They're changed. Different somehow. They're under attack."

Robby Healdton stood joyously in the demonic form provided by the total immersion virtual reality system he was wired into. If he hadn't known better, hadn't realized all the advances technology was capable of, he might have believed he really was in another world and in the middle of a war between demon races.

He stared down into the craggy valley where the Dorinogs, the race of demons he was currently a member of, battled the Kaliths, a rival demon race. They fought for control of the world they lived on, a place called Ollindark.

Harsh broken land lay in all directions, always a ragged tumble of jagged, crusty rock, shifting yellow alkaline sand that cut like powdered glass, and incendiary boulders. Oh, yeah—and the frequent pools of turquoise acid that could leech the flesh from bones in seconds. Robby had seen that happen a number of times. No vegetation grew on Ollindark. Everything that lived on the world was a carnivore. That fact suited Robby just fine. Shooters and twitch games were his specialty, and combined with a multiplayer RPG format, the game he was currently play-testing totally rocked.

A fat blue sun hung in a green sky that got steadily greener as it neared the horizon. Sunsets and sunrises tended to look like festering wounds on the horizons, and nights were as black as a George Lucas villain's heart. Red and orange mountains rose up from the yellow land unexpectedly, as if shoved through from the dying core of the world.

"Searfire!" Robby shouted, warning the rest of his troops as the threat neared.

A *searfire* was what he and some of the other gamers had named the unpredictable gusts of wind that tore across the world, lifting a small cloud of sand from the harsh terrain. The whirling yellow blitzkrieg of agony, as Robby liked to think of the phenomena, whipped toward him.

"Lock down! Lock down!" Robby ordered. Curling his long, prehensile toes, he drove his hard talons down into the barren rock, hooking in solidly. As Dorinogs, all of the players had the ability to dig in with their hind talons as he had.

The *searfire* grew closer and larger, standing nearly twenty feet tall now—twice as tall as Robby in his new body—and was nearly sixty feet long. The familiar growl of the sand cutting through air filled his ears, cutting off all other sounds.

Robby stretched out his great, leathery wings. They were a darker purple than the rest of his body and were nearly fifteen feet long. Still, for all their length, the wings folded up compactly on his back when he wasn't using them, and whatever they weighed, they were nothing to him. He wrapped himself in the wings in his hunkered position, creating a protective dome of leathery flesh that was as hard as chain mail.

In the darkness, he waited. The *searfire* came along too quickly for his liking. That was one of the minor faults he saw about the game's artificial intelligence. The AI controlled the wandering monsters' encounters, but there was plenty of patrolling and scouting of the enemy Kalinths to keep Robby and his fellow gamers occupied.

Most of all, there were the bones to find that were the objective of the game quest. Torqualmar's bones, Dredfahl called them. Dredfahl was the game's designer, and that was the only name that he'd given.

Robby knew the Dredfahl name was an alias. The designer was probably really a guy named Mark or Eric or Jerry. Just an ordinary guy with a chance to build the first truly interactive on-line world.

He hoped that the other players stayed put, hoped that the strict admonishment Dredfahl had given them would hold them in place. In a total immersion game like this, Robby and the other gamers found it hard not to test the game AI. In some of the other video games on the market, the death effects had been cool, and sometimes he'd let his character die just to watch the effect.

Dredfahl had warned them all during the briefing on the game that anyone who intentionally got killed wouldn't be allowed back into the game. Likewise, anyone who got slain during the current campaign also wouldn't be allowed back in until the maiden campaign was finished.

He felt the needle pricking of the *searfire* battering him, but none of the razor-edged sand penetrated his wings. Gradually the howling wind died away. Cautiously, because *searfire* swirls didn't always come alone, Robby parted his wings and gazed out.

Outside the safe embrace of his wings, nothing moved. Robby furled his wings, pulling them in close and tight against his back now. Early sessions within the VR simulation had taught him how to use his new body.

"Come on, you gold-brickin' grunts!" Robby yelled to the rest of his team. He did his best to sound like Nick Fury, one of his favorite comic-book characters. All he needed, he felt, was a cigar stub to chew on and an eye patch. "It's a good day to go kill sumpin'!"

He surged to his feet, grabbing one of the nearby boulders in one huge, three-fingered hand. Glancing over his shoulder, he saw that the other nine men on his team were getting to their feet as well.

The other players inhabited bodies that were ten-foot-tall Dorinogs as well. With wings, three-fingered hands, and three-toed feet with razor-sharp talons, the others looked like Robby. The purple hue of their skins varied a little, but not much. All of them had huge, round heads, squarely set on broad shoulders, and all of them were primarily upper bodies balanced over stumpy, muscular legs.

Their faces consisted of two small slits for nostrils, a wide slash filled with fangs for a mouth, sleek bald heads, and chins as wide as their foreheads.

"Here they come," one of the players yelled.

Robby turned, hoisting the primitive club he'd fashioned from one of the straight rock formations. The club was seven feet long and a foot thick at its widest end.

But the greatest weapon in his arsenal was his ability to transform some of the boulders found throughout the hellish landscape into fireballs. He recognized the boulders were incendiary through the large crystalline content they had that made them gleam in the sun, but also through some natural affinity for the boulders.

He concentrated on the boulder he held, squeezed it in his hand, and shoved power into it. The boulder burst into flaming slag.

The Kalinths thundered up the side of the valley. They stood half again as tall as the Dorinogs and vaguely resembled buffalo. They stood on four legs thick as tree trunks and ending in thick, callused pads, and they had human-shaped torsos and six thin arms that made them look something like a praying mantis. Wedge-shaped heads five feet long and tapered at both ends could be used as spears at the front and back and as blunt weapons if striking from the side. Hard chitin covered the Kalinths. They could also shoot force beams from their third eye that could bruise, break bone, and sometimes kill outright.

"Strike!" Robby roared as the Kalinths came toward them. "Now!" He effortlessly threw the flaming mass that had been the boulder, watching in gleeful satisfaction as the missile struck one of the lead Kalinths on the head and shoulders.

Slammed by the mass of burning rock, the Kalinth didn't even have a chance to scream in pain. The Kalinth tumbled end over end, rolling back down the hillside.

The Kalinths outnumbered Robby's team three to one, even counting the NPCs, or non-player characters, the computer game provided. The live-action gamers were only about twenty-five percent of the Dorinog army. The NPCs acted like real demons and didn't have much to do with the gamers, but the NPCs followed orders—if they were explained clearly enough and the NPCs were reminded regularly. One of the things Robby intended to suggest was making the NPCs' AI a little smarter.

Confident of the coming success, the Kalinths closed in, never knowing they were playing into Robby's plans. As a devout gamer, starting out with board games—going on to pen and paper RPGs, and moving into computer and platform gaming—Robby knew all about scheming and planning. He'd studied military operations from Sun Tzu's *The Art of War* to current small-unit Special Forces strategies.

"They're going to overrun us, Robby!" one of the players yelled.

"Hold that line, Chris!" Robby bellowed. "Don't you move! We have to keep them in a group!" He found another boulder, lit it up, and threw it at a Kalinth that raked the mountainside with a force beam from his third eye.

The green force beam caught one of the players in the chest and blasted him backward. The player screamed in pain as he tumbled head over heels.

Man, Robby thought, *you gotta love the VR feedback.* The whole encounter seemed so real. Laughter erupted from his lips before he knew it. The whole experience was just so . . . so *awesome.* There really was no other word for it.

Then the flaming boulder he'd flung caught the Kalinth in the side, bowling the creature over in a tangle of waving limbs.

One of the Dorinog players attempted to leap from the ground and fly away to avoid the coming Kalinth assault. *Stupid move,* Robby thought an instant before a green eye beam blasted the fleeing Dorinog. The demon's wings shredded like confetti, and broken bones showed through the dark purple flesh.

Robby didn't even see the winged demon fall because that was when the first wave of Kalinths rolled over him. He swung the club with both hands, shattering the thick legs of the Kalinth that bore down on him. The creature screamed, but his hands reached for Robby. Shoving the Kalinth's hands away, Robby swung the stone club again, crunching his opponent's skull. All three of the Kalinth's eyes dimmed.

"Die, Dorinog scum!" another Kalinth yelled as he hurled a spear at Robby.

Robby leaped to one side, slamming into another Kalinth that barreled through the position the players were trying in vain to hold on the mountainside. Reaching up instinctively, Robby grabbed the arm of the Kalinth he bumped into, ran three steps, and vaulted up onto the creature's back.

Reversing the stone club while riding his opponent, Robby slammed the small end through the Kalinth's back. There'd been no information on where a Kalinth's heart might be, but the blow seemed to do the trick. The running Kalinth stumbled, falling down as he died.

Gathering himself, grateful for having the Dorinog's short legs, Robby pushed down with one hand and levered himself to his feet on the Kalinth's back. Robby leaped from the dead Kalinth an instant before the creature crashed into the ground.

Standing for just a moment, surveying the destruction and death that he had planned, covered in the blood of his enemies, Robby felt elated. *Man, this game is good. When it comes out, it's going to sell millions.* He was determined to make his play-testing report the best that he could. There were going to be sequels to the game, an expansion kit soon, and maybe he could wow whoever was designing the game into letting him help. He planned on delivering a paper on suggested tweaks and ways to cut down on the real-time action.

The Kalinths had no problem overwhelming the Dorinog position. That was exactly as Robby had planned. The Kalinths had taken casualties too. They wouldn't easily give up the pursuit.

Time to close the trap, Robby thought. He dropped his club at his side for a moment, cupped his hands around his mouth, and yelled, "Retreat! Retreat! Back up the mountain!"

Like a well-drilled special ops team, the players turned and fled. Despite their shorter stature and stubby legs, the Dorinogs could cover ground more quickly than the Kalinths. But only over short distances. In the long run, the Kalinths would run them all aground.

Robby grabbed his club and a boulder and fled up the mountain with the Dorinog pack. The ground shivered and shook beneath him as the Kalinths regrouped and pursued. Robby glanced over his shoulder and couldn't help grinning. Okay, everything was working so far.

The Kalinths were nearly on their heels when they reached the mountain ridge. Yellow dust glimmered green in the blue sunlight, swelling and shifting like rolling fog.

Robby topped the ridge and threw himself down. The other side of the mountain was nearly sheer, covered with a thin layer of sandy crust that made for treacherous footing. Even with the Dorinog's superhuman balance and agility, Robby couldn't keep his footing. He slipped and fell, skidding along the mountainside at least fifty yards, narrowly avoiding the stone stakes that he and the other players had put into place. He reached out and caught one of the stakes, then pulled himself to his feet.

The Kalinths came on across the mountaintop, too quick and too heavy to stop suddenly. Several Dorinog players lost their footing and fell, but others were crushed or injured by the Kalinths that tumbled down the ridge.

At the end of the long fall, the stone spikes stood upright. The spikes pierced even the Kalinths' chitinous skins easily. Bright red blood, holding a purple cast under the blue sun, spilled across the yellow sand. Only a few Kalinths stopped short along the mountain ridge, and even a few of them tumbled down after other demons slammed into them from behind.

Robby dropped the boulder he'd managed to hang on to, then lifted his fingers to his mouth. Neither a Dorinog's blunt fingers nor crude mouth had been intended for the purpose that he used them for, and it had taken hours to get the effect he wanted. He whistled, and the shrill sound filled the mountainside.

More Dorinogs, all of them live-action players—bringing the numbers up to ten or twelve dozen, the most that Robby had ever seen—erupted from hiding along the mountain ridge behind the Kalinths. They blasted the Kalinths with fireballs and stone spears, driving them over the mountain or killing them where they stood.

Absolute and total carnage prevailed, and Robby Healdton loved every minute. *This game so totally rocks!*

Chapter Ten

Now that I think about it, Xander told himself as he stood outside Robby Healdton's room in the Intensive Care Unit at the hospital, *this is so really not a good idea.* Heart hammering, he peered around the corner at the cadaverous man in the electric-blue suit standing at the foot of Robby's bed.

The ICU room was dark except for the orange, green, and blue lights of the various monitors hooked to Robby. The room was also silent, except for the chirping peeps of the equipment.

The cadaverous man's snow-white hair picked up color from the machines monitoring Robby. He spoke again in the coarse whisper he'd used on the woman at the nurses' station.

"Manik," the cadaverous man whispered. "Wake."

He's in a coma, buddy, Xander thought. *And why would you think he's some guy named Manik?*

Robby slept in the middle of the hospital bed. Round patches of adhesive attached sensors to his head and chest. Restraining straps bound his arms and legs to the bed rails.

Xander wondered why the Sunnydale police department hadn't left an officer to watch over Robby. He knew from past visits to the hospital that they sometimes did that with drunk drivers or victims that survived drug overdoses or suicide attempts.

A muted walkie-talkie bleated, breaking into the chirps and hums of the hospital equipment. Following the source of the unexpected noise, Xander slid a little farther around the doorframe and peered into the left corner on the opposite side of the hospital room.

A Sunnydale police officer sat in a chair in the corner. A reading light played over one shoulder, falling onto the *Guns & Ammo* magazine lying on the carpeted floor at his feet. The police officer leaned heavily against the nearby wall. His eyes were wide open and didn't see a thing.

Xander didn't know if the police officer was alive or dead. But Xander was certain he knew who was responsible.

"Manik," the cadaverous man said with a little more force. He inscribed a sign in the air that glimmered for just a moment. "Wake, or I'll peel the flesh from your bones in this world and the other."

Okay, Xander thought grimly, *this is the part where all smart heroes bug out and go find help. Even Lassie knew when to go get help for Timmy.* Before he could move, though, Robby opened his eyes and looked at the cadaverous man standing at the foot of his bed.

"Dredfahl?" Robby croaked. "Master?"

The old man waved Robby to silence. "Shut up, Manik. You'll not win me over with any attempts at false subservience now."

"But, Master—"

"No," Dredfahl said. "You had orders. Once we had this boy's body, you knew where you were supposed to go."

Although every nerve in him screamed to leave, to go find Buffy or Giles, Xander remained frozen at the doorway. Robby was his friend, and by the time Xander got back with help, he was sure something bad would have happened to Robby.

"If this boy were not so valuable on the other side," Dredfahl continued, "I'd kill you now. But twinning him with another would take more time than I want to give. There are other things I must do if Torqualmar is to be returned to this world."

"Yes, Master. I apologize. My only defense is that I was unprepared for the experiences this body has brought me. It is so unlike anything I've been used to."

"You have no defense." Dredfahl stood ramrod stiff despite his infirmity. "You were chosen as one of the elite, Manik, and because you knew to disobey me was to forfeit your life."

"Yes, Master."

"This body you now inhabit is useful to me, but it is not as strong as your true form."

"I know that now, Master." Robby looked glum and ashamed. "There were so few humans, and yet they took me." Then a wicked smile curved his mouth. "But you should have seen them, Master. You should have seen the way they scattered and ran before me. Had I been in my true form, I promise you there would have been a blood-letting. I don't know if I even managed to kill any of them tonight."

"You will get your chance," Dredfahl promised. "There will be other humans to kill before all of Torqualmar's bones are recovered."

"Good," Robby said. "They chased us from this world, and made our people live in that grave pit with only the Kalinth to destroy for thousands of years."

"Those times are almost over." Dredfahl gestured at the bed. The restraining straps pulled free of Robby's arms and legs. "Once Torqualmar is in this world again, more gateways will be open to us."

"Then there will be a bloodletting." Robby pushed himself out of the bed and stood in the flimsy hospital gown. He pulled the sensors from his head and chest. "And I can leave this puny body and reclaim my own."

"Remain with me," Dredfahl ordered. "You will have to give the appearance of being human for a few days while I prepare for Torqualmar's return. His bones have been scattered in this world as well as given to the Kalinths in the other. You need to clothe yourself."

Robby crossed the room to the prone police officer. "These will fit." He started undressing the police officer, then noticed the pistol holstered at his side. He pulled the pistol free enthusiastically. "A weapon, Master. Now humans will have more reason to fear me."

"Hurry," Dredfahl snapped. "The humans in Ollindark are about to deliver another of Torqualmar's bones to me. I must be there."

"Of course, Master. I am embarrassed that they are somehow able to do what we could not." Robby squatted down and began stripping the police officer.

In the hallway Xander turned to go, and he ran head-long into what he at first believed to be a brick wall. Only the brick wall wore a trenchcoat. He glanced up past the impossibly wide chest to the impossibly hideous face on the head atop the chest. The face was full of angles and bone ridges around the eyes that echoed the mouthful of fangs in his cold grin. Xander didn't know what kind of demon had quietly come up on him, but he knew it was a demon.

"Eeep," Xander squeaked, regretting it at once because there should have been something more heroic or brave he could have uttered.

"Spy," the demon accused in a low, rumbling voice.

"Actually," Xander said, thinking quickly now, but he never had the chance to say anything else because the demon's big hand suddenly wrapped around his throat. Lassie never had problems like this. *Timmy fell in the well. Much easier than telling the folks that a demon ate Timmy.*

The demon lifted Xander from his feet in one huge hand. Trying to keep his neck from snapping, Xander grabbed the demon's wrist in both his hands, helping support his own weight. The demon handled him like he was a kitten, striding into the ICU room.

"Master Dredfahl," the big demon said. "You were spied upon."

The cadaverous man focused on Xander. "Who are you, boy?"

The demon's grip loosened on Xander's throat. "Lost," Xander said. "I was in an accident earlier." At least, after the fight at the Lamplighter Theater he certainly looked the part. "Came to in one of the other rooms. Wanted to check on my girlfriend."

Robby—or Malik, Xander thought—looked at him curiously. For a moment Xander was afraid the demon was going to recognize him. For the first time, Xander noticed the demon's lavender eyes. They were pale and cold, not Robby's eyes at all.

The demon wearing Robby's body stepped forward and aimed the pistol at Xander's head. "Do you want me to kill him, Master?"

"No," Dredfahl said. "Killing him will only draw more humans into the hunt for us. Leave him."

Xander almost breathed a sigh of relief. Then Malik slammed the pistol butt into Xander's forehead. Pain crashed through Xander's skull, and everything went black.

"I see demons," Derek Traynor said.

Tara watched the *Othersyde* host rocking on his knees, staring with sightless eyes up at the bright stage lights. In the last few months of watching the show, Tara had never once seen Derek lose his composure. He'd been touched by sadness on occasion as stories had unfolded during the taping, but never the hysteria that gripped him now.

Chaos reigned in the studio. Most of the audience had chosen to bail and headed for the exits singly or in small groups. The security guards stood in a ring around Derek.

Susan Kane left the studio control room and crossed over to Derek. She knelt and wrapped her arms around him, then looked up at the closest security man. "Get a doctor. He's in shock."

"Yes, ma'am." The security guard clicked the Handi-Talk handset on his shoulder and spoke over the radio link.

Tara felt the power surging within her, knowing that her own witch ability somehow made her sensitive to the mystical forces at play. They hadn't been there during the earlier session Derek had performed.

Giles stood beside her, ever watchful.

Guess that was kind of what Giles was trained to do, Tara thought.

"I see demons," Derek said again. "They're everywhere."

"Calm down, Derek," Susan Kane urged. She put a hand to his forehead. "He's burning up with fever. Get me an ice pack from the first-aid kit."

One of the security guards sprinted for the control room.

"I see demons," Derek said again.

Amy, the girl who Derek had been talking to, pushed forward, held back by two of the security guards who were working just as hard not to hurt her as they were to restrain her. Tears tracked her angry features.

"What about Donny?" she demanded. "What about Donny?"

"Donny's dying," Derek said.

"Noooooo!" Amy shouted, and her anguished cry echoed throughout the studio.

"Robby."

Still excited, feeling the sting of the wounds that his enemies had inflicted on him, Robby leaned on the stone club, driving the sharp end through the heart of the Kalinth that had fallen prey to the stone spikes in the trap.

"Fool!" The Kalinth grabbed the club. Blood trickled from his mouth.

"Game over, pal," Robby said. "We came, we saw, we kicked your ass."

Pain showed in the dying Kalinth's eyes.

Robby hoped the game editor featured options that allowed players to edit out the long death scenes. They weren't to his taste. He preferred enemies that simply disappeared once they were defeated. All the hanging on to life, gasping and hurting like they were real, was just a bit too much.

"Dredfahl is using you," the Kalinth gasped.

And that, Robby felt, was odd, too. Although game designers always put little in-jokes in a game, not many of them used themselves in direct mission-oriented text or even subtext. Maybe the Dredfahl reference would be taken out later.

"You're just . . . just pawns to Dredfahl," the dying Kalinth gasped. "You're going to . . . to loose a great . . . great evil into your own world." Then, with a choking, gargling gasp, the Kalinth died. After a final shudder, he went limp.

"Man," Robby said, feeling a little disgusted, "that was just a little too creepy, you know?"

The Dorinog beside him nodded. "Yeah. Creeps me out too."

Robby looked at the Dorinog. They really needed to get some individual markings or something going so they could tell each other apart quicker. "Chris, right?"

"Yeah. It's me."

"What's up?"

"It's Donny, man. Looks like his game is over." Chris gestured back toward the stone spikes.

At once Robby spotted the Dorinog that had to be Donny. Somehow during the melee, Donny had fallen on one of the spikes himself, or maybe he'd been thrown by one of the rampaging Kalinths. The sharpened end of the stone stuck up from Donny's midsection, holding him about five feet from the ground—about waist-level on a Dorinog.

"Now there's a fatality," Robby said. "He's still alive?"

Chris nodded. "Barely. He asked for you."

Robby shook his head. "I hate these death scenes."

"Me too. Maybe they're realistic, but they're entirely too weird for a shooter game." Chris shrugged. "I mean, unless the guy is scripted to give you some kind of cryptic message that's a game hint."

So far, though, the teammates that Robby had seen die had only screamed in agony before finally going quiet and still. Once, when they'd been encamped waiting further directions from Dredfahl, Robby had watched the site of a past battle. The bodies there, both Kalinths and Dorinogs, hadn't disappeared. They'd been removed piece by piece by carrion-eaters until only bones remained. Robby's team, in turn, had feasted on the carrion-eaters. That had been a truly gross experience— just one step removed from cannibalism.

Robby stepped in front of Donny, watching as the other player's eyes rolled in their sockets and finally focused on him.

"Hey, Donny," Robby said. The game's brief instruction sheet hadn't been exactly forthcoming about what to say during these times.

"Robby, dude," Donny whispered hoarsely. "This isn't a game. I'm dying. I can see the white light. Man, my grandfather is talking to me, and he's been dead for ten years." He coughed and spat up blood.

"Sorry, man," Robby said sincerely. "It's game over for you. Maybe the designers will re-up you for the next beta test."

Donny shook his head. He held on to the stone spike sticking through his guts as if to keep from sliding further down. "Not a game. Are you listening to me?"

"I hear you." Robby hated the fear in Donny's voice. The sound gave Robby the willies. He knew Donny from back in Sunnydale. Sometimes they said hey to each other in the comic shop or the game shop, or every now and again an on-line game when they recognized each other's pseudonym.

Donny wasn't a whiner.

Man, Robby thought, *the death experience through the VR must be totally rad too.* He almost wanted to try it himself. He knew from experience, like the wounds that he bore now, that the game AI definitely knew how to pass on pain. But what did it feel like to die?

"Does it hurt?" Robby asked.

"Yeah," Donny gasped. "Hurt more a little while ago." His eyes rolled again. "But this is *real*, Robby. Dredfahl, whatever his name really is, he lied to us. This isn't a game."

Touched by the honest fear Donny had, Robby put a hand on the other player's head. "Hey, man, don't be freaking out. In another minute or two, you'll be back in the VR chair in whatever warehouse Dredfahl and his people are hiding us. Then you'll be ticked off 'cause you lost and aren't playing anymore."

"No!" Donny shouted. "This isn't a game! This is real! Dredfahl—" Without warning, he shivered and went still. His eyes glazed over.

"Is he dead?" Chris asked.

"Yeah," Robby said.

"Man, I'm glad. That was really starting to get on my nerves."

"Donny whining like that, you mean?"

"No. This stuff's too real, Robby. You think some of the other computer games and platform games have had PR problems? That ain't nothing like what this gaming system is going have."

"I know."

"But it's kind of scary, too."

"What do you mean?"

"Think about it," Chris said. "You and I have both been around gaming systems all our lives." He waved at the battlefield around them. "We're talking full-immersion VR here. You want to tell me how anybody's going to be able to afford a setup like this? Let alone however much the game people decide to charge for the games."

"No, man," Robby said. "They said the same thing about the PlayStation 2. A lot of people said it would never sell, and then when there were all those supply problems? A lot of people thought the PS2 would tank. It didn't. That's 'cause there's one rule and one rule only when it comes to gamers: Gamers game. If designers can find a way to produce it, gamers will find a way to play it."

"I just don't know," Chris whispered. "But I think maybe I'm going to be glad to get out of here."

"If that's what you want to do," Robby suggested, "all you gotta do is fly up into the air and drop down on one of these stone spikes."

Chris hesitated. "Naw, man. I think I'll game a little more first. Besides, if this isn't a game, what else could it be?" He turned and walked away.

The other player's words haunted Robby even after he left. *If this isn't a game, what else could it be?* The question echoed in Robby's head as he looked down at the bright patch of blood on his hand. That had been Donny's blood.

If this wasn't a game, Robby decided, whatever this world *really* was had to be too horrible to contemplate. He wiped the blood off his hand with the yellow alkaline dust, then turned back to his troops.

"Search the Kalinths," Robby ordered. "Dredfahl said this group had one of Torqualmar's bones. Let's see what it is."

"Something's wrong with Willow," Buffy said as she clung to the bucking bone bridge that spanned the abyss between her world and the demon world from which the Craulathar was attempting to summon his mate. Buffy peered at the other end of the bridge at the portal. Fog obscured the view of the cavern beneath the mausoleum.

"We got our own trouble, Slayer," Spike said. "If this bridge collapses, we're going to fall into the abyss below."

Buffy listened to Spike and knew what he said was

true, but everything in her screamed to get back to Willow. "We've got to help Willow."

"That bloody portal's not going to work," Spike said, flattening on the bridge and holding tightly to the sides as the structure continued to whip about. "I was wrong about Willow. She's not strong enough to hold the portal open on her own. We don't have much time here."

Bones rattled and cracked as the bridge shook and shivered.

"The only way we're going to help Willow," Spike continued, "is by helping ourselves."

"How?" Buffy asked. But she was suspicious as well. Spike's agendas always put Spike's survival ahead of everything and everyone else.

"By slaying the Craulathar demon," Spike replied. "He's working the spell that's attacking Willow and causing this bridge to act possessed. If we kill the demon, we should be able to get back."

Gazing back through the portal, Buffy watched as the fog momentarily lifted. Willow was still on her knees, her arms lifted before her. Firelight glistened over Willow's arms, and Buffy realized that they were encased in something. *Ice? But that's not possible.*

"Buffy," Spike called.

A shadow moved from the darkness in back of Willow, heading straight for her.

"Someone's back there with Willow!" Buffy yelled to Spike. She started back along the bridge.

Spike grabbed her arm. "You can't help Willow now."

Buffy turned, one hand already drawn back to punch Spike. "Let go of me."

Spike released her arm and took a step back. "Fine. Throw your life away. While you're at it, throw Willow's life away as well. Because that's what you'll be doing if you don't listen to me."

Buffy stared at Spike.

"But I bloody well won't stand idly by and let you throw *my* life away." Spike pointed at the demon on the island that hung out over the dark abyss. "Killing that demon is the only chance we have. Do you hear me?"

Slowly Buffy nodded. She felt confused and tried to focus on Spike's words. Since her mom's death, everything had seemed confusing and too hard. Life was supposed to be simple part of the time, but it was like that part had disappeared a long time ago.

"Then let's get on with it," Spike snarled, morphing into full vampire face.

Holding the battle-ax in one hand, Buffy gathered herself and crawled along the bridge, staying as low as she could. Incredibly, the bridge shifted and strained, swinging violently from side to side. Caught off guard, she slid across the uneven surface of the bones and tumbled toward the darkness that lay beyond the safety of the bridge. She missed grabbing hold with her free hand, but managed to wrap a leg around one of the railing supports, hoping that the railing would hold her weight. When her fall stopped, she swung herself forward, caught the railing, and pulled herself back onto the bridge with Spike's help.

Near the end that was attached to the floating island, the bridge stopped swinging so wildly. Pushing up from her stomach, trusting her skills, Buffy ran the last few steps, then hurled herself toward the small island of barren stone.

She studied the small stone building the Craulathar demon had prostrated itself in front of. The architecture was Gothic in a sense, thick and palpable, but the style was also alien, featuring small demons cavorting through flames and the entrails of unidentifiable monsters. Symbols appeared to be etched in the stonework by acid, none of them looking familiar to Buffy. Something was missing from the scene.

"Where's the demon?" Spike growled as he landed on the island beside Buffy.

Okay, Buffy thought, turning her attention to the island's perimeters, *now I remember what's missing.*

Spike pressed himself flat against the building. He gripped the mace in both hands, then peered around the corner.

"He's around here somewhere," Spike said. "I can still smell him."

Shadows shifted at the top of the building. Glancing up, Buffy spotted the Craulathar demon crouched on top of the structure. Before she could yell a warning or even ready herself, the Craulathar demon leaped down at her, smashing into her and driving her away.

Buffy fell and rolled, propelled by the creature's greater bulk. The Craulathar demon was incredibly strong. Buffy put her hands out and tried to stop her fall, but the barren rock that formed the island slid away from her. She was over the side before she knew it. One last frantic grab at the island's edge won her a hold, but she dangled over the waiting darkness.

Unwilling, but unable to stop, Buffy glanced down. The darkness seemed to fold in on itself below her, like a dust cloud getting sucked into a vacuum cleaner. The motion reminded her of a mouth, a hungry mouth. The darkness waited in greedy anticipation, and she knew the malignant force would have her if she slipped free of the island.

She swung and tried to find a way to pull herself up. Then she found herself staring into the ugly face of the Craulathar demon glaring down at her.

"You're too late, Slayer," the demon taunted. "Time for you to die." He lifted one massive foot, intending to drive his boot down onto her unprotected fingers.

Buffy swung the battle-ax even as she tried to slide her fingers out of the way. The demon's foot slammed into rock instead of her fingers, but she couldn't maintain her grip. Her fingers slid free and she started to fall. Then she felt the battle-ax catch on the island's edge. She held onto the haft, feeling the ax head grate precariously on the stone.

The Craulathar demon raised his foot again, then staggered as Spike attacked him from behind. Spike wrapped both hands around the demon's head, poking his fingers into the demon's eyes and catching him under the chin for leverage. Staggering back, the demon reached up to grab Spike's arms.

"Hurry!" Spike yelled. "I'm not going to be able to hold him much longer! He's too strong!"

Buffy pulled on the ax haft, caught hold of the island's edge with her free hand, and pulled herself up again. Despite the action going on with the demon, she couldn't help glancing back at the portal that framed Willow back in the mausoleum.

The fog parted, and she saw that someone had stepped beside Willow. At least he didn't appear to be offering her any harm. Looking back at the bridge, Buffy saw that a few of the bones were breaking free, tumbling through the blackness and disappearing from sight.

"Buffy!" Spike yelped.

Switching her attention back to the demon, Buffy saw Spike go flying. Luckily, Spike only smacked up against the building in the center of the island. Rock cracked from the impact, and Spike slid down to the ground. A dazed look filled his eyes.

The Craulathar demon cocked his big head and grinned at Buffy. "Now it's just you and me, little girl," the demon crowed, stepping toward Buffy.

Without hesitation Buffy whirled the battle-ax in front of her. The demon stayed out of reach, circling her.

When she was ready, Buffy swooped toward the Craulathar demon, bringing the razor-edged ax at knee level. Effortlessly the demon leaped over the swinging blade. A grin darkened his face.

However, Buffy had figured that the demon would avoid the first blow. She stood her ground and reversed the ax, bringing the weapon back in a flashing arc. The demon barely got an arm up in time to block the blow. The ax haft broke with a harsh snap, and the ax head sailed out over the island's edge.

"Give up," the demon suggested. "I can make your death quick."

"No," Buffy answered, twirling the long wooden haft in her fingers. The Craulathar demon shot a fistful of talons at Buffy's face. She reversed the ax haft and batted his hand away. The fierce talons caught briefly in her hair, then sliced on through. Spinning away, Buffy brought the ax handle up and chopped down. The hard wood crashed into the demon's knee, breaking bone.

The demon growled in pain and anger, hobbling a little to turn to face Buffy. Still in motion, Buffy took the ax haft in both hands and used it to block the demon's claws again. She kicked her opponent in the side a half-dozen times, feeling the impact shiver along her leg. Shifting quickly, she ducked under the Craulathar demon's backhanded blow, slid her hands together on one end of the ax haft, and swung for the demon's head. The ax haft caught the Craulathar demon along his broad jaw, snapping his head back. He took two stumbling steps backward, but quickly recovered.

Roaring in rage, the demon charged, arms outstretched. Buffy backpedaled swiftly, knowing she was headed for the island's edge. She gripped the ax haft tightly, then threw herself to the left—less than three feet from the drop-off. The Craulathar demon tried to stop, jamming his feet down and skidding across the rock.

Probably, given the broad feet and his incredible agility, the demon would have managed to stop, but Buffy didn't give him the chance. She jammed the ax haft between her opponent's ankles as she slid on her side, hoping that she wouldn't careen over the edge as she held on. The Craulathar demon tripped over the wooden haft and came down face first. He thudded into the ground and kept going, rolling out of control and flailing his arms.

For a moment, Buffy thought she was going to be safe. Then the demon's arm smacked into her and sent her tumbling over the island's edge. She lunged for the edge as the demon fell past her, twisting end over end into the abyss. Arm outstretched, she knew she could get her fingers over the edge, but she wasn't sure if she'd be able to maintain her grip.

Her fingers brushed the stone.

Chapter Eleven

Then, before Buffy's weight could even reach the end of her arm and test the grip she had with her fingertips, Spike's hand closed around her wrist.

"I've got you," Spike said. As he spoke, his face changed back to human features. He lay flat on the ground and Buffy knew he'd thrown himself toward the edge in an effort to save her.

Buffy glanced down, watching the Craulathar demon disappear into the darkness below, listening to his howls of fear growing more and more distant.

Carefully Spike pulled her back onto the island. As Buffy stood, she felt tremors start shuddering through the island. The building with the alien Gothic designs started glowing. One wall suddenly burned white, and something moved inside.

"What is that?" Buffy asked.

"The frustration of interrupted *amore*," Spike answered. "The Craulathar demon's girlfriend isn't taking kindly to you killing her guy. She's breaking off the spell that's holding the way station together."

"Got that." Buffy moved, stepping away from one of the fissures splintering the island. She glanced at the bone bridge, watching more pieces fly away as the structure came apart. "Come on." She grabbed Spike's arm and pulled him toward the bridge.

When they were no more than two strides down the bridge, the building on the island blew up. The force from the explosion knocked Buffy and Spike down and caused the bridge to swing even more wildly.

At the other end of the bridge, the portal leading back to the mausoleum started to close.

Buffy struggled to get to her feet but found the effort almost impossible on the unsteady bridge. More bones flew from the structure, leaving gaping holes in the path as the portal dwindled and grew smaller.

Then a blues guitar riff tore through the thunder of the explosion. Almost immediately, the bridge steadied and the portal opened a little wider.

On her feet now, running before her next heartbeat and knowing that Spike was on her heels, Buffy saw the portal clear. Willow peered at her through the opening.

"Buffy!" Willow called.

A guy dressed in a snap-brim fedora and a long coat stood beside her. He played an acoustic guitar with silver and ivory inlays.

"Come on, girl," the guy yelled. "Ain't no time to be dawdlin' now."

Buffy ran, feeling the bones loosen beneath her feet, knowing the bridge was falling apart even as she powered across. The portal wavered, blinked out of existence, then blinked back in as she covered the last few feet. She threw herself forward, putting her arms out in front of her, feeling the numbing cold as she passed through the portal. Then she slid across the stone floor over the symbols Spike had drawn and knocked the candle away.

She turned over, looking back at the portal, wondering if Spike had made his escape as well. As Spike dove, the portal blinked, disappearing for a heartbeat, then opening back up as Spike sailed into the room and thudded up against Buffy. Burning bones dropped onto the ground beside him.

On the other side of the portal, the bone bridge fell apart, scattering into the dark void like ivory toothpicks. In the next moment, the cavern around Buffy started to shake.

Buffy got to her feet and saw the guy with the guitar help Willow to hers. "We've got to get out of here," the guy said. "Whatever voodoo that demon used on this place, it's about all used up."

Spike seized a burning leg bone from the pyre the Craulathar demon had built and used it to lead the way up the spiral stairs. Buffy grabbed one of Willow's arms while the guy with the guitar held Willow's other arm. They kept her between them, hurrying her along faster than she could have run on her own.

A liquid rushing hiss sounded behind Buffy. She glanced over her shoulder and watched as the cavern started to swirl and fold in on itself.

"It's goin' away," the guy with the guitar said. "Goin' back wherever that demon hoodooed it from."

"Yeah," Buffy said. "Figured that one out." She kept running, following the now-familiar twists and turns of the labyrinth the Craulathar demon had created.

Less than a minute later they were outside, listening to the liquid rush turn to pounding thunder that caused the ground to shudder.

"Get down!" Spike yelled, throwing himself onto the ground.

Buffy pulled Willow down behind a headstone.

The thunder ended in a sudden rush of dust and rock debris that spat from the mausoleum and rattled across the nearby gravestones.

Spike unwrapped his arms from his head and stared up at the mausoleum. The building stood as if nothing had happened.

"Well now," Spike grumbled, "that was somewhat anticlimactic."

"Personally," Buffy said, getting to her feet, "I could use anticlimactic at this moment."

"Me too," Willow said. She stood and brushed the hair from her eyes.

Buffy looked at the guitar guy but spoke to Willow. "Who's your friend?"

"We didn't exactly get around to mentioning names," Willow admitted.

The guitar guy lifted his snap-brim hat, which had somehow managed to stay on his head during the running and diving. "Bobby Lee Tooker, ma'am. But all my friends call me Bobby Lee. Pleased to meet you."

Buffy folded her arms. During her career as the Slayer, she had stopped trusting easily—even for someone who might have saved her life.

"Nice to meet you, too, Mr. Tooker."

"It's Bobby Lee," the guitar guy said. "All my friends call me Bobby Lee."

"We're not exactly friends," Buffy replied.

After a short hesitation, Bobby Lee nodded. "Yes, ma'am. I reckon that's so."

"Buffy!" Willow chided in a whisper directed only at Buffy. "If he hadn't come along and done what he did, I'd have lost you."

Spike leaned irreverently against a headstone and smirked. Cupping his hands, he lit a cigarette and blew smoke out. "Now, there's the Slayer I've come to know and love."

Buffy glared at him.

"You've got a right to be suspicious," Spike said. "This bloke came lookin' for you at the Alibi earlier."

A chill raced through Buffy as she regarded Bobby Lee. "Is that true?"

Bobby Lee nodded. "Yes, ma'am."

The honeyed tones of his Southern accent sounded relaxed, but Buffy ignored them. "I don't know you," she said. "Why would you come looking for me?"

"Because you're the Slayer," Bobby Lee said.

His words surprised Buffy, even though a lot of people knew about the Slayer, or at least about the myth of the Chosen One. The demon world was bigger than she'd even imagined when she'd first encountered it. "How would you know that?"

"My family," Bobby Lee said, "we've been involved in fightin' demons for a long time."

"There's plenty to go around," Buffy said.

Bobby Lee grinned, and the effort was charming, even a little disarming. "Yes, ma'am. That there is for sure."

"Where are you from?" Buffy asked, knowing from the accent that Bobby Lee wasn't from Sunnydale, and probably not even from the West Coast.

"Louisiana, ma'am," Bobby Lee answered. "From down near New Orleans, but out in the bayou country."

"Why did you want to see me?"

"Need some help, ma'am."

"You helped Willow keep the spell intact to save the portal so we could get out," Buffy said. "I couldn't do that. So if it's that kind of help you're needing, you've come to the wrong place."

Bobby Lee shrugged good-naturedly. "Aw, that

hoodoo wasn't much. Just somethin' my Tante Camille taught me. Music, it kind of strengthens some spells and such. That spell your friend put up, why I couldn't have done that."

"Then what brings you here?" Spike demanded in a harsh tone.

"A demon," Bobby Lee said.

"The one that I fought?" Buffy asked.

"No, ma'am."

"Okay," Buffy said. "Enough with calling me ma'am. You're making me feel incredibly old. Call me Buffy."

"All right," Bobby Lee said agreeably.

"How did you get here?"

"Saw you at the Alibi," Bobby Lee said. "I had talked to a few demons that told me what you looked like. Seein' you at the Alibi, I figured I knew who you was. Followed you out here."

"Why?"

"This demon I come out here for," Bobby Lee said. "He's from New Orleans. His name's Dredfahl, an' he's got history with my family that goes back generations. He's a small-change demon lookin' to go big-time right here in Sunnydale."

Spike shot Bobby Lee a mocking smile. "Because you and your family chased him out of New Orleans?"

"Out of Pierre's Mule," Bobby Lee said. "That's where I'm from. A little place in the Bayou Teche. An' no, we didn't chase him out of there. Figure when Dredfahl finishes up what he's doin' here, why, he'll go back there again. There's a lot of bad blood between him an' my family."

"What's Dredfahl doing here?" Buffy asked.

"Resurrectin' a demon that's been dead a couple thousand years or so," Bobby Lee answered.

• • •

Dawn Summers glanced at the Magic Box when she reached the curb. Lately, the shop had been as much of a home to her as the house where she'd lived with her mom and sister. Buffy always seemed to be here—whenever she wasn't out hunting demons and vampires.

Moving with athletic grace, Dawn crossed the street at a jog. She was tall and lean—unkind people would call her thin—with long dark hair and intense eyes. She wore jeans and a navy blue sweater under a long leather jacket.

A car's headlights pinned her in the street for a moment, but Dawn was jogging and reached the curb before the vehicle even got close to her.

"Hey, girl," someone called from the passing car.

Dawn turned and looked at the car, watching as the brake lights flared ruby red for a moment. Whoever had yelled at her sounded male and young.

Guys can be such dorks, she thought. At least, she hoped it was a normal flesh-and-blood guy and not some creep of the night. Of course, guys her age weren't exactly normal either.

The car hesitated at the corner half a block away.

Probably thinking of something really clever to say, Dawn told herself. *Could be a long night for him.* She took her key to the Magic Box from her pocket and opened the door. After she stepped through and closed the door, she looked back and watched the car drive away.

"Is there a problem, Dawn?"

Breath catching in her throat for just a moment before she recognized Giles's voice, Dawn turned around. "No. Everything's just fine."

The Watcher gazed at her with concern. He'd taken her mom's death pretty hard too, Dawn knew, and he felt responsible for both the Summers girls.

"What are you doing here?" Giles asked.

"Came to see what all the excitement was about."

Dawn looked past Giles and saw the table set up in the center of the room. Soft yellow light from nearby lamps lit the table and Tara, who sat in one of the chairs. As usual, whenever there was trouble, books littered the table.

"There's no excitement," Giles replied. "And I don't think Buffy would approve of your being here. You've got school to think about. Homework. Tests."

"All done," Dawn countered, crossing her arms and showing a little defiance. "Buffy wasn't much older than me when you started keeping her up all night to go out slaying."

"That's different," Giles said. "Buffy is the Slayer. Her physical constitution is different from that of a normal person."

"Stronger. Faster. Heals really quick." Dawn sighed. "Yeah, I know. I got that. But Xander and Willow weren't exactly more than human, were they?"

"No," Giles said. "They weren't." He looked like he was trying to find something else to say.

Dawn sighed, knowing from past experience that the Watcher was susceptible to adolescent sighs. "My homework's done, and I'm a better student than Buffy was."

"All right. Won't you join us?" Giles led the way back to the table.

"Got any munchies?" Dawn asked, shrugging out of her coat.

Seated at the table, a thick book open before her, Tara offered a cylindrical package. "Mentos?"

"Sure." Dawn hung her jacket on the back of the chair across from Tara, sat, and took the offered goodies. She popped one into her mouth and gazed at the books, always amazed at the number of books Giles had managed to accumulate. "What kind of demon are we looking for?"

"We don't know yet," Tara admitted.

"Where's Buffy?" Dawn asked. She tried to downplay the anxiety she felt, but with her mom gone, the stark realization that she was probably going to lose her sister someday soon because of the whole Slayer thing was constant. After all, Slayers didn't live forever.

"She's on patrol with Willow," Giles answered. "Can I get you some tea?"

"I'm good." Dawn took one of the books from a tall stack. "So if we don't know what kind of demon we're looking for, what *are* we looking for?"

"Tales and legends about mediums," Giles said. "Apparently, Derek Traynor went a step beyond his customary perusal of the afterlife and peered into a demon world. We're trying to ascertain which one."

"Didn't you ask?"

"The security people shoved the audience out the door."

"The trouble is," Tara said, referring to a notepad beside her, "there are dozens and probably hundreds of instances involving mediums and seers that have looked into demonic dimensions."

"Kind of like finding a needle in a haystack," Dawn suggested.

"We'd have better luck finding the needle," Tara said. She quickly relayed the events that had unfolded at the television studio. During that time, she and Dawn called in for pizza.

"I guess they won't be airing *that* episode of *Othersyde*," Dawn said when Tara had finished. "What happened to Derek Traynor?"

"I suppose he's staying at his hotel."

"Maybe we could ask him what he saw," Dawn said. "You know, show Derek some pictures of demons or do some kind of composite sketch the way they do on *NYPD Blue*."

"I got the impression from the way the security people surrounded Derek Traynor tonight that getting to him would be next to impossible," Giles said.

Dawn didn't point out how impossible the task of finding the demon world they were searching for would be without some idea of what they were looking for. Giles had been doing this kind of thing since before she was born. "Does Buffy know?"

"I don't know," Giles answered. "We've not had any contact with her."

"Oh." Dawn's worry increased.

The door rattled as someone worked the lock, drawing all of their attention. A moment later, Anya stepped into the shop, looking angry.

"Boy," Anya said, "when I catch up to Xander Harris, I'm going to let him have it. Do you know what he did?"

Dawn kept silent, knowing Tara and Giles remained quiet as well out of self-defense. Despite the fact that she was no longer a demon, Anya could still show a considerable temper. Maybe Anya didn't understand *all* the finer points of being human and part of the socialization of being such, but the temper part was an area she was definitely qualified in.

"First of all," Anya declared, "Xander took me to a movie marathon. Hours and hours of 'Beam me up, Scotty,' when we could have done something I wanted to do. I tried to be the brave little teapot, you know. The whole, 'this is my handle, this is my spout' thing, trying to be supportive."

"Little teapot?" Dawn asked, not getting the reference.

"Brave little toaster?" Anya asked.

Tara shook her head.

"Whatever," Anya grumbled. "Anyway, I'm at this movie and one of his friends comes in and tries to kill everybody."

"Who?" Dawn asked, knowing there was a chance she might know the person because she sometimes caught rides with Xander when her mom and Buffy had been too busy. Xander had taken Dawn to some of his hangouts and introduced her to some of his friends.

"Some guy named Robby," Anya said. "So Xander's all worried about Robby because he's ranting and raving—"

"Xander's ranting and raving?" Tara asked.

"No, Robby is." Impatience flickered across Anya's face. "Aren't you listening?"

"I'm trying to," Tara said. "Just trying to keep all the pronouns straight."

"Robby's ranting and raving, saying he's going to kill everybody and going to curse people so that their women are barren and their cows go dry."

"Now, *there's* something you don't hear every day," Giles commented.

"That's what I said." Anya smiled. "All the really good curses are being forgotten. This guy sounded like a demon. I mean, if I hadn't known he was a human, I'd have thought he was a demon."

"What made Robby go spacey?" Dawn asked, remembering the quiet guy Xander had introduced her to in the comics shop.

"I don't know," Anya said in exasperation. "The next thing I know, Robby's girlfriend comes up to us. Xander offers to give her a ride to the hospital where the police took Robby. While I'm standing there, doing my best to comfort this girl who's suddenly realized she's got a homicidal nut-job for a boyfriend, Xander leaves."

"Leaves where?" Tara asked.

"Me. The girlfriend. The hospital. All of it." Anya blew out her breath. "He said he was going to go get us something to drink. Then he disappeared."

"That doesn't sound like Xander," Giles protested. "Something must have happened." He glanced at Tara. "Was Robby the name of the boy Derek Traynor claimed he was channeling tonight?"

"No," Tara replied. "That was Donny."

Giles nodded and scratched his chin.

"If it's the same Donny that Xander has introduced me to," Dawn said, "Donny and Robby are friends."

"Derek did say that Donny was wherever he was with friends," Tara said. "And Xander's friend must have had some reason for wigging out."

"Maybe Xander knows," Anya said. "When I get finished with him, you can ask." She looked at the back of the shop. "Is he hiding back there?"

"Xander hasn't been here," Giles said.

Anya looked exasperated. "He *has* to be here. He wasn't at the hospital and he wasn't at home. Where else could he be?"

"I don't know," Giles replied. "Perhaps we might consider talking to his friend at the hospital."

"We can't do that," Anya said. "Robby knocked out the police officer guarding him and escaped from the hospital a little while ago."

"Before Xander disappeared?" Giles asked.

Anya shook her head and tapped her foot impatiently, glaring at the shop door as if in readiness for Xander to step through at any moment. "After."

Slowly, Anya's foot stopped tapping, and Dawn knew she was starting to realize what everyone else was already thinking.

"Hey," Anya asked worriedly, "do you think something happened to Xander?"

Chapter Twelve

Xander's head banged against something hard and metallic, and in that instant he came awake. He knew he wasn't at home, because he didn't usually sleep sitting up. And only then with the accompaniment of late-night programming on the cable stations.

Suddenly he remembered the events in Robby's ICU room at the hospital. He also felt some kind of restraint around his chest and another one that bound his wrists. *Wherever I am,* he thought, *I'm in trouble.* He didn't have to work hard to do the math on that one.

The whir of tires on pavement remained constant. From the noise and the motion, Xander surmised he was in a vehicle of some kind. But why would anyone take him from the hospital if he were badly hurt? And if he were badly hurt, how had they gotten him—unconscious—past the people at the hospital without being stopped?

Then he remembered the power that the man in blue had used on the receptionist at the nurse's station.

Voices, low and rumbling, spoke only occasionally. Mixed in with the guttural half-baked attempts at conversation were strains of music and . . . and *video games*?

"Hey," one of the voices said. "Did Dredfahl say what we were going to do with the human?"

The human? As in a singular *human?* Xander's mind worried frantically at the term. *If there's only one human here, then that's gotta be me!* He remembered Robby, or the demon in Robby's body, addressed the man in the blue suit as Dredfahl.

"Dredfahl hasn't said anything about him yet," another voice growled. "You ever seen a human before?"

"Not me."

"Me either," someone else said. "I heard stories about them. You know, from when our people used to live in this world too. I always heard about how bad they smelled, but I wouldn't ever have thought it was this bad."

What you're smelling, Xander thought helplessly, *is pure, abject fear.* He could feel his pulse throbbing at his temples and in the hollow of his neck. Heat burned through his face. What he wanted, more than anything, was for Buffy to show up. She always saved the day.

"Maybe they don't taste too bad," the first voice said.

Xander thought he recognized the voice as that of the demon inhabiting Robby. That line of thinking got him to wondering about Robby and where his friend had ended up.

"Do you think we should eat him raw or cook him first?"

"Bake him in a pie. My grandmother told me human was always best served baked in a pie with iced blood on the side."

Without warning, someone grabbed Xander by the hair and yanked his head up from his chest.

"You aren't fooling anyone," a deep voice said, "by pretending to be asleep."

"Ow!" Xander cried, glancing up at the person that held him by the hair.

Robby, or at least it would have been Robby if Robby were still knocking around inside his body, stared down at Xander and grinned. The lavender-colored eyes made a definite statement that Robby wasn't home.

"You know me," the demon said. A wicked smile that Xander had never seen on Robby's lips fitted itself to the familiar face.

"I don't know you," Xander said, putting a little defiance in his voice. Actually, the defiance was more like a thin crust over the fear that filled him and threatened to burst.

"But you know the person whose body I wear," the demon said.

"Yeah," Xander replied. "I'd like to know what you did with him too."

The smile never flickered, but the demon cocked his head to one side. "You were his friend."

Xander didn't dignify the question with an answer.

"Did you play video games too?" The demon's question was mocking for some reason.

Xander glanced past the demon that wore Robby's body, seeing four other guys in the back of the large cargo van. Carpet cleaning tools occupied one side of the van, and a wire mesh wall cut the driver's area off from the cargo space. The four guys looked human, sitting around in jeans and shorts and concert T-shirts and superhero shirts. Two of them even wore caps advertising video games. Three of them had Walkmans and the fourth had a GameBoy Advance that shined light back over his features as he played with inhuman speed. Xander was certain he'd seen three of the guys hanging out at the comics shop or the arcades. *At least, I saw the bodies of these three guys.*

All of the guys now had lavender eyes, and Xander was sure that hadn't been the case the last time he'd seen them.

"I asked you a question," the demon wearing Robby's body said. "Do you play video games?"

"Yeah," Xander said.

"You any good?"

The demon with the GameBoy looked up and laughed.

"I'm good," Xander said.

"Sure you are," the demon said.

Xander held the demon's lavender gaze and tried not to let his voice crack. "Do you have a name?" Names were good. Sometimes a lot of power went with knowing the name of someone or something. Besides that, having a name to look up in one of Giles's books would be great. *After I make my escape,* Xander reminded himself.

The demon considered, then said, "Manik."

"Terrific. Nice to meet you, Manik." Xander remembered the name from the hospital now. He turned and glanced through the front van windshield as the driver drove the vehicle into a warehouse. Beyond the edge of the warehouse, Xander caught sight of the dark sea and the running lights of a few boats out in the harbor. "Where are you taking me?"

Manik ignored him. The driver cut the lights and everything went dark inside the warehouse. Metal screeched as the warehouse door lowered behind them. A moment later, soft electric light flooded the warehouse.

One of the other demons opened the van's side door and stepped out. He growled something in a language that Xander couldn't understand.

Realizing that the demons had their own language and didn't have to speak his, Xander hoped that the whole conversation about eating humans had just been to frighten him because they'd known he'd still been pretending to be knocked out. Of course, they might have said that to frighten him before they ate him too.

"Get up," Manik ordered. He released Xander's hair and grabbed the gray duct tape binding Xander's wrists.

"Where are we going?" Xander asked. Visions of giant ovens and gingerbread houses trimmed in candy danced in his head. *Not a good thought*.

"Where I tell you to," Manik growled. "And if you keep asking questions, I'm gonna twist your head off and squeeze your guts out."

Xander clenched his jaw, ready to resist any impulse to ask questions. He followed Manik, having trouble keeping up with the demon's long stride because his legs still felt a little numb.

Docktown, Xander mused. *Gotta be in Docktown*. The stink of fish, salt, and industry furthered that impression.

Docktown was the part of Sunnydale that lived off the ocean, a place of poverty and fishermen and canneries and dark things that slid out of the sea to kill people on land. Xander had been there a few times on patrol with Buffy, or following the trail of some demon-spawned creature that had left carnage spread all over the downtown area. He didn't care for the place, and he'd only dreamed about being a pirate for a few days one summer.

The warehouse was run-down, probably one of the abandoned structures in the area. Back in the days when the canning industry was booming, space was at a premium. Now there were a lot of empty places, like rotten teeth just waiting to be drilled out and replaced or capped. But no one had anything they wanted to build in those places.

Fishing nets, bags of trash, and a couple of broken johnboats that had been scrapped for parts occupied the main warehouse floor space. Smoke reeked from a few fifty-five-gallon drums. Xander guessed that a few of Docktown's homeless or teens looking for a place to party had used the warehouse on occasion.

Manik pulled Xander up rickety steps that led to the warehouse's second floor. As he gazed back at the electric lighting breaking the darkness in the warehouse, he realized that Dredfahl's operation had to have been underway for some time. Xander doubted that the warehouse had been constantly supplied with electricity. Now that he listened for the sound, he heard generators throbbing in the background. *Pocketa-pocketa-pocketa-pocketa.*

At the top of the stairs, Manik pulled Xander into the office space, tripping him so that he sprawled onto the floor.

"Stay down," Manik ordered.

Xander nodded, his attention drawn to the room's walls. They were all white as snow, covered in some kind of slate material. The whiteness of the room was jarring in one regard, but also relaxed Xander to a degree. If the room had been used for killing humans—or even tenderizing them to bake in pies—that would have showed.

Manik crossed his arms over his chest and leaned against the wall beside the door.

Xander remained prone, knowing that with his hands bound that getting up would be at least a little difficult. Before he managed the feat, he was sure Manik would kick him in the ribs or break his fingers. Getting up wasn't worth the effort.

A few minutes later, the man in blue walked into the room. *Dredfahl,* Xander reminded himself.

The cadaverous old man stopped in front of Xander and gazed into his eyes.

Xander tried to look away but couldn't. There was something mesmerizing about Dredfahl's gaze.

Remembering the action the old man had performed at the hospital, Xander tried just to close his eyes. But he couldn't do that, either.

"You know some of the young men that were brought here," Dredfahl said in his heavy accent.

"Yes," Xander found himself saying before he even knew he was going to speak.

"You know the boy whose body Manik now wears."

"He's a friend," Xander answered.

Producing a small black bag, Dredfahl opened it and took a single black candle from inside. He rubbed his forefinger against his thumb. A yellow flame stood up from his thumb and he lighted the candle.

"I'm going to return you to your friend," Dredfahl promised. "You will aid them in their quest." He dripped melted wax onto the floor, then placed the candle on the waxy spot, waiting till the melted wax hardened enough to hold the candle.

"Wouldn't it just be easier if you brought him here?" Xander asked.

Dredfahl smiled, but the grudging effort was in no way humorous. Then he took a pinch of powder from the black bag and sprinkled it over the candle flame as Manik switched off the light with the switch by the door. Catching fire less than an inch above the candle, the powder exploded with a loud *bamf!*

A sour stench filled the room. Smoke curled up toward the ceiling, and that was when Xander noticed that glowing symbols in bright neon colors now filled the ceiling, the walls, and the floor. Dredfahl sprinkled more powder over the candle flame and got the same result, only larger this time.

As the smoke rose to the ceiling, Xander saw the symbols start shifting on the walls. The symbols spun and orbited around him, growing faster and faster till they blurred.

Xander felt himself floating free of his body. He struggled against the feeling, trying desperately to anchor himself to his flesh.

"You can't stay here," Dredfahl said. "There is much you can do on the other side. And one can come to serve me in your body."

"No," Xander said, but the denial sounded like it came from someone else very far away. He slid free of his body and thought the feeling was probably what a banana felt leaving the peel—if the banana didn't want to go. He had one totally weird birds-eye view of his body sprawled across the floor of the darkened room in front of Dredfahl.

"Go," Dredfahl commanded, his words growing more faint with each syllable. "Serve me well. Perhaps, if I am so inclined after Torqualmar returns to this world and gives me the power I know he will, I'll be generous toward you. Then again, maybe not."

The old man's mocking laughter chased Xander, pursuing him into the darkness that consumed him.

"His name is Dredfahl," Bobby Lee Tooker said.

"No last name?" Buffy asked.

They all sat around the table in the Magic Box while sparse traffic passed on the street outside. After the showdown in the cemetery, Willow had driven them back to the shop so they could have a place to talk to Bobby Lee about the demon he'd come to Sunnydale to hunt. Bobby Lee had ridden with Willow and Buffy, but Spike had insisted on bringing his motorcycle.

Buffy had been surprised to find that Tara, Giles, and Anya were already at the shop, and that Xander was currently among the missing. Buffy had been even more surprised to find Dawn there. Especially after the importance of homework and a good night's rest speech series she'd been giving.

"If there ever was a last name for Dredfahl," Bobby Lee said, "record of it was lost long ago."

Giles turned his attention to one of the books. Buffy caught a glimpse of the title *Lore of the Demons of West Africa*. The Watcher flipped through the pages with a practiced thumb. "I don't recall Dredfahl in my readings."

"Most of Dredfahl's activities," Bobby Lee replied, "have been among African people. My family fought him several times."

"If your family fought him so often," Spike said, "why didn't you just kill him and be done with it?"

"Some things, unlike vampires," Bobby Lee said, "are hard to kill a final time. My ancestors killed Dredfahl on four different occasions. The last time was in the 1940s in New Orleans. My grandpa faced Dredfahl in battle an' slew him, givin' his own life to do it. My grandma was pregnant with my daddy then, an' he grew up never knowin' his father except from the stories he was told."

Giles laid the book open before him. "How was your father trained if your grandfather wasn't there to train him?"

"Mostly," Bobby Lee said, "my daddy's skills against demons an' other night folk was natural. Kind of a feelin' he got about what he should do an' such. What my daddy didn't know, he found out from other people he done business with." He nodded at Giles. "Daddy shared a little information with the Watchers Council in his day. That's how I come to know about the Slayer."

"If your grandfather killed Dredfahl," Spike said, "then what makes you think Dredfahl is here now?"

"Because Dredfahl come back from the dead," Bobby Lee said. "Ain't no surprise. He's up an' done it before. He always finds himself a rabbit hole for when things up an' go bad on him."

"And you're here to kill Dredfahl again?" Spike asked in a mocking tone.

"Five months ago," Bobby Lee said in a flat voice, "Dredfahl murdered my daddy." He locked eyes with Spike. "I'm gonna do worse than kill Dredfahl. You can make book on that, bloodsucker."

Chapter Thirteen

For a moment, Buffy thought Spike was going to launch himself at Bobby Lee. The guitar guy sat easily, but Buffy noticed that he was carefully balanced, sitting in the chair with most of his weight centered over his knees and toes, his elbows resting lightly and slightly forward on the table. Buffy was certain Bobby Lee would have been up and out of his chair before Spike reached him.

Maybe if Spike hadn't still been carrying the Initiative's chip in his skull, he would have made the attempt. Instead, he grinned. "The way I see it, the faster I get you to Dredfahl, the sooner I get to watch you die. I'm up for that."

Not exactly a glowing Martha Stewart endorsement, Buffy thought. "What is Dredfahl doing here?" she asked. "Back in the cemetery, you said something about Dredfahl coming to Sunnydale to resurrect a demon."

Bobby Lee nodded and looked back at Buffy. "Back in West Africa all them years ago, Dredfahl had started tryin' to piece together the bones of Torqualmar, who was one powerful demon."

"I've heard of Torqualmar," Giles said. "He's a very deceitful demon. He commanded armies of believers in his day and attempted to conquer Africa."

"We found him in one of the books when we were researching earlier," Tara added. She reached for one of the books, pulling it from the stack and flipping through it. "I remember reading about Torqualmar tonight because the book said witches used to follow his teachings."

"I didn't know that," Willow said, looking interested.

"Me neither until tonight," Tara said. "When we go to the West African art exhibit next week, we'll have to see if anyone there has heard of him."

Anya leaned in. "Xander," she said pointedly. "Remember him?" She paused. "*Missing.* I want him back."

"We know," Willow said, chastised. "It's just kind of a coincidence, you know. The exhibit being here at the same time that Dredfahl blows into town is kind of well, you know . . . coincidental."

"Too coincidental," Giles agreed.

"It's not coincidence," Bobby Lee said. "Dredfahl came to Sunnydale because of the exhibit, an' because of the Hellmouth. That Craulathar demon you guys found tonight?"

Buffy nodded.

"That portal spell he was usin'?" Bobby Lee asked.

"Yeah," Willow said.

"Way more powerful than he should have been able to manage on his own," Bobby Lee said.

"The Craulathar demon had help," Buffy reminded. "You know: 'single male evil demon seeks single female evil demon for wanton destruction and devastation.'"

Bobby Lee shook his head. "Not even with help. The

Craulathar demon got that portal up an' goin' because Dredfahl's got some spells already locked down in place around here."

"Sympathetic magick?" Willow asked.

"Yeah," Bobby Lee said.

"What's sympathetic magick?" Dawn asked.

Willow brushed hair from her face. "If a really big spell is going on somewhere, sometimes a sphere of proximity is created. The odds of getting a similar spell to work—and with less magick input—increase. Kind of like sympathy pains. When you have a toothache, pretty soon it feels like your whole jaw is one big mass of pain."

"All of which means that while Dredfahl is up and running his world-hopping spell, more demons in other worlds are likely to cross over into our world," Buffy said.

"Not just into our world," Bobby Lee said. "When they come through, they'll be comin' through Sunnydale."

"As if Sunnydale wasn't already the gateway to the weird, lethal, and vicious," Dawn said.

Everyone looked at her.

"Sorry," Dawn said, looking down. "That sorta just slipped out."

Buffy watched her sister and immediately felt guilty. Was this any way to bring someone up? Talking about demons and world dominion? Something had to be done. Buffy felt a little angry then, and the feeling saved her from some of the guilt. She'd told Dawn not to be there. It wasn't her fault Dawn was at the Magic Box talking about this. At least, not *all* of it was her fault.

"Dredfahl is building a gateway?" Giles asked.

Bobby Lee nodded.

"Why?"

"What do you know about Torqualmar?"

"As you said, he was a demon from the West African

coast," the Watcher replied. "He had some sort of ancestry involving snakes."

"In some circles," Bobby Lee said, "Torqualmar is considered the father of *Damballah-Wedo,* the Great Serpent."

"According to the voodoo belief," Giles said. "But followers of Torqualmar spread throughout several religions."

"An' Torqualmar had more enemies than he did followers," Bobby Lee said. "Ultimately, demons an' humans stood against him an' killed him."

"As I recall, Torqualmar's conquerors burned his body," Giles said.

"They did more than that," Tara said, studying the book in front of her. "According to this, once Torqualmar's decapitated corpse was burned, the victors smashed the Torqualmar's skeleton to pieces, and the bones were scattered across worlds."

Bobby Lee grinned. "Makes it sound like there was a lot of worlds, doesn't it? But there weren't." He held up two fingers. "Actually, they only used two worlds. This one, an' a place called Ollindark. See, Torqualmar had this deal going on with a race of demons called the Dorinogs. Their world, Ollindark, is a real hellpit. Nothin' but desert, an' everything that lives on Ollindark spends its whole day figurin' on eatin' everything else. What Torqualmar was doin', he was bringin' Dorinogs across into our world to serve him."

"And that was a good deal for them?" Buffy asked.

"The Dorinogs evidently thought so. See, the Dorinogs ain't exactly rocket scientists. They're big on thumpin' things and killin' anybody Torqualmar told them to, but when it came to brains, the Dorinogs were pretty much left holdin' the bag."

"So what's the purpose of bringing the Dorinogs here?" Buffy asked.

"The Dorinogs listened to Torqualmar. An' they took orders. He wanted somethin' burned, they burned it. He wanted somebody killed, they killed somebody."

"Foot soldiers," Spike said.

"But Torqualmar couldn't bring the Dorinogs physically into this world on account of their sun bein' blue and ours bein' yellow. An' that was a good thing, because the average Dorinog demon stands about ten feet tall an' is built like a Sumo wrestler with wings."

"But they can't come here?" Willow asked.

Bobby Lee shook his head. "There's something about yellow sunrays that melt Dorinogs down into protoplasmic puddles. But Torqualmar could bring the Dorinogs through another way. He used his magick to give the Dorinogs new bodies here."

"Through consciousness transference," Giles mused. His eyes danced with excitement. "The legends about Torqualmar said that he had the power to drive men mad, to make them forget themselves and lose themselves in him."

"You're talking about possession," Buffy said, not nearly as appreciative of the process as the Watcher evidently was. The thought of demons inhabiting the bodies of humans disgusted her. Not out of any xenophobic reaction, but out of a sense of claustrophobia. She remembered being trapped in Faith's body while Faith had paraded around in her body not too long ago. A person's body was supposed to be his or her own.

"Yeah, but Torqualmar's spell was weak," Bobby Lee said. "The humans he used, they had to be willin' to cross over an' swap bodies with the demons. He couldn't just force a deal like that on folks, except for maybe one or two at a time. In order to raise an army, he had to have folks that was willin'."

"No human would willingly trade his body for that of a demon stuck in some hellpit of a world," Willow said.

"No," Bobby Lee agreed. "No human would."

"So Torqualmar did what every demon does," Spike said. "He lied to the people that believed in him."

"Yeah," Bobby Lee said, nodding. "Torqualmar told his believers they were bein' visited by spirits. Once the Dorinogs possessed the humans, they showed some healing powers and a limited ability to forecast the future. The other people, the ones that didn't get possessed, they looked at those that did an' thought maybe being possessed for a little while wasn't so bad."

"They were obviously patterned after the voodoo rituals," Giles said. "Under the direction of a voodoo priestess, participants dance and drink, praying to Damballah and the elder gods for a *loa*—a spirit, if you will—to take over their bodies. But the possession—the *riding of the host*, as they call it—doesn't last more than a few minutes."

"Some people," Bobby Lee said, "say Torqualmar's practices began the voodoo rituals that are still in use today. Me, I think they come out of other things. Maybe Torqualmar took what was goin' on then and bent it to his own uses. You know, a lie covered in truth."

"So Dredfahl is trying to bring Torqualmar back," Buffy said. "Why?"

"Once Dredfahl has all of Torqualmar's bones back together," Bobby Lee said, "the story goes that Torqualmar will come back to life."

"One of your ancestors helped kill Torqualmar?" Spike asked.

"Yeah," Bobby Lee said.

Spike leaned forward slowly and grinned. "Doesn't anyone your family kills stay dead?" he asked in derision.

Bobby Lee stared at Spike. "We killed a whole lotta vampires," Bobby Lee said. "New Orleans used to be rife with them." He paused, and a slow smile spread across his face. Buffy spotted the cruelty that was possible in the handsome features. "Ain't that way no more, is it?"

"I wouldn't know," Spike said. "Maybe, once this is over, it would be interestin' to find out."

"If you got the guts to buy into this mess," Bobby Lee said in a quiet, tense voice, "an' if you get lucky enough to make it through, come on down. I'll keep a candle burnin' for you. We'll find out if you tango as well as you talk."

"I'm getting bloody bored," Spike protested. "So we know that Dredfahl is tryin' to bring back Torqualmar, but we don't know why. So he can be Torqualmar's toady again? And Dredfahl came back from bein' dead himself for that?"

"Dredfahl plans on killin' Torqualmar," Bobby Lee said. "Then takin' his power from him."

"Oh, come on," Spike exploded. "Bring him back just to kill him? Where's the bloody sense in that?"

A smile covered Bobby Lee's face. "Dredfahl, he's probably not very happy about that his ownself. If he's successful at killin' Torqualmar, he gets more power. But if Dredfahl ain't successful, he gets his old boss back, an' maybe he gets killed, too."

"Either way," Buffy said, "we've got trouble. Sitting here isn't going to solve that. We need to find Dredfahl. If we stop him early enough, we don't have to worry about Torqualmar."

"I agree," Giles said. "We need a plan. The first thing we need to do is to secure whatever bones might be at the West African exhibit Willow mentioned."

Buffy nodded. Planning was good. Knowing the enemy was usually good too. But planning was next to action.

"You're sure that some of those bones are there?" Giles asked.

"Yeah," Bobby Lee answered.

"I can look for the bones," Buffy offered.

"I'll go with you," Bobby Lee said.

Buffy gazed at him.

"I know what Dredfahl looks like."

Buffy considered that, then nodded. "What about this television guy?"

"Derek Traynor of *Othersyde*," Tara said.

"Right," Buffy said. "Him."

"What about him?" Giles asked.

"Is it me, or did the whole 'I see demons' thing just seem too weird and come too close to everything else that's going on. I mean, the guy's supposed to see ghosts."

"Yeah," Tara agreed. "Derek said Donny Williford was somewhere else, and that he was changed somehow. That kind of sounds like the body-swapping thing."

"Consciousness transference," Giles corrected automatically.

"Did you say Donny Williford?" Anya asked.

"Yes," Tara answered. "Now, and a few minutes ago when I was telling this story."

"I wasn't really listening," Anya confessed. "I was more interested in discussing Xander's disappearance and what we were going to do about it. I was kind of irritated at all of you because you wanted to talk about this whole Dredfahl thing instead of getting out there to look for Xander."

"Anya," Buffy said quietly, "it's going to be all right. We're going to get Xander back."

For a moment, Anya looked like she was going to argue, like she was going to give in to the doubts that filled her. Then she said, "Promise?"

The pained innocence in Anya's eyes made her impossible to lie to.

"Yes," Buffy said. "I promise."

"Okay." Anya dabbed at her tears.

"Why did you ask about Donny Williford?" Tara asked.

"Because he's a friend of Xander's," Anya said. "He and Xander talk sometimes at Matt's Comics or the arcades."

"Donny's a gamer?" Willow asked.

Anya nodded. "Big-time. Writes columns on comic books and games for Web sites."

"Does he have a girlfriend?" Tara asked.

Anya looked confused. "Yes."

"What's her name?"

"What does this have to do with anything?"

Exasperated but trying desperately to be tactful, Buffy said, "Just answer the question, Anya."

"Amy," Anya said. "Her name's Amy."

Buffy looked at Tara, who nodded.

"Giles and I saw Amy on the set of *Othersyde*," Tara said.

"So we have a tie to Derek Traynor," Buffy said.

"Apparently Derek's gift somehow ties him into the spell Dredfahl has set up to bring Torqualmar back from the dead," Giles said.

"Tara and I will try to contact Derek Traynor," Willow offered. "If he can see into the demon world, maybe that would be a good thing."

"You should be looking for Xander," Anya declared.

A pained, guilty expression filled Willow's face.

"She will be looking for Xander, Anya," Buffy said in a stern voice. "In the demon world, if she can talk to Derek."

"Fine," Anya said. "But I'm coming with you to the museum."

"Actually," Giles said, "you'd probably help better by searching through the books with me. I'm sure we'll need more information on Torqualmar and whatever spell Dredfahl is planning to use."

"I can't," Anya said. "Not with Xander missing. One of us would go absolutely crazy if I stayed here."

Giles didn't hesitate. "Then by all means, you should go."

Buffy shot the Watcher a glance to let him know how unhappy she was.

Out of Anya's sight, Giles lifted his shoulders slightly and dropped them.

"What about me?" Dawn asked.

Buffy shifted her attention to her sister. "What about you?"

"What am I supposed to do?"

"You," Buffy said, "stay here. We've talked about this."

"Homework's all done," Dawn protested.

"Then you should get to the sleeping part of the night," Buffy replied.

"I could help," Dawn said. "I could help you watch your back at the museum. Or I could help Giles with looking up stuff in the books."

"No," Buffy said. "This stuff is off-limits. All of it. You've got school and rest to tend to."

"But, Buffy—"

Buffy folded her arms over her chest. "No buts. All out of buts here. Consider me but-proof."

"I can't sleep with Xander missing."

"Try harder," Buffy suggested.

Dawn sighed, deep and heavy.

Nice attempt, Buffy thought, *but tonight I'm sigh-proof, too.* Still, she didn't like having to be the bad guy, but having Dawn involved in this thing, as dangerous as it was sure to get, was unacceptable. "Get home. Wait. I'll be there by morning to let you know the status regarding Xander."

"We need to talk," Dawn said. "Alone." She got up

from the table and walked to one of the rear rooms in the shop.

Having no choice, Buffy followed her sister into the back room of the Magic Box.

Hard, callused flesh scraped along stone.

Xander Harris blinked his eyes open and regretted it instantly when the harsh green light stabbed deep into his brain. For a moment, he believed some kind of napalm bomb had gone off inside his head.

The scrape sounded again, a little more tentative, and Xander felt his senses coming alive. A prickling feeling scurried across the back of his neck. *Okay, those are definitely my Spidey senses tingling.*

Xander stared out at the yellow sand and rock in front of him. The yellow alkaline desert stretched for miles, rising slightly the way the ocean did far off into the horizon. The land ended in jagged, toothy mountains, and the green sky rose above them. High in the sky a blue sun burned down, baking into Xander's body.

Definitely not in Kansas anymore, Toto.

The scrape of callused flesh along stone sounded closer and turned into the rasping scrabble of talons against rock and baked sand. Heart exploding in his chest, Xander pushed himself up on his arms and rolled to one side.

A lizard the size of horse dropped onto the sandy patch where Xander had been lying. The creature resembled a gecko because of the slender, long-legged, long-tailed body, but the long snout filled with serrated teeth reminded Xander of an alligator. Instead of green, the lizard was brindle-colored in at least six different yellow, amber, and orange hues that matched the shifting sand and the rock. The iridescent scales glistened in the sunlight and rolled over sleek muscle.

The thing hissed angrily, turning its long head sideways to focus on Xander with one rolling eye.

"Oh, man," Xander yelped, stepping back. His back twitched in a manner he'd never before experienced. Wings popped out on either side of him. A quick glance showed him that he was no longer human and must have been one of the demons Stephie had described from the VR game Robby had been testing. Only Xander knew this was no game.

The lizard rushed him again, hammering widely spaced, spatulate fingers down against the sandy crust. Dust clouds flew up behind the creature, and if the situation had not been so dangerous, Xander might have laughed at the sight. Instead, Xander turned and fled, hoping that whatever he was turned out to be faster than the lizard-thing.

The lizard slammed into Xander's legs and knocked him sprawling. Instinctively, he furled his wings as he fell, managing to push himself up to his knees as the lizard darted again, jaws open wide to tear at Xander's throat.

Xander threw an arm up, hammering the side of the lizard's head. Overpowered, the lizard dropped to the ground, rolled, and pushed up. The creature stood, and for the first time Xander saw that there were six legs instead of four. The lizard's tail curled and flexed in a hypnotic fashion.

"Go on," Xander yelled. "Beat it. You don't want to pick a fight with me. You'll make me angry." He flexed his arms and shoulders, making the big body he wore appear even bigger and Hulk-like. "You won't like me when I'm angry." He raised his voice. "Xander smash! Xander crush!"

Apparently, the lizard hadn't grown up on comics the way Xander had, and didn't have a clue about warning dialogue. Muscles twitched, then the lizard sprang forward. Defending himself, Xander seized the attacking creature's long neck in both hands, going over backward as the lizard knocked him from his feet. The broad, spatulate feet came equipped with curved, black talons that ripped into Xander's flesh.

Working to strangle the lizard, Xander rolled, throwing himself on top of his opponent and going flat so the thing couldn't scratch him anymore. The lizard hissed and spat. Harsh, gross breath washed over Xander's face and triggered his gag reflex. Still, he maintained his hold, hoping to choke the lizard down.

The creature's neck snapped like a brittle twig. Convulsive shivers ran through the lizard. The six legs flailed uselessly at Xander, leaving bloody scratches in their wake but not much real damage. A moment later, the lizard went limp and the eyes rolled emptily in their sockets.

"Cripes," Xander said. Tentatively, he released his hold on the lizard's neck and pushed himself up to his knees, straddling the long creature. He'd been fighting demons and vampires too long to believe easily that things always died when they appeared to.

But the lizard was dead.

Slow, mocking applause sounded, carrying over the expanse of sandy desert.

Craning his neck, Xander glanced back and saw a bald, earless gargoyle with furled wings sitting on a rocky outcrop thrust up from the ground only a short distance away.

"Xander smash!" the gargoyle said, putting his hands down and grinning.

At least, Xander *hoped* the grim rictus on the gargoyle's face was a grin.

"Xander crush!" the gargoyle shouted, then shook his head. "Man, that is so lame. I kept waiting for you to shout, 'It's clobberin' time!'"

"Anyone who reads comics knows that's The Thing's battle cry," Xander said automatically.

The gargoyle crossed his arms over his knees. "You're new here."

"Yeah."

"Just get in the game?"

"Yeah," Xander said, remembering how Dredfahl had forced him from his own body.

"Wow," the gargoyle said. "Didn't know they were letting anybody else in. This late in the game, I mean."

"Special invitation," Xander replied. He had to restrain himself from screaming out that the whole thing was a demon world, not a game at all. He wondered if he would find anyone willing to believe that. Most of the gamers he knew would rather believe in virtual reality.

"Cool. Who invited you?"

"Dredfahl."

The gargoyle smiled again. "Man, that's what he tells everybody his name is. My name's Dylan."

"Good to meet you, Dylan. Is Robby Healdton around?" *Please,* Xander thought, *don't let Robby be dead.*

Dylan pointed back toward the mountain. "That way. There's a valley along the way. You just can't see it from here."

"Thanks." Xander turned and started walking in the direction that had been indicated.

"Hey!"

Xander turned, thinking it would probably be just about right that he'd be under attack from something again. He scanned the green sky around the blue sun but didn't see anything. He stood stock still, waiting for tremors to shoot through the ground beneath his feet to let him know something was burrowing up to get him. "What?"

"Can I have that?" Dylan pointed at the lizard's corpse.

"For what?"

"To eat."

"Eat?" Xander looked at the lizard's corpse. *Okay, that just exceeded the gross barrier.*

"Yeah, man. That's how we store up energy in the game." Dylan hopped off the outcrop and used his wings to coast over to the lizard. "I think it's pretty cool, but it keeps tripping my gag reflex, you know. But if you don't eat, you get weak and you don't heal as fast."

Nauseated, Xander watched as Dylan bent down, clawing the lizard open. Blood spilled, and intestines slithered around inside the corpse. Dylan lowered his head and started feeding, and the sucking, slurping noise was stomach turning.

Taking a quick break, Dylan turned to Xander. Blood dripped down the gargoyle's face, dropping from his chin to his chest. "You sure you don't want any of this?"

"No," Xander said.

"Suit yourself." Dylan shrugged and went back to feeding.

Xander continued in the direction Dylan had pointed. *Okay, and that's totally stomach wrenching. I am not staying in this place long enough to eat dinner.*

Chapter Fourteen

"**I** can help with this. I'm not a little kid."

Buffy looked at Dawn, wishing she had all the words she needed to explain. Their mom was always so much better at dealing with communication things. At least, she had been after Buffy had started listening. Her mom had dealt with the Slayer bit, and even dealt with the cancer better than Buffy had.

And she'd probably have dealt better with my death than I'm doing with hers, Buffy couldn't help thinking. Or maybe she was being a little selfish there because being dead would have meant not having to feel confused or hurt—or responsible for anybody else.

Dawn stood in the back room of the Magic Box. She had the whole sullen teenager thing going on, and for a minute Buffy was blown away by the attitude. She'd seen the attitude in her friends before, but that had been cool because she'd been their age and they were all on the same side then.

Now, Buffy realized, she was on the other side of the attitude. The experience was awful.

Buffy folded her own arms, feeling foolish arguing with her sister in the semidark room. "No," Buffy said, carefully enunciating the word and surprised at her own skill. "You can't help."

"I'm good at this, Buffy. I've helped on other things."

"I shouldn't have let you," Buffy said. Letting Dawn help at other times had been easier then than it was now. Before, losing someone hadn't seemed so . . . so permanent.

"Why?" Dawn demanded.

"Because I don't want you getting hurt."

"I won't get hurt."

"You don't know that."

"You might get hurt," Dawn said.

"I'm the Slayer," Buffy said simply. "I get hurt, I heal quickly. One of the perks."

"You could still be killed. Slayers get killed. Or don't you remember that?"

"I know that," Buffy stated calmly. All those times she'd argued with a parental or authority figure, she'd never known how hard staying cool was. Being calm in the face of someone's verbal attack and visceral hatred of the authority being imposed was a lot tougher than it looked.

"You can't just tell me what to do," Dawn said.

"I can. I will. I am."

"It's not fair, Buffy. You're not fair."

"I'm not about being fair," Buffy said. "You're my sister, Dawn. All the family I've got left." *Except for a father that doesn't take time out of his day to call and check on us.* "I won't lose you. That's just not going to happen."

"So you expect me to just stay here like a good little girl?"

"That," Buffy agreed, "would really help me out here."

"And if I don't?"

"If you don't," Buffy said, "then I ask Giles or Tara to be your baby-sitter. I can't stay. I've gotta slay."

Dawn shook her head.

"Of course," Buffy said, "you'll make it harder for Giles or Tara to help out, and make my job harder—if not impossible." *Or suicidal.* She chose not to play that card, thinking that would be way over the top and cruel. If something happened tonight, she didn't want Dawn ever to think somehow she was responsible for her death.

"This sucks, Buffy."

Buffy tried to think of something to say, but couldn't. The silence dragged out between them.

Footsteps sounded outside the doorway. "Buffy," Giles said. "I don't mean to interrupt."

"Sure you do," Buffy said. "But it's cool." She never took her eyes from Dawn. "We were just about finished here."

Dawn glared at her.

"So what's it going to be, Dawn?" Buffy asked. "Stay here like a big girl? Or do you need a sitter?"

"I don't need a sitter."

Dawn stalked by Buffy, and if Giles hadn't been standing in the doorway, Buffy was sure her sister would have slammed the door.

"Don't die tonight," Dawn called back. "We're not through with this discussion."

"Sure," Buffy said.

Giles rubbed his chin and tried to appear as though he hadn't heard the exchange between the sisters.

"Kids," Buffy said in a mock grump, trying to keep some of the hurt from touching her and knowing that it wouldn't work. "What are you going to do?"

"If I may offer a bit of advice," Giles began.

"If I say no," Buffy said, "you'll just wait until later to say whatever it is you're going to say. I might as well hear it now." She crossed her arms and waited, then realized she was striking pretty much the same pose that Dawn had. "Sorry." She dropped her arms to her sides.

"You're not Dawn's mother, Buffy, and she's not your daughter. You're sisters."

"Right."

"I just think you might want to keep that in perspective when you talk with her."

Buffy waited.

Giles looked at her, then looked away, then looked back at her.

"That's it?" Buffy protested. "That's your pearl of wisdom?"

Giles stuck his hands in his pockets. "I'm afraid so."

"Gee," Buffy said, "all of this has gone really well. I hope Dredfahl and his demons are at the museum tonight. I really feel the need to get back into something I don't suck at."

Xander found Robby and his group camped out down in the valley. Most of the gargoyle creatures— *Dorinogs, Robby had informed him*—were feasting on the remains of the buffalo creatures—*Kalinths*—and acting like they were in the middle of a tailgate party. Kalinth bones, stripped of flesh, went flying only to be carried away by small scavengers.

"You sure you don't want anything to eat, X-Man?" Robby asked Xander.

"No," Xander answered. "Really. I couldn't eat a bite." *Not without throwing up. And the really disturbing part is that if I did throw up, these guys or someone else would probably fight over it.* Xander's borrowed stomach lurched. He didn't know if the reflex came from the demon he'd invaded or was his own feeling of revulsion. *Maybe it's both of us.*

"So how did you get into the game so late?" Robby asked.

Xander considered his answer. He'd listened to all the excited conversations of the gamers in the bodies of the demons around him. All of them were in gamer heaven, killing and conquering.

"Haven't you felt anything strange about this game, Robby?"

Robby picked a piece of gristle from between his demon's teeth. "Man, this game is awesome, dude. I mean, look around you. Even when we talked about VR in gaming, did you ever think it was actually going to turn out like this? This is like a whole new world." He pointed a bone at a large group of Dorinogs off to one side feasting by themselves. "The only thing I'd change are those guys."

Xander had noticed the schism in the group. The larger group of Dorinogs were sullen and totally antisocial. Xander also had the sneaking suspicion that this particular group of Dorinogs were real demons that hadn't had their conscious minds replaced by human gamers from Sunnydale.

"Who are they?" Xander asked.

"NPCs," Robby said. "And they really suck. I mean, they're stupid and can't hardly follow orders. Those guys couldn't think their way out of a wet paper bag."

Xander let out a breath. *Okay, they're demons. And we're camped right in the middle of them. Terrific.* "Does everybody think this is a game?"

Robby looked at Xander, blood dripping down his face. If they'd been back in Sunnydale and Robby had been wearing his own face, Xander knew a challenging expression would have been there.

"What are you talking about?" Robby demanded.

"I mean," Xander said, "this isn't a game."

"Are you working for some other side?" Robby asked. "Is that what this is all about? You've been sent over here to undermine our confidence? Because the game documents didn't say anything about spies being involved in the play."

"I'm not a spy," Xander said. "It's just that not everything here is what you think it is. Dredfahl isn't who he says he is. Dredfahl is a demon. The reason I'm over here now? I heard his plans, and he shoved me over here so I couldn't tell anyone."

"Dredfahl's not his real name," Robby said. "I know that. Who would have a name like that?"

Xander took a deep breath and felt his wings shift across his back, which was kind of a weird feeling because he wasn't used to the sensation. "This game is real, Robby. These demons, the body you're in. All of it."

Robby stood and flexed. Scabbed wounds tracked his body, testifying how close he'd come to dying any number of times. Some of the scabs broke open as he moved, and fresh drops of blood threaded down his arms, legs, chest, and back.

"Man, I hate bleeding." Robby bent and scooped up a handful of sand to rub in his wounds. "You can smell the blood in the air in this place."

"I can't smell anything," Xander said.

"Take my word for it, buddy. Once you get acclimated to the VR interface, you'll smell blood too. And once the scent of blood gets in the air, everything that lives in this world comes hunting you. If one of those predators thinks it's big enough to kill you and eat you, it tries. If it thinks you're weak, it hangs around until you drop." Robby grinned a gargoyle smile at Xander. "Of course the upside is that if whatever it is that's stalking you drops first and you know it's there, you get to eat it."

Xander shook his head. "Think about it, Robby. Who would design a game like that? When we talked about a VR game, we talked about hunting and fishing, but we never imagined a world like this. This place is harsh, man."

"The environment," Robby said defensively, "is user-friendly to system specs. It won't eat up the operating space in your system."

"C'mon," Xander said, stepping forward and putting some steel in his voice, "what system is capable of doing the stuff you see around you?"

"None. None that I know of."

"And how much do you think a system would cost that would do something like this?"

"A design company with a deep R and D pocket could do it," Robby said stubbornly.

"That's the gamer in you talking, pal. That's the kid that grew up on Nintendo and Sega and moved on to PlayStation, PlayStation 2, and Dreamcast. You're a computer programmer too, Robby. Tell me what kind of system requirements it would take to maybe—*maybe*—create something like this."

Robby was silent for a while. "Military Crays. At least third and maybe fourth generation. Xander," he continued in a quiet voice, "I know this is weird, okay? I mean, as soon as I woke up here, I knew this place was weird. Even the preliminary exercises we did here."

"I didn't do any exercises," Xander said. "Dredfahl just threw me in here."

"That doesn't make any sense."

"I found out about him," Xander said. "I saw him in the hospital when he came after the demon that's in your body."

"What?" Robby sounded incredulous.

"It's true, man. This guy Dredfahl, he's a demon of some sort. Got the power to trade minds with people. This place we're in? It's real."

Robby paced, shaking his head.

Watching the hulking goliath, the pacing habit was the only thing that Xander recognized about his friend.

"Why did Dredfahl put you in here?" Robby asked.

"Maybe he wanted another demon in a human body," Xander said.

"This doesn't make any sense."

"And having a computer system capable of creating a VR environment like this does?"

Robby spread his arms to encompass the world. "A game like this, Xander? Man, this is all a lot of us used to dream about. We've almost got the technology down." He held his thumb and forefinger a fraction of an inch apart. "We're this close. So when somebody comes up to me, offers me a chance to test hardware and programming like this, I'm going to say yes."

"And you're going to believe," Xander said. "I know. There's nothing wrong with that. But this isn't hardware, and this world isn't digital gaming."

Robby started pacing again. "I knew you hung out with some strange people, X-Man. The old guy that used to be the librarian at your high school. That girl, Buffy, who always seemed to be around true weirdness."

"Demons live in Sunnydale," Xander said. "So do vampires. And those that don't live there come to visit. The guy that did this? I think he's from out of town."

"This is crazy. This is just a game." And without another word, Robby stalked off.

Xander stood there, not knowing what to say. How could he convince Robby that what he was experiencing wasn't a dream-come-true gaming environment, but a monstrous other world instead?

• • •

Buffy roamed the shadows of the museum room that held the West African artifacts. The exhibit was big enough to rate a private room. Most of the exhibit was still packed in wooden crates filled with Styrofoam peanuts, but some of those crates lay open with vases, pottery, and even a couple of canoes.

The center of the room held a miniature reproduction of a village, straw and mud-thatched huts sitting on the bank of an ocean. Small lights burned in the center of artificial bonfires where tiny villagers cooked and danced. They'd lived on a narrow strip of sandy and rocky land between the ocean and a thick jungle.

Trapped between harsh environments, Buffy thought. And she felt it was a lot like trying to be responsible for a sister like a parent is and trying to be a peer at the same time. *Not much margin for error.* Her head wasn't filled with happy thoughts.

Getting into the museum hadn't been hard. Bobby Lee had broken through the locks, and Spike had bypassed all the security systems. Once inside the museum, Buffy had divided them up into two groups. Spike and Anya patrolled the rest of the museum, and Buffy remained with Bobby Lee. They'd started rummaging through the exhibit boxes at once.

"How you doin', *chèr?*" Bobby Lee asked.

"Cher?" Buffy looked at Bobby Lee. "Am I supposed to call you Sonny?"

Bobby Lee smiled. He sat loose and relaxed on crossed legs. He held the guitar in his hands across his lap, and his fingers danced silently across the strings, strumming an unheard melody.

"*Chèr,* that's just a term of friendliness back where I come from, Buffy," Bobby Lee said. "Meant nothin' by it. I apologize if I done somethin' wrong."

"No," Buffy said. "It's okay. Maybe I'm just a little uptight."

"'Bout your sister?"

Buffy turned to face him a little more. "You've got some nerve, you know that? You show up here, bring all these demon problems, and now you want to question me about my personal life?"

"Looks like I'm bound an' determined to get on your bad side. I'll leave it alone. My apologies again."

Buffy sighed, feeling guilty, knowing she should have been feeling focused. "It's not your fault. It's mine. All I have are bad sides tonight."

"Maybe not. You're here now. Getting ready to do what you been born and trained to do."

Buffy glanced at her watch. They'd been inside the museum for over an hour. Standing and waiting was horrible. She never had to wait that long for action in Sunnydale's cemeteries. And usually while she was there, she had company she could talk her problems over with.

"You got your sister on your mind," Bobby Lee said.

Buffy didn't say anything. If she was going to talk to anybody about the strain between her and Dawn, it was going to be Willow or maybe Spike. He'd gotten in the habit of showing up and talking to her at the back of her mom's—*her and Dawn's*—house. He was the one person Buffy didn't feel responsible for, and that was nice for a change.

"That's okay," Bobby Lee said. "We don't have to talk about it if you don't want to." His fingers brushed the guitar strings, and Buffy heard them ring ever so slightly. The melody was haunting and lyrical, sad but somehow hopeful.

Buffy stared out into the darkened room for a while longer. "I was sorry to hear about your dad. Sorry to hear about your grandfather, too."

"Thank you. It's hard losin' someone."

"I know," Buffy said. "I . . . I lost my mom not too long ago."

"That," Bobby Lee said, "would be a hard one to go through."

Buffy remained silent, willing herself not to cry. God, she'd cried enough, hadn't she? Surely there couldn't be much left. But all she had to do was think about her mom, and she'd feel the tears trying to break through.

"Your daddy ain't around much?" Bobby Lee asked.

"Not much," Buffy said, wishing that Bobby Lee would find something else to talk about.

"So it's just the two of you."

"I have my friends, and she has her friends."

"Yeah, but how many of them friends do you see bein' responsible for your sister?"

"If something happened to me, they'd look after Dawn."

"But you wouldn't want them to have to do that, would you?"

"No," Buffy said irritably. "Because if they had to do that, it would mean I was kind of dead."

"It's more than that, *chèr*. It would mean you wasn't there for your sister when she needed you to be. An' maybe you're a little afraid if somethin' happens to you, maybe it'll happen to Dawn, too. If she's around you and in your business."

"You're wrong," Buffy made herself say.

"Maybe," Bobby Lee conceded unexpectedly. "But if I am, I'll be mighty surprised." His fingers rang quietly against the guitar strings.

"And what makes you so sure you're right?"

"After my daddy got killed," Bobby Lee said, "that's how I felt about my sisters."

"You have sisters?"

Bobby Lee nodded. "Two. Chenille and Taffy. Chenille, she's seventeen now, but Taffy's only nine. See, after my daddy died, I tried bein' a daddy to them. Tried tellin' them what to do, how to act, keep their grades up, who to see, who not to see. Now, you see, that was the wrong thing to do."

"They didn't like it."

Shaking his head and frowning but with a self-mocking glint in his eyes, Bobby Lee said, "Not even a little bit. That's when my momma told me I was too much into their business. She told me that we'd all lost a daddy, an' she'd lost a good man, but my sisters didn't need me tryin' to be a daddy to them. Oh, my momma agreed as how it would help out if I kind of watched over my sisters a little more than I had been, but she said what they really needed was a brother who cared. See, if I kept on tryin' to be a daddy to them, they'd probably come to resent me. Then they'd have lost their daddy, an' with me constantly remindin' them of that, they'd lose their brother, too."

"So how are things between you now?"

Bobby Lee smiled. "My sisters, they got the best brother that sisters could ever want to have."

"You mother sounds like a very smart lady."

"Oh, she is," Bobby Lee agreed. "An' she'd be the first to tell you that. She was what kept my daddy in line."

"And what about the demon hunting you do? Do your sisters know about that?"

"Yeah."

"Doesn't that worry you?"

"Some," Bobby Lee admitted. "But you got to remember what I got is family business. My family, we been handing down this responsibility for a long time now. Everybody in the family knows what the risks are. But we are in it together. Like you and your friends are."

"I can't keep them out of it," Buffy said. "I've tried."

"That's 'cause they're your friends. And your sister? Why, Dawn should be the closest one of them. Especially now that it's just the two of you. What you don't understand is that while you're all busy tryin' to take care of her, she's all busy feelin' like she should be takin' care of you. You try to push her into the safe parts of your world, there won't be no part of you left to hang on to. What you are, *chèr*, is what you are. Ain't no way you can divide that up."

Buffy was silent, thinking over what Bobby Lee had told her. Then, as a sudden chill stole down her spine, she knew they were no longer alone in the museum.

Chapter Fifteen

"I don't think this is really a good idea, Willow."

Trying not to sound irritated because she knew Tara had a hard time dealing with other people's anger, Willow glanced up. "Didn't we try calling Derek Traynor's hotel room?"

Reluctantly, Tara nodded. She sat on the floor of their dorm room and didn't look happy.

"And didn't we try sneaking into the hotel where he's staying?" Willow asked, finishing laying out the chalk line that constructed the protective circle they'd need for what she had planned.

"Yes."

"I thought after hotel security threatened to call the police, that going back there might not be such a good idea," Willow said. She put the chalk away in the bag of witchy things she had.

"But this?" Tara said. "I'm really not that comfortable with a séance."

"I don't see that we have a choice," Willow said. She pushed herself up and went to the center of the protective circle. The dorm room was dark around her, but down the hall she could hear stereos and televisions playing.

"Magick isn't something you do every time you have trouble," Tara said. "Magick's supposed to be something you experience and share." She frowned. "You use witchcraft . . . maybe a little too much."

"Tara," Willow said, "how can you say that? I've never used my powers out of greed or laziness the way some witches try to do. I've only used them to help my friends."

"You're starting to use your power more and more often to help your friends," Tara said.

"Well," Willow said defensively, "my friends have been needing more and more help lately. Kind of balances everything out."

Tara pointed at the rat in the hamster cage sitting on the dresser. "Amy Madison got a little too into her witchcraft. Now look at her."

The rat, as if sensing the discussion was about her, stuck her nose toward them. Only a few years ago, Amy Madison had been a high school student. Now she was just one of those Missing-in-Action from Sunnydale High.

"I'm not doing any morphing spells," Willow said. "Just an old-fashioned séance to summon up the ghost of Donny Williford."

"He might not even be dead," Tara said.

"You're doubting Derek Traynor?" Willow made herself comfortable in the center of the protective circle.

"No, I didn't say that. It's just that Derek might be mistaken."

"There's only one way to find out," Willow said. She got out a lighter and glanced at the five candles she had placed near the circle's perimeter. "Are you coming in, or are you staying out? Once I get this spell going, you can't cross the circle till I'm finished. And you can't be in this room outside the protective circle."

Tara had an unhappy look on her face as she stepped over the circle, careful not to break the line. She sat down in the center facing Willow.

"I could probably do this alone," Willow offered, already feeling a little guilty that she had forced Tara to accompany her.

"No," Tara said. "I don't want you in here alone if anything goes wrong. And we're strong together."

Feeling warm and cheery inside at Tara's words, Willow leaned forward and gave the other girl a quick hug. "We'll always be strong together."

"Let's just be careful," Tara said.

"We will," Willow promised. She leaned forward and started lighting candles. She lit three of them, then Tara stretched out her hand for the lighter and lit the remaining two candles. After Tara gave the lighter back, Willow dropped it into her bag.

The smoking flames danced atop the candles, and the scent of magick was in the air.

Willow's witchy senses quivered in anticipation. *There is just something so* cool *about magick.* She took Tara's hands in her own, holding them with tight reassurance. "Are you ready?" she asked.

"Yes," Tara replied, giving a hesitant nod.

Breathing out, Willow relaxed and concentrated. Since real world tactics weren't going to get them to Derek Traynor, she'd decided the only way to get to the television personality was through magick. Because Derek had some mystical ability of his own, Willow didn't think the connection would be hard to make. All they had to do was stay in touch with Derek long enough to convince him that they were real, and that the problem

facing them was real. Then he'd come to them willingly.
At least, that was the plan.

Willow just hoped that none of them would get killed
in the process.

> *"Like still waters running deep,*
> *Inky shadows from night,*
> *Bend to my will*
> *And give me the sight*
> *Of the one I want*
> *So that I may continue the fight."*

Power swelled within Willow, expanding quickly.
She felt Tara's hands in hers, felt the other girl tightening
her hold.

In the next instant, gray-white fog surrounded the
protective circle drawn on the floor. When the wispy
layer got so thick that she could no longer see the rest of
the room, a face pressed out of the fog.

The face belonged to a guy that Willow didn't know.
He had a narrow, pinched face and long hair that hung
down over one eye. And he was ghostly, pasty pale
almost like a reversed film negative.

He twisted his head around, searching, then stared at
Willow and Tara. With an inarticulate cry of feral rage,
the ghost rushed at Willow, arms outstretched as he sailed
out of the fog.

Despite the rebellious and hurt feelings that snarled
within her, Dawn still felt a little guilty as she entered the
arcade only a few blocks from the Magic Box. Staying
there hadn't been an option, and she'd gladly bolted as
soon as she was able. She turned her attention to the
sights and the sounds of the arcade, wanting something to
drag her thoughts away from Buffy and whatever demon

she was probably going up against right now.

Whatever demon might be killing her right now.

Dawn's heart almost froze in between heartbeats. She made herself stop thinking thoughts like that. Or, at least, she tried to. The problem was that she knew what Buffy did and what risks Buffy took. And Dawn knew that at any moment Buffy might be ripped away from her the way her mom had been.

That knowledge was almost too much to live with. And it was certainly too much for her to just sit home with or concentrate on homework or hang on the phone with her friends.

Dawn walked through the aisles of the arcade. The machines held a cornucopia of games. Colorfully clad mutants fought armies of bad guys and sometimes each other. Special federal agents blasted demons and ghouls and aliens, while other law-enforcement personnel went after more mundane criminals—mundane although equipped with weapons that delivered absolute carnage. Other machines held racing games featuring stock cars and eighteen-wheelers. And there was a whole plethora of military assault vehicles that featured different fighter jets and tanks.

Xander sometimes brought Dawn there on nights when Buffy was out late on a solo patrol. Those visits weren't very often, though, because Xander spent most of his time with Anya. But Dawn and Xander had enjoyed good times battling their way through various scenarios and combating each other.

Dawn wasn't there for a good time, though. After listening to Anya's talk about Robby Healdton and Tara's discussion of Donny Williford—both of whom Dawn knew through Xander—Dawn had decided there was only one place to find demons seeking out gamers to do the whole mind-swap thing with them.

Actually, though, there were several places to look

for demons. Sunnydale had a lot of arcades and comics places, but most of them—including Matt's Comics where Dawn knew she'd seen Robby Healdton on more than one occasion—were already closed. Despite the long night and the meeting at the Magic Box, the time was now only 1:47 A.M. Shooter's Other Worlds, the arcade place, closed at two in the morning.

Dawn walked through the rows of machines and felt kind of hopeless. Hearing about Donny Williford dying in the other dimension had been horrible, but Dawn had figured Donny hadn't been the only guy to die. If gamers were dying in the demon world, it had to mean that recruits would be needed.

That was the plan Dawn had come up with at the Magic Box. But she'd known that Buffy wouldn't listen, and if Buffy had listened, she would have asked someone else to check it out. Coming here like this, even though she knew there was a chance she would fail, Dawn at least felt useful. She wasn't being pushed away or treated like some little kid.

However, if the demons looked like everybody else in the arcade, Dawn wasn't sure how she was going to find them.

She wound through the games, speaking to the few people who noticed her and moving quickly on. None of the arcade visitors was a real friend. They were more people that Xander knew. Dawn's friends wouldn't have been in the arcades because being there as a high-school girl was just way too geeky.

The times Dawn had come with Xander had been out of boredom and desperation to get out of the house while Buffy was gone, and she would hope that no one saw her. Xander had been cool with that because he understood. He even kind of helped her hide out and kept her in snacks and near-food things.

Xander. Dawn's breath locked at the back of her throat. *Please, please don't let anything happen to Xander. How could Buffy even think I could just go home with Xander missing?*

Dawn rounded the air-hockey table, which usually only had a little action. Sometimes the older crowd played air hockey, but generally the game was used as a gossip corner. Two guys were there now, obviously macking on three girls who clearly had no interest in them.

Taking the short flight of steps up to the second level of Shooter's, Dawn stopped by the "Jurassic Park" game that was mocked up like a touring SUV from the first movie. Two guys were inside, cursing and blasting the dinosaurs that attacked them. The second level of the arcade gave a good view of everyone in the lower level, as well as the entrance.

Dawn stood and watched, telling herself she'd made the right choice. The only other gaming store open was Realms, a shop that specialized in collectible card games and pen-and-ink dungeon crawlers. Dawn was hoping that Dredfahl was more tuned in to platform and arcade gamers than guys that played CCGs and RPGs.

1:52 A.M. The minutes rushed by. Dawn's stomach growled as she watched the entrance and the players. She remembered the pizza she'd left back at the Magic Box, and remembered that she hadn't eaten at home. She'd forgotten to. Without Buffy there, life kind of consisted of television shows, trying not to think about Mom, homework, and the occasional semi-interesting phone call from one of her friends.

Living at home since Mom had died was pretty much pathetic. Dawn figured that Buffy felt the same way. *That's why Buffy's never home.*

"Hey, Dawn."

Dawn turned and saw Eric Rogers, one of the geeky

gamers from junior high. He was thin and awkward, with blond-and-magenta hair in a skater cut and wire-rimmed granny glasses. He was dressed in a Mighty Mouse T-shirt that made him somehow look cute.

"Hey, Eric," Dawn said.

"Did you sneak out of the house?" Eric asked, stopping in front of her.

"Yeah," Dawn said. *This is* so *like the last thing I need right now.* She peered past Eric. Had someone just entered the arcade? She wasn't sure, and that was frustrating and scary.

"Cool," Eric said. "Been doing it long?"

"Every now and again," Dawn said.

"As wiped out as I've seen you from time to time in school," Eric said, "I figured you probably were."

Great, Dawn thought. *Guess makeup hasn't been quite covering those dark circles from not sleeping.*

"Just haven't seen you around Shooter's much," Eric went on.

"I don't usually come here," Dawn admitted.

"Oh?" Eric looked interested. "You usually go to parties?"

Well, that might be a reputation enhancement, Dawn decided. "Yeah."

Eric nodded. "Cool, cool." He hesitated. "Maybe sometime we could hook up, you know?" He absently fiddled with the cell phone hanging from his waist.

"Maybe," Dawn said.

"When?" Eric pressed.

Dawn hesitated, not wanting to offend Eric but not wanting to promise anything she wasn't going to go through with either.

"Attention," a feminine voice blared over the PA system. "Shooters will be closing in five minutes. Please finish the games you're on."

A multitude of groans filled the arcade, along with a few curses.

"I'll talk to you about it soon," Dawn promised, hoping she'd never have to.

Eric shrugged. "Okay. Maybe I could walk you home."

Before Dawn could reply, she spotted four guys entering the arcade. She knew they were gamers because they wore the attire: comic book T-shirts on two of them, and two of them dressed in Goth-style long black trenchcoats.

The four gamers moved through the crowd without saying a word, but a few of the other gamers came over to them immediately. Some of the new arrivals were turned away at once, but a few of them were allowed to join the group. They continued to cycle through the arcade. Some of the guys chosen to join the group high-fived each other and talked enthusiastically.

Excitement and nervousness filled Dawn in a rush, flooding adrenaline through her system. These were the guys. They had to be the guys.

"Do you know those guys?" Dawn asked Eric.

"They're creeps," Eric said in disgust. "I've played against them, and they're all top-of-the-line gamers. Haven't seen them in here much, though, and their names are starting to disappear from the top rankings on their favorite games. Figured that would draw them back."

"Where have they been?" Dawn asked. "Some of the other arcades?"

"Uh-uh," Eric replied. "I haven't seen their names there, either. It's like they vanished off the face of the earth. Somebody told me they've been beta testing some new game platform that's supposed to be coming out, but they could have started that rumor themselves."

Confidence soared through Dawn as she watched the

gamers add two more guys to their collection. *They're recruiting.*

"Shooter's is now closing," the female voice announced over the PA. "Thanks for coming, and we hope to see you again tomorrow."

Instantly, lights and arcade games in the back of the building began going dark. A potpourri of game-over music poured from the speakers, a homegrown blend of losing riffs from dozens of popular games.

As Dawn watched, one of the first four gamers turned in her direction. The guy never broke stride but he stared at Dawn.

For the first time, Dawn saw the guy's lavender eyes. Even in the dimming light of the arcade, the virulent purple stood out starkly. Two of the other guys looked at her as well, and she saw that they had lavender eyes too.

"Purple eyes," she whispered, remembering Bobby Lee's story that the demons that had swapped bodies with humans were marked by the trait.

"Yeah," Eric snorted. "Purple eyes. All of them have them. Like maybe the game design company they're doing the beta testing for is handing out contact lenses, too."

Thinking maybe she was drawing too much attention for whatever reason, that maybe the demon had somehow gained access to the possessed guy's memories and remembered seeing her with Xander, Dawn turned and hugged Eric. They looked like a couple, like some of the other couples kissing good night at the arcade.

The move also hid her face.

And it nearly blew Eric Rogers's mind.

"Hey," Eric gulped. His arms hung out around her but he didn't make the effort to close them.

Dawn kept hold of Eric till the gamers left the arcade. "Hey," she said, "I'll see you at school tomorrow."

"Sure," Eric said, his voice cracking. "Maybe I'll—maybe I'll catch you around here again."

Dawn felt bad as she left him. She also slid his cell phone into her jacket pocket. Tomorrow, she'd return the cell phone, say something about how the phone must have fallen off his belt and into her jacket pocket somehow.

She was almost running when she reached the arcade door. Stepping outside, she looked down the sidewalk in the direction she'd seen the gamers go. She stayed in the shadows under the neon sign advertising Shooter's Other Worlds Arcade and watched as the group loaded up into an unmarked black cargo van parked near the street corner.

None of the gamers looked back.

Senses alive, feeling jittery because she was certain she'd stumbled on to something—*This will show Buffy I can help!*—Dawn scanned the street. There was no way she could keep up with the van on foot, and not knowing where it was going was next to useless. If the van had at least been marked, given some clue about where it was going to end up, Dawn knew she could have lived with that. But coming this close and not knowing? The idea was intolerable.

The van engine turned over, then the lights came on. Another moment and the reverse lights flared, white in the center of the ruby brake lights.

Heart hammering, knowing what she had to do in order to pursue the demons and regretting every second of it, Dawn broke from cover and sprinted toward the van. *Don't look in the mirrors! Don't look in the mirrors!*

The van stopped, and the transmission *clonked* while changing gears. Then the vehicle edged forward, gaining speed.

Dawn ran, jamming the cell phone down into her

jacket pocket. She focused on the utility ladder affixed to the outside rear of the cargo van. Her breath burned her throat, and for a minute she didn't think she was going to be fast enough to catch the van. Then her fingers curled around the van's ladder.

She leaned into the van, taking longer and longer strides, letting the vehicle take more of her weight rather than jumping onto the back. If she'd jumped onto the van all at once, she was sure someone would have heard her. She was also sure that if she fell at the speed she was going, she was going to be seriously hurt.

Taking a final long step, almost falling in spite of her best efforts, Dawn pulled herself onto the ladder. The darkness that covered Sunnydale masked her from sight. She was fairly certain that she blended in with the black color of the van. The wind whipped her hair around, causing her to blink rapidly. She also knew after a couple minutes that if the ride lasted much longer, she wasn't going to be able to hang on. Carefully, she clambered up the ladder and stretched out prone across the top of the van, hoping that she didn't make enough noise to be heard.

Facing forward, Dawn watched as the driver wound through Sunnydale. From the direction he was headed, there was only one place he could be going: Docktown. But Docktown was still a big place. Docktown, Dawn decided, wasn't specific enough to give Buffy as proof of her worth as a Slayerette. Grimly, Dawn lay flat on the van and waited, rolling into Docktown and toward the black Pacific Ocean in the distance.

The twenty-six intruders that initially broke into the Merriwell, Haggard, and Burroughs Museum consisted of demons and demon-possessed humans with lavender eyes. Buffy crouched in the shadows of the ersatz cave wall and watched as the group fanned out quickly.

The demons and demon-infested humans attacked the crates at once with crowbars and long knives. Nails squealed as they pulled free of the wood. Irreplaceable plates, vases, and pottery shattered against the floor.

Bobby Lee put his guitar to one side and shrugged out of his coat. He took two *escrima* from his guitar case. The way he twirled the martial arts fighting sticks told Buffy he was well versed in their use.

Demon-hunting with spells and music must have been all right, Buffy thought. *But somewhere along the way you upgraded your fighting techniques, Bobby Lee Tooker.*

The wholesale destruction of the West African exhibit continued. Buffy knew if the alarm system hadn't been shut down that the clang and clatter would have set Klaxons screaming in warning.

"C'mon," a Fraxian demon snarled. He was tall and incredibly broad through the chest. His red hair made a lion's mane around his head, which looked deformed because of the blunt maw that jutted out from his face. "We don't have all night. Dredfahl wants those bones."

How many bones? Buffy wondered. Bobby Lee hadn't known, nor did he know how to tell which bones were Torqualmar's.

Buffy leaned down close to Bobby Lee. "I don't want them all dead. We need to know where we can find Xander." *If Dredfahl actually took Xander from the hospital.* They still weren't even sure of that, and the lack of knowledge ate at Buffy. If Xander had somehow gotten in the way of Robby Healdton's abduction from the hospital, there weren't any guarantees that he was even still alive. *No negative thoughts. Only happy thoughts here.*

A flashlight shined out in the hallway.

Rising to her feet, Buffy stopped and stood still, just another layer of the ersatz rock covered in replicated prehistoric cave paintings.

The light flicked over the demons who were hard at work destroying the exhibit. Then a man's loud voice demanded, "What do you think you're doing, Nossif?"

The Fraxian demon turned, holding up an arm and squinting against the harsh light that flooded over him. "Get that light out of my eyes, Webber," Nossif growled.

A heavyset man in a blue security guard's shirt and tie strode into the room. Reflected light glinted from the badge he wore on his shirt.

Well, Buffy thought, *that explains how the demons got in.*

"Didn't you listen when we talked today?" Webber complained.

"You said the last of the shipment arrived today," Nossif replied. "The stuff we were hired to get has to be in that shipment."

Webber crossed the room angrily, shining his flashlight around as the Fraxian demon crew and lavender-eyed demons that looked like humans stopped working.

"I told you the crates that came in today had yellow shipping tickets on them," Webber grumbled. "Man, the kind of mess you and your boys are leaving here, I'm gonna get canned for sure."

Moving swiftly, Nossif grabbed the security guard by the throat and yanked Webber from his feet. With one lithe move, Nossif had Webber pinned on the display table amid the clutter of the destroyed model village.

Webber groaned in pain, cursing and flailing uselessly as he tried to escape.

Nossif stuck his muzzle to the security guard's nose. The dropped flashlight rolled across the floor, but the diffused light glinted off the Fraxian demon's long fangs.

"You were well paid to keep us informed about these

shipments," Nossif growled, "and to let us in tonight." The demon grinned. "But we don't need you after tonight, Webber." He opened his jaws, leaving no doubt what he intended.

Even though Webber wasn't one of the good guys, Buffy couldn't stand idly by and watch the man get killed. She glanced at Bobby Lee. "You heard about the yellow tickets?"

"Yeah." Bobby Lee's eyes narrowed in suspicion. "What are you—" Understanding dawned in his eyes. "No, you're not. Not for that guy. He's not worth—"

"I don't make decisions like that," Buffy said. And she broke from the darkness, running toward the Fraxian demon and the security guard. She raised her voice. "Hey!"

Face masked in predatory hunger, not even remotely human now, Nossif glanced up. His feral gaze focused on Buffy, and he flung out an arm. "Stop her!"

Two lavender-eyed demons in human bodies reached out for Buffy. She shrugged them off before they could close their hands on her. They fell to the floor behind her, stunned by the short jabs she delivered as she passed. Then she left her feet in a flying kick.

Chapter Sixteen

Nossif tried to draw back from Buffy's attack, but the bestiality that fired through him wouldn't permit him to lose the security guard as his prey.

Centering herself behind her feet, Buffy lashed out with her left foot as she neared Nossif. Her foot caught the demon on his right temple and she drove the kick hard, turning his face to the left. If Nossif had been human his neck would have broken from the impact and driving force. Instead, the demon lost his grip on Webber and stumbled back.

Stopped by the demon's great bulk, Buffy fell backward, throwing herself into a quick back-tuck so that she landed on her feet. She raised her fists in front of her.

"You just picked the wrong fight, Slayer!" the Fraxian demon roared. "I thought you might try to deal yourself into this, and I'm prepared for you!" He turned to the other demons. "Get her!"

The demons hesitated for just a moment, then rushed Buffy. Webber, the security guard, didn't hesitate in taking advantage of the distraction and heading out of the room. Buffy doubted the guy would be around for questioning in the morning.

At first, Buffy retreated from the group of demons pouring at her. If she'd tried to stand her ground, and even if she'd managed to take some of them out of action, she knew she'd have been mired in bodies and swept away. She caught the first demon with a spinning backfist, turned her momentum into a rolling block that knocked another demon into the two humans behind him, and sent them all down.

Another Fraxian demon stepped forward, carrying a feathered spear Buffy was certain had been snatched from one of the exhibits. The demon rammed the spear at Buffy, who sidestepped the blow and swept her right arm around, bent at the elbow so that the inside of her forearm slammed into the spear haft and deflected both the weapon and the demon.

Before the demon could recover, Buffy grabbed the spear in her left hand, braced herself, and kicked the demon in the face. Powered by the strength that came from being the Slayer, the kick lifted the demon from his feet. Buffy turned and ran, still holding on to the spear, staying only inches ahead of the mob that was howling for her blood.

She caught a quick glimpse of Bobby Lee fighting for his life against a half-dozen attackers. The *escrima* sticks created a lightning-fast wooden wall of pain and agony as Bobby Lee stabbed, slapped, and hammered his opponents. He was holding his own, but he definitely wasn't making any headway.

Buffy ran straight for the ersatz wall covered with the replicated cave paintings. She lengthened her stride and took up the spear in both hands. Even with her speed, she was only a couple of quick steps ahead of the mob that pursued her. Never breaking stride, the Slayer ran up the stone wall, listening to the creak of support wires protest the unaccustomed and violent weight.

As she made the third step and hunkered into the wall to get as much traction as she could for as long as she was able, Buffy felt gravity pull at her. She pushed off the wall into a long, triple back flip that carried her over the heads of the demons and lavender-eyed possessed. Still holding the spear in both hands in front of her, she landed on her feet, watching as the demons and possessed swung back around and came at her again.

Breathing out, keeping loose and relaxed, Buffy launched her attack. She stepped forward, ramming the spear tip into a demon's neck, already on the move again as he clutched at his ruined throat. Swinging sideways, Buffy brought the spear in close and slammed the butt into the temple of a possessed, rendering him unconscious before he hit the ground.

Circling, using the unconscious man as a shield, Buffy lifted the spear and blocked an overhand knife blow. Before the demon could retract his knife and hand to try again, the Slayer swept the spear around and butted him in the mouth, breaking his fangs. Kneeling, Buffy swept another enemy's legs, upending him and dropping him to the floor.

A demon's fist caught the Slayer in the face, driving her back a stumbling step. She ignored the pain, willing herself to keep focused and to keep fighting. Reversing the spear, Buffy thrust it through the demon's eye, killing him. The crowd before her started to slacken, no longer as certain of their victory.

"Buffy!"

Glancing over her shoulder, Buffy saw Spike enter the room with Anya at his heels. Sprinting to reach her side, Spike morphed into full vampire-faced mode, his features turning horrific. He fought with blind fury, fists and feet thudding into the demons like a whirlwind.

"Vampire!" one of the demons shouted in surprise. "Nossif, you didn't say there were vampires!"

Before he could stop himself—or maybe he didn't even try, Buffy thought—Spike smashed a fist into one of the lavender-eyed humans. As soon as the contact was made, Spike dropped to his knees in agony, the pain caused by the chip inside his head.

"Kill the vampire!" one of the demons shouted. He tore a broken shard from a nearby wooden crate and rushed toward Spike, who was still somewhat disoriented on the floor.

Before the Fraxian demon could reach Spike, Bobby Lee took up a defensive position. The *escrima* sticks flew, batting aside the wooden shard, then trapping the makeshift weapon and tearing it from the demon's grasp.

"Don't kill the vampire," Bobby Lee said.

As he got to his feet, Spike glanced at Bobby Lee grudgingly. "Thanks."

"Don't mention it," Bobby Lee said. "You'd have done the same for me."

"Not bloody likely," Spike muttered.

"The crates," Buffy yelled.

Anya took up a club from one of the unconscious humans. "Which crates? There are crates everywhere."

"The crates that have yellow tickets on them." Buffy scanned the exhibit room, searching for Nossif. The demons and possessed humans stayed out of her reach but still ringed around her. A moment later, she spotted the Fraxian demon rooting around in a crate on the other side of the room.

Nossif clutched a rocket launcher in one hand. Smiling, the demon turned and fled for the entrance on the same side of the room.

Taking a fresh grip on the spear and holding it in two hands in front of her, Buffy rushed forward. The spear slammed into the crowd of demons and possessed humans, bowling them backward. But they caught the spear and held on, stopping her forward progress.

Swinging quickly, Buffy held on to the spear and flipped over her opponents. At the apex of her swing, she released the spear and sailed through the air another ten feet, past the knot of demons and possessed humans. She landed, bending her knees to absorb the shock. From the corner of her eye, she saw her attackers turn and rush toward her. But by then she was two steps ahead of them, then three, and was rushing through the debris with the speed of an Olympic athlete.

Buffy caught the door frame and swung herself around into the next exhibit area, certain she was closing the distance between herself and the Fraxian demon. She saw her quarry in the hallway, speeding toward the exit door.

The Fraxian demon didn't even bother trying to open the glass door. He just lowered his head and burst through the glass, tearing out the frame. Buffy gained two steps on the demon. A convertible roared up to the exit, rolling over the curb and the grounds outside.

Buffy scanned the car as she closed on the fleeing demon. A demon was driving, and another Fraxian stood up suddenly in the convertible's back seat and raised a tube to his shoulder.

For an instant Buffy thought the tube was another mailer or container like Nossif had taken from the exhibit. Then flames belched from the tube.

Rocket launcher! Buffy identified the weapon in a split second. Without her speed, she would never have been able to turn and flee back down the hallway before the rocket smashed into the side of the museum. She felt the concussive wave of the explosion even as she threw herself into a headlong dive back into the group of demons and possessed that had followed her out into the hallway.

The explosion drove Buffy into their midst like an arrow, then swept them all up and threw them to the far end of the room. Heat swarmed over Buffy as she fell into a tangle of arms and legs. Senses reeling, she fought her way back to the top of the heap, knocking out two possessed humans and a demon as she stood.

"Buffy!" Spike's voice was filled with worry.

Hurting, scared, and angry, knowing that some of the possessed humans had died and she wasn't quite sure what that meant to the original owners of the bodies, she pushed herself to her feet. "I'm here."

Smoke filled the hallway, and flames licked at the gaping hole that had been a doorway leading out of the museum.

Spike rushed over to Buffy, grabbing her by the arms and looking her over. He still wore his vampire's face, and somehow his interest wasn't as reassuring as it might have been.

"Are you all right?" Spike asked.

"Yes," Buffy said, then she had a coughing fit from the smoke that pained her bruised ribs. She hurt everywhere and knew this was going to be a night that she'd be glad to have the Slayer's amazing recuperative powers. "But we lost the Fraxian."

Spike morphed back into his human features. "It's all right. We've got some of his little demon friends here, an' some of the possessed humans as well. Give me a few minutes alone with one of them an' we'll know where Dredfahl has his little hideout."

Sirens split the night air, echoing inside the museum.

"Sure," Buffy said. "But we've got to get out of here

before the police arrive. Otherwise we're going to be here for a while answering questions."

Despite the protective circle she'd drawn and beefed up with her witchcraft, Willow screamed a little as the ghost sailed toward her with an insane look on his face.

Then the ghost slammed into the invisible magick barrier that protected the two witches from the supernatural powers they'd called from the ghost roads. Instantly furious, the ghost beat at the mystic shield with both hands. Rainbow-colored sparks shot from the shield, and a whirlwind ripped through the dorm room. The winds caught papers and sent them flying, and yanked at the curtains. Still, the wind never touched the candles inside the protective circle, offering proof to Willow that the spell she and Tara had created stood against the ghost's power.

At Willow's side, Tara hunkered down.

Ghosts didn't always return from the other side sane, and most of them were angry about what had happened to them in the mortal realm.

"Stop," Willow commanded. Tara had never been truly comfortable with the power her friend was able to command, and Willow knew it. In the beginning, Tara had demonstrated more control over her craft, and probably still did, but she'd never matched the raw energy that Willow could command.

The ghost continued beating against the mystic barrier.

"Donny," Willow called. "Donny, stop."

"No!" the ghost howled.

Willow saw the fear in the ghost's face that outweighed the rage and hurt. She felt sorry for him. "Donny, listen to me. We can help."

"How?" the ghost demanded. He struck the protective barrier one last time, then stepped back. Even though he was dead and didn't need to breathe, his chest heaved with the raw emotion coursing through him. "I need to talk to Amy. I gotta make her understand."

"You can't help her," Willow said. "And she won't be able to see you. In fact, if it wasn't for my spell, you might not even be able to manifest in this world."

"What are you talking about?" Donny crossed the room and stood before Willow again.

"Where were you before you got here?" Willow asked.

The question froze the ghost for a moment. "I don't know. Some place I'd never been. It was all white, filled with voices I couldn't quite understand. At first, I thought I was dreaming." Hope filled his face. "Maybe I'm still dreaming. Maybe me dying in that game was just a dream too."

Willow shook her head, feeling bad about what she had to tell him. "That was no dream and that was no game."

"You were all lied to," Tara said gently. "There's this guy, actually he's a demon, named Dredfahl."

"Dredfahl was the codename for the sys/op," the ghost said. "The gamemaster of the VR RPG we were testing."

"He's a demon," Willow said. "And he's got the power to send people over to that world."

"Why?"

"The bones that you were looking for?"

"Torqualmar's bones," Donny supplied.

"Right. They really belonged to a demon that Dredfahl's trying to resurrect. I need your help."

Donny laughed, a harsh, dry derisive noise that hung in the dorm room and was about as welcome as a scab on a cupcake. "What could I possibly help you with?"

"Derek Traynor reached out to you tonight," Willow said.

"So?" Donny rubbed at the silvery tears on his face. Control was starting to come back to him.

"We were hoping," Tara said, "that you'd be able to contact Derek. We need to talk to him."

"Why?"

"Because we want to stop Dredfahl before he gets more people killed," Willow said.

"We've tried to contact Derek ourselves," Tara added. "We can't get to him. After the experience he had on the set tonight, his staff has sequestered him away in his hotel. I don't know if he's even going to do the show tomorrow."

"You said Dredfahl really is after Torqualmar's bones?" Donny asked. "Just like in the game?"

Willow nodded.

"Then we don't have much time, because Robby had led us to all but two of the bones. They might even have those by now."

Willow thought about the museum where Buffy and the others had gone, wondering if they'd been able to locate one of Torqualmar's bones there. *Doesn't matter,* she decided. *We still have to do this.*

"Do you know Xander Harris?" Willow asked. Fear trembled through her on cat's paws. They still didn't know what had happened to Xander.

"Yeah, I know Xander."

"Is he . . . is he over there?" Willow asked. "Has something happened to him?"

"Xander wasn't in the game as far as I know," Donny said. "I know Robby and Chris and Travis were there, a few other guys Xander probably knows, but I never saw Xander."

Willow breathed a sigh of relief, then lost the feeling immediately when she considered the alternatives. If she'd known Xander had been swapped out with a demon, at least she'd have known that he was alive.

"You said I could help you get to Derek Traynor," Donny reminded.

"You can," Willow said. "I'm sure of it."

"How can I do that?"

"Because you're a ghost and he's a medium," Tara explained. "You should be drawn to each other like iron filings to a magnet. You just gotta get within reach."

Donny snorted. "How am I supposed to find him?"

"I can help you find your way," Willow said. "But you're going to have to help me."

"How?"

"Take me with you." Willow felt Tara looking at her.

"No," Tara objected.

"It's the only way," Willow said.

"I can't even touch you," Donny protested. "How am I supposed to take you with me?"

"Not me exactly," Willow answered. "My astral self."

"Your astral self?" Donny repeated. "Like Dr. Strange? You can do that?"

"Yeah," Willow said, taking pride in her abilities. "I can do that."

A tentative smile flickered across Donny's face. "That's cool."

"A little," Willow said, flushing with embarrassment.

"It's also dangerous," Tara pointed out. "You could get lost out there."

Willow took Tara's hands, holding them tightly. "No," she told the other girl calmly. "I won't get lost. I can't get lost with you here looking over me and waiting for me."

"Willow—" Words failed Tara, choked with emotion. She shook her head and went on in a thick voice. "You act like this is nothing."

"I'm acting," Willow said, "like this needs to be done."

"There are consequences to magick, and you use it like . . . like it's cable TV or something."

"Tara," Willow said softly, "I have to do this. Dredfahl has to be stopped." She paused, seeing the tears form in Tara's eyes. "I know you're scared. I'm scared too. But one thing I've learned from Buffy after all these years is that you work through your fears. If you give in to them, if you don't do the things you know you have to do, then you're not really living your life."

"Buffy is the Slayer," Tara said.

"I'm a witch," Willow insisted. "And you're not going to let anything bad happen to me. Right?"

"Willow—"

"Do this for me," Willow said. "Just be here for me. Help me find my way back if I get lost."

Wordlessly, unable to speak, Tara nodded.

Willow hugged Tara tightly, mastering her own fear, then she turned to Donny and pushed out her hand. Donny mirrored the movement automatically. Their hands met through the mystic barrier. The rainbow colors rippled out from their joined palms, pooling wider and wider across the barrier's surface.

"Ready?" Willow asked, feeling the connection between her and Donny Williford growing stronger.

"Yeah," the ghost said.

Then Willow pushed herself from her body, passing through the barrier and standing beside the ghost. She hadn't done the out-of-body experience often, and the feeling was amazing. She felt as light as marshmallow fluff. While continuing to hold Donny's hand, she turned to Tara.

Tara sat beside Willow's flesh-and-blood body, a worried look twisting her features.

"I'll be right back. Try not to worry." Willow didn't know what else to say. Turning, she walked with Donny, and their first step took them from the dorm room and across half of Sunnydale.

Chapter Seventeen

"We questioned the guy we took from the museum," Buffy told Giles. They sat at the table in the Magic Box, surrounded by the others. "We didn't get anything."

The Watcher looked harried and exhausted. "He wouldn't talk?"

"Oh, he talked all right." Spike spun a chair and sat in it reversed. He folded his arms over the back. "He just didn't have anything to say that we wanted to listen to."

"The guy we took from the museum didn't know anything about Xander," Anya said. A pained, worried expression filled her face. "This is all his fault."

Buffy looked at Anya, certain that she was so tired she hadn't heard right.

"It's Xander's fault," Anya repeated, her voice cracking a little. "If he'd just stayed with me and gone out to dinner like he promised, he wouldn't be missing right now."

Okay, Buffy thought, *not going to try to argue logic points.*

"The person you took," Giles said to Buffy, "was one of the possessed?"

"Yeah," Spike answered. "Lavender eyes an' all."

"But he talked?"

"Sure he talked," Spike said. "After all, it was me askin' the questions."

"I don't understand why you didn't get any information then," Giles said.

"Gotta remember the gamer is over in Ollindark or whatever the demon world is called," Buffy said. "The demon guy here? He doesn't read English, and nobody ever bothered to tell him where he was, and he had no clue how to get back to the hideout. He was never one of the drivers who ferried the gamers out to the site. He just referred to wherever the place is as Dredfahl's fortress. Not exactly a lot of help there, because we're not going to be able to find it on a Sunnydale map. They don't have roads or streets back where he comes from."

"Dredfahl's fortress?"

"From the way he described it," Spike said, "the place sounds like a warehouse of some sort."

"I don't know how you got that," Anya said, "with all the screaming and yelling that was going on."

"He did say the place was by the 'big water,'" Spike said.

"Big water?" Giles asked.

"Probably talking about the ocean," Buffy said. "Didn't you say there weren't any lakes or rivers in the demon world he was from?"

Giles adjusted his glasses. "Yes. Yes I probably did. Well, this is certainly most unfortunate."

"You said those Doorknobs—"

"Dorinogs," Giles interrupted.

Buffy ignored the interruption. They all knew who she was talking about. "—were pretty lame in the thinking department, but I didn't know they were this bad."

"That's why some of Torqualmar's bones were placed in that world," Giles said. "The Kalinths and the Dorinogs species are both predatory. Anyone who made his way into their world would be viewed as an enemy and summarily killed on the spot. And that's why Dredfahl had to go to the lengths he's gone to in order to get those bones." He glanced at the yellow legal pad in front of him. "However, I think I have found a solution to getting rid of Dredfahl once and for all."

"Listening," Buffy said.

"Dredfahl has somehow tied his energy to this world," Giles said. "That's why Bobby Lee's ancestors have had such a hard time dealing with him, and he keeps coming back when they think they've done away with him. But Dredfahl's own chosen course of action suggests the method, and the texts I've researched during your absence bear this out."

"What?" Buffy asked.

"If, when we find him," Giles said, "we're able to shove Dredfahl into the demon world on the other side of the portal, we should be able to defeat him. In that world, whatever wards and spells that tie him to the world here will be at their weakest."

"Defeat him there, in that world," Bobby Lee said, "and he won't be able to return to this world. Kill him there, and he's dead."

"That is the plan," Giles agreed.

"No one has ever thought of this before," Bobby Lee said.

"There probably haven't been many chances to confront Dredfahl close to a means to reach another world."

"Terrific," Buffy said. "Now if we knew where

Dredfahl was and could catch him with the door to the other world open, we'd be just dandy."

Everyone looked at her.

"Okay," Buffy said, "maybe feeling disheartened and stressed here. Being shot at with a rocket launcher tends to wig me. A little. But the point is we haven't found this guy yet."

"And we haven't found Xander, either," Anya added.

"Have you heard from Willow?" Buffy asked. "Maybe she's had some luck tracking down Derek Traynor."

"No," Giles said. "Neither Willow nor Tara have called."

"Maybe we should call and check on them." Buffy got up and went to the counter. She dialed their dorm number, then listened to the phone ring as the call went unanswered. She cradled the receiver. "No answer."

"Maybe Willow and Tara aren't there," Giles suggested. "Perhaps they're following up on a lead."

"By themselves? With this much weirdness going on?" Buffy shook her head. "No. Something else is going on." *I just hope they're all right.* The quietness of the Magic Box suddenly registered with her. Despite all the confusion going on, one voice was missing. "Has anyone seen Dawn?"

"She *was* here," Giles said.

Feeling suddenly alarmed, Buffy stood and quickly searched through the shop. Drawn by her apprehension, the others joined her. In frantic seconds, the verdict was clear.

"She's not here now," Buffy said, looking at Giles.

"I'm sorry, Buffy," Giles said. "I've been occupied with the books and the research. She must have sneaked out when I wasn't looking."

"Maybe she went home," Bobby Lee suggested.

"No way. Not after the fight we had tonight. She was mad. She would have felt she had something to prove." Buffy walked to the front door and gazed out at the nearly empty street, knowing that wherever her sister was, Dawn had chosen to pursue a dangerous course. And Buffy knew the fault was all hers.

Derek Traynor was in the bathroom in his hotel suite when Willow arrived with Donny Williford. Willow knew this because the television medium wasn't in the king-size bed in the opulent room—and sneaking up on a man she didn't really know in bed had been a creepy enough thought. Seeing the steam coming from the bathroom and hearing the shower running was way beyond where Willow wanted to go. Even on a world-threatening quest.

Willow balked, stopping outside the bathroom door while the ghost pulled at her hand.

"What?" Donny asked.

"He could be in the shower," Willow whispered.

The hiss of the shower echoed throughout the room. Aerosmith played on the stereo system. Vases of flowers and cards filled the dresser and the floor. Abandoned clothing hung from chairs and littered the floor, making a definite path toward the bathroom.

"So what?" Donny asked.

"I'm not comfortable with barging in on a guy taking a shower."

"We're here to save Sunnydale," Donny said. "Maybe the world."

"Maybe saving the world could wait a minute," Willow said nervously. "Or two. I mean, he can't shower forever, can he?"

Donny looked mad and frustrated. "I got killed today, then pulled out of wherever you found me and yanked here to help you get to Derek Traynor, and you're going to let a shower scene stop you?"

Willow took a deep breath. "No. No, I'm not. You go on in there and tell him I need to speak to him."

Shaking his head, Donny strode through the bathroom door. He returned almost immediately. "It's safe," he said. "He's wrapped in a towel."

"Then that means he's almost through," Willow said. "Shouldn't be much longer now."

"You've seen this guy's hair?" Donny asked. "This guy's all about his hair. No way is he going to bed with it wet. He's going to be in there for a while." He grabbed Willow by the wrist. "We're not waiting."

Willow didn't even have a chance to steady herself before Donny yanked her through the door. She covered her eyes with one hand as bright light flooded her vision. Cautiously she widened her fingers and peeped out.

Derek Traynor stood at the huge vanity and stared into a steam-covered mirror. He was naked except for the towel wrapped around his waist. In the mirror's reflection, he looked dulled and listless, with dark circles under his eyes. Willow knew he'd been in the bathroom for a while, because droplets of condensation dappled the walls and ran down the mirror.

"I see ghosts," Derek mumbled tiredly.

"Um," Willow said, fighting against Donny who was behind her and pushing. "Actually, I'm not a ghost."

"Then maybe you can explain how you just walked through my bathroom door."

"He's a ghost," Willow said, pointing at Donny. Then she indicated herself. "And I'm a witch. Kind of in my astral projection phase right now."

"You're a peeping tom who hangs out with dead guys?" Derek asked, still looking at Willow's reflection in the mirror.

"No," Willow answered, feeling terribly embarrassed. "I'm not a peeping tom, and I don't hang out with dead guys." Then she remembered Angel and Spike. "Okay, I'm not a peeping tom."

"That's real interesting. Maybe you could leave now."

Willow couldn't help noticing how the steam just drifted through her and Donny. The effect was fascinating.

"We're not leaving," Donny said. "We're here for an important reason."

"Of course you are," Derek said. "You ghosts seem to think I've got nothing to do all day except sit around and take dictation for you guys. 'Hey Derek, tell my wife I knew about her having that affair.' 'Hey Derek, tell my grandson I saw what he did to the cat. That'll really freak him out.' 'Hey Derek, tell my wife there's an insurance policy I've got hidden in my home office that she didn't know about.'" He frowned. "Of course, that last one was a trick. I almost got sued over that one. I didn't know that she'd killed her husband and the police hadn't been able to prove it. But her husband is feeling a little better because the wife is going crazy trying to find an insurance policy that doesn't exist."

"No," Willow said, then took a deep breath. "We're really here for an important reason."

"Why?" Derek challenged.

"Because," Donny said, stepping forward, "the demons that killed me—"

"Who are you?"

"Donny Williford."

Derek shook his head. "Nope. I heard Donny Williford is up walking around. His parents called me, then the parents of Donny's freaked-out girlfriend. My lawyer tells me he's going to be a busy guy, and my producer has liked me a lot more in the past than she does now."

"I *am* Donny Williford," Donny insisted. "The other guy is a demon that has taken over my body."

Derek looked at Willow.

Willow nodded. "It's true."

"A demon has your body?" Derek asked. "You see, I'm going to run right out and tell the judge that, because I know that's going to help my case so much. Probably get fitted for a straitjacket and a rubber room. At the very least I'll be getting sued for even more." He sighed. "You two need to get out of here. I've had a really terrible day." He took a champagne bottle from an ice bucket on the vanity. From the looks of the bottle, he'd been drinking for a while.

"We need your help," Willow said.

"I can't help you."

"You saw into the demon world," Willow said. "That's how you saw Donny get killed."

Derek poured himself another drink, then gulped it down. "I didn't really see into the world. The connection was bad. And I see demons, too. There's just not much money in that. And they generally don't like to be noticed." He waved his empty glass around. "They're everywhere in this place. Almost as bad as they are in L.A. If I'd known that, I wouldn't have come here. But I kept feeling drawn, you know?"

"You're going to help us," Donny protested. He took a step forward.

"No," Derek said flatly, "I'm not. I'm going to drink too much, then go to bed. The headache I get in the morning will make sure I don't see ghosts. At least for a few hours."

"I died today," Donny said. "And the demon that was responsible for that is going to get his butt kicked."

"I'm sorry," Derek said. "Maybe it's not working out for you, but your parents, your girlfriend and her parents, and the demon walking around in your body are probably going to get some fat cash out of this. That's what Saul is telling me anyway. He's my attorney."

"Listen to me!" Donny reached for Derek, but his hand passed through the man.

Derek didn't even flinch. "Don't you think ghosts threaten me all the time? Some say they're going to haunt me. Other's say they're going to mess me up. Only every now and again do I come across a true poltergeist—a ghost that's able to physically manipulate the world. That's pretty rare. Then I go have them exorcised. Got a juju woman in Brooklyn that I use all the time. Boy, the ghosts are really sorry after she gets through with them, I tell you."

"The demon we're after," Willow said, "isn't just taking over bodies of people here. He's after this whole world domination thing. He's bringing back this really bad demon named Torqualmar so he can take over Torqualmar's body and have even more power to bring demons into our world. And probably worse."

"What worse?"

"I don't know," Willow said. "We haven't gotten that far yet. But with demons like this, there's always worse."

"Of course there is." Derek poured himself another drink. "I'll be glad to sit and listen to you until the champagne starts kicking in. Then after that, you'll vanish like a bad-anchovy-pizza nightmare." He waved bye-bye to her.

"You're going to help us," Willow threatened, "or—or—or—" She thought quickly. "Or I'll turn you into a rat."

Derek laughed as if what she'd said was the funniest thing he'd ever heard. He spilled his drink. "You'll turn me into a rat?"

Willow made herself look all confident and threatening. "Yes."

"You've turned people into rats before?"

"I've—I've seen it done before." After all, Amy the rat back in her dorm room was proof of that.

"When I grow whiskers and get a craving for cheese that won't go away," Derek mocked, "maybe I'll be scared then."

Angrily, Willow pointed at a bar of soap on the vanity. She willed the soap to turn into a butterfly, thinking that would be proof enough.

Instead, the soap bar exploded with a loud bang. Chunks of soap flew through the air and stuck to the shower-sweat clinging to the walls. Slowly, the soap chunks started sliding to the floor.

Derek gazed at the soap remnants in total surprise.

"And . . . and," Willow struggled to add, "if you don't help me, I'm going to give you the worst acne you ever saw. We'll see how your television career goes then."

Derek put his drink down. "Okay. You've got my attention."

Tara sat in the darkened dorm room and worriedly kept watch over Willow's abandoned body. The five burning candles barely lit the room and provided no warmth. Tara felt chilled.

She glanced at her watch. Willow had only been gone five minutes, but the time seemed like forever. Tara glanced at Willow again, sitting there cross-legged with her eyes closed like she might wake up at any minute. Her pulse throbbed at the side of her neck.

Tara wished Willow would come back. She hated the fact that Willow sometimes got so lost in magick. As for her own interests, Tara had always been drawn to witchcraft because she wanted to better understand herself and her place in the world. Her mother had been a witch too. She'd grown up believing, and had turned out to have some skill at the craft.

Just not as much power as Willow, Tara thought.

A hot, electric buzz thrilled through Tara. She straightened and automatically looked at Willow's body. *At Willow,* she made herself remember. *That's Willow. Not just her body.*

With her eyes still closed, Willow said, "Tara."

Knowing that Willow was still far away and was only using her physical body to communicate, Tara said, "I'm here, Willow. Are you all right?"

"I'm fine."

Willow sounded far away, and Tara hated the distance that was between them. "Have you found Derek?"

"I have. I need you to call Giles and see if Buffy's there. We need to coordinate how we're going to deal with Torqualmar."

Tara looked at the phone sitting between the twin beds. "The phone's outside the circle of protection."

"It'll be okay," Willow said. "Get the phone and call Giles."

"All right." Tentatively, Tara stood and stepped out of the circle of protection. The candles guttered for a moment, but everything within the circle held steady. She picked up the phone and punched in the number to the Magic Box. "Maybe you should come back to your body now."

"I can't," Willow said. "I'm going to try to contact the demon world. We need to know what's going on there."

Tara ran her hand through her hair. Some days she hated Willow having so much power because having that power seemed to constantly place her life in danger. "You know, there's a chance that something might happen to you."

"It'll be okay."

You don't know that, Tara thought. *You can't know*

that. And if you believe that, you may get killed over there just like Donny Williford. She blinked back tears, knowing she'd never get Willow to see that now. Willow was too far into the spell, locked too much into the belief that she could make everything work.

"Hello," Giles answered after the fourth ring.

"Giles," Tara said, knowing her voice sounded all wrong. "It's Tara."

"Is everything all right?"

"I hope so," Tara said. But the truth was, she didn't know—couldn't know—if everything was all right until the demon-bashing was over.

Buffy sat on the bed in Dawn's room. The *made* bed in Dawn's room. Buffy tried to remember when the last time was that she'd made her own bed. Sometimes she never even bothered to climb under the covers. She'd come in from patrol, kick off her shoes, and pass out. After a quick shower and a change of clothes in the morning, she was usually ready to go.

Dawn wasn't as messy as Buffy was. She was more the "keep order and keep things moving" type.

"Hey."

Buffy looked up from the bed and saw Spike standing in the doorway. When she'd left the Magic Box, he'd offered to drive her on his motorcycle, and she'd agreed. She hadn't been able to think of anywhere else to go, and she'd had to go.

"You doin' okay in here?" Spike asked.

"Oh, yeah," Buffy said. "Just peachy. A demon's trying to take over Sunnydale and make it a transit station for more demons. Xander's missing, maybe dead. And my sister decided not to come home tonight and is God-only-knows-where because I'm not a good sister and I'm an even worse stand-in for a parental unit."

"We'll find Dawn," Spike said. "And when we do we—*you* will give her a good talkin' to. Out at all bloody hours of the night, what's up with that? She can't just be roaming the streets."

"It's my fault."

"No, it isn't. Part of this is Dawn's fault. An' part of it is nobody's fault."

"If I was here more often," Buffy said, "if everything was more normal—"

"If frogs had wings, they wouldn't bump their butts against the ground when they hopped," Spike said. "See, what you're forgettin' is that you are doin' the best that you can. Now, me, for instance, I'd walk off and leave problems. Or kill them."

"Killing problems," Buffy said. "Now there's a real original solution."

"At the time," Spike said, "it kind of seemed like the thing to do."

Buffy nodded. "I can't do that, and I can't just walk off, either."

The phone rang.

Buffy scooped up the receiver. "Dawn?"

"Sorry," Giles said. "It's me. I take it you haven't heard from Dawn."

"No."

"Perhaps she's just staying over at a friend's house," Giles suggested.

"No. I've already called the few I know." Buffy took a deep breath, calming herself. "You called. What's up?"

"I just had a phone call from Tara. Willow has contacted the medium. She's trying to use Derek Traynor's link to the demon world to track down Dredfahl. Perhaps she'll be able to."

"I hope so. In the meantime, I'm going to head to the docks. Tracking down the 'big water' lead."

"Do you think that's wise?"

"I can't just stay here. I'll call you in fifteen minutes to find out if anything's changed. I've got to be doing something." Buffy broke the connection. Save the world or make peace with her sister? Both needed to be done.

Then a horrible thought hit her. God, what if one day she had to decide which she had to do, choosing one over the other? She wanted to curl up into a fetal ball, but she was the Slayer. She didn't have that luxury. She got up and got moving.

Dawn tensed when the cargo van slowed as it approached the warehouse in Docktown. A faded sign, black on white, read HERMAN'S MARINE SALVAGE. From the broken glass of the windows and the rusting corrugated tin sides and roof, she doubted the building was in use anymore.

The van's tires crunched through loose gravel as the driver steered for the open bay. Shadows moved inside the building, and flashlights came on.

Glancing around, heart hammering at the back of her throat, Dawn knew she couldn't ride the van inside the building. The demons would find her. As the van trundled toward the building, she rolled to the left and dropped from the vehicle. She hit the ground on her feet and nearly fell in the gravel. Moonlight and a few security lights painted a dozen shadows around her. All the shadows went into motion as she ran toward the edge of the building.

I'm invisible! Dawn told herself. *No one saw me! No one saw me! Pleaseletnooneseeme!* She plastered herself to the building's side, listening intently for a cry from one of the people inside the warehouse.

No one shouted. No one seemed to have noticed. Still, her breath came rapidly, tearing through her lungs, filled with the salt stink of the sea and the thick musk of diesel fuel.

She pulled the cell phone from her jacket. On the way over, almost freezing in the night wind, she'd programmed the number for the Magic Box into the phone. She punched redial, trying to regain her breath.

She'd found the demons' hideout. Now she just had to live long enough to tell someone. Turning, she headed to the back of the warehouse, staying low and under the cover of the shadows.

Giles answered. "Hello?"

"It's Dawn," Dawn said. "I found the demons. Tell Buffy. Their hideout's at a warehouse down in Docktown. A place called Herman's Marine Salvage."

"Dawn, you need to get out of there."

I know that, Dawn thought. "Did you hear me?"

"Herman's Marine Salvage," Giles repeated.

"Great."

"Get out of there, Dawn."

"I'm going," Dawn said. "I'll leave the rest of the hero stuff up to you guys. Just tell Buffy."

"She's worried about you," Giles said. "She went home to look for you."

"Instead of looking for these demon guys?" Dawn couldn't believe it. "She can't do that. She's the Slayer."

"I think tonight she was also very concerned with being your sister. I'll call her and let her know that you're safe."

Before Dawn could respond, someone grabbed her from behind, flipped her up hard against the metal side of the warehouse, and knocked the phone away. Dawn screamed before she could stop herself. The cell phone shattered against the ground.

Xander pinned her against the wall. A cold smile framed his mouth.

Dawn tried to talk, but Xander's hand was too tight around her throat. She couldn't believe he was holding her like that.

Three more guys flanked Xander. All of them had lavender eyes.

For a crazy moment, Dawn thought maybe Xander was only pretending to be one of the bad guys. Like he was undercover or something. Then she saw the lavender color of his eyes.

"See?" Xander asked. "I told you I thought I saw someone drop off the van."

Chapter Eighteen

When Spike stopped the motorcycle on the promontory overlooking the Docktown service piers, Buffy pushed off and took out the infrared binoculars that she'd gotten from Riley Finn. As part of the Initiative, Riley had access to much cooler technology than Buffy did. And for tonight, she'd figured the IR binoculars would come in handy.

She crossed the ground at a run. Giles had called her immediately after Dawn had called him. *I don't know if she's all right, Buffy,* Giles had said. *She screamed, then the phone went dead.* A chill ran through Buffy as she took up a position next to one of the trees along the promontory. The forest bits had been saved as part of scenic Sunnydale.

"You okay?" Spike asked.

"No, I'm not okay," Buffy said. "My sister is somewhere inside that place with a majorly bad demon."

Spike started to pat her on the shoulder.

Buffy looked at the vampire.

Spike took his hand back but didn't look like he entirely knew what to do with it. "We're here now. Everything's going to be all right."

Unless Dawn is already dead. Buffy refused to give voice to the possibility. Saying it might make it real. She lifted the binoculars and scanned the warehouses.

Nearly two dozen ramshackle buildings, only some of them still in use—though many of those were no longer being used for their original business—occupied the beachfront. Herman's Marine Salvage was in the middle of them.

Buffy used the regular binocular view at first. A few men stood at obvious guard posts around the warehouse. All of them were armed with pistols as well as swords. Evidently Nossif, the Fraxian demon munitions supplier, had been busy making money. Surprise flooded Buffy when she realized one of the guards wore Xander's body.

Clicking on the binoculars' infrared function, Buffy watched the scene dissolve into a chromatic display that spanned the rainbow's colors. With the IR working, the men outside the warehouse looked humanoid, filled with red and yellow patches because of their internal body temperatures. The surroundings, both the warehouses and the landscape, registered in cooler colors and black. The IR also permitted X-ray vision of a sort. She was able to see through the warehouse walls and scan the people inside the building.

Twenty or twenty-five people milled around inside the warehouse. Buffy had a hard time knowing for sure how many there were because most of them kept changing positions, and the vision through the binoculars sometimes blurred.

A few people were upstairs in other rooms. One of those rooms showed a weird glowing turquoise pattern.

In another room, a figure wriggled on the ground as if fighting restraints.

Dawn!

Although Buffy couldn't see any further details through the binoculars, she was certain the struggling figure was her sister. Buffy stilled herself with effort, sipping her breath for a moment because she was too tight to take a full breath. She lowered the binoculars.

"Is Dawn in there?" Spike asked.

"Yeah," Buffy said. "I think so."

"Where?" Spike stared at the building.

"Second floor. In a room by herself." *By herself.* The words haunted Buffy.

"And she's . . . ?" Spike let the unfinished question hang.

"She's alive," Buffy said. "That's all I know."

Rubber whirred on the narrow access road, drawing closer.

Buffy glanced up and saw the Gilesmobile coming down the street with its lights off. She felt a little more hopeful. "The cavalry has arrived."

Giles, Bobby Lee, and Anya got out of the disheveled Citroën. All of them carried weapons and wore grim faces. Dawn's call had caught them all off guard.

"Dawn," Giles said.

"She's in there," Buffy replied, then shifted her gaze to Anya. "Xander's in there too."

"What's he doing?" Anya asked, walking over to peer down at the warehouses.

"Guard duty," Buffy answered.

"That means that Xander's probably off in the demon world," Giles said.

Buffy nodded. "Maybe Willow will find him. If she managed to get over there through Medium Guy."

"We'll know soon enough." Anya brandished the cell phone she carried.

"Call Tara," Buffy said. "Have her tell Willow to try to enter the world through Derek Traynor's connection."

Anya nodded and dialed the number.

"Perhaps we should plan our attempt to get into the warehouse a little better," Giles suggested.

"I don't have time to build a wooden horse," Buffy said. "We go in. We kick demon butt . . . and," she looked at Spike meaningfully, "we remember that those lavender-eyed guys that look like humans *are* humans and we don't want to overly hurt them. We save Dawn and Xander. And we defeat Dredfahl once and for all before he can resurrect Torqualmar." She paused. "Sounds like a plan to me. Any problems with that?"

"Except for the we-all-may-get-killed part of that," Anya said, "I'm good."

"Then let's do it." Buffy led the way down the side of the promontory, staying within the shadows.

A moment later, Spike joined her, moving as silently as Buffy did. "Anya talked to Tara. Willow's on her way."

"Let's hope she can do it," Buffy said.

Spike looked back at the three people coming down the hill behind them. "Let's just worry about our part and get Xander and the kid back."

Buffy kept going, reaching the rear of the warehouse next to Herman's Marine Salvage. She glanced over her shoulder as Spike joined her at the back of the building.

Giles, Anya, and Bobby Lee carefully made their way down the hillside. A moment later, all of them were at the back of the warehouse.

"Two groups," Buffy said. "Bobby Lee and Spike, go around the other side of this building. Try to create a diversion at the front of the warehouse and draw as much attention as you can. After that, you're on your own. Giles, Anya, and I will try to get in from the back and surprise Dredfahl."

Everyone nodded.

Buffy led the way, staying in the shadows. She crouched at the back of the building and looked across the empty space separating the building where she was hunkered down from the marine salvage where Dredfahl was hidden away.

The three human-demon guards patrolling the area weren't totally committed to the job and spent most of their time talking to each other at the corner of the building so they could see the alley between. Still, the distance between buildings was considerable.

Buffy waited until the human-demon guards were involved in conversation, then darted across the alley between the buildings. Giles followed next, making himself flat in the tall weeds behind the building. Only a short distance beyond the weeds, the dark surf lapped at the rocky beach with gurgling slaps. Farther out, the drone of diesel engines chugged, and voices carried over the water.

"Back door," Buffy whispered, pointing up the short, rickety steps leading up to the main ten-foot high steps.

Giles went up the steps while Anya waited at the other building to cross.

"It's unlocked," Giles whispered back.

Good, Buffy thought. *Something's working out for us.* Still, worries and guilt about Dawn persisted. If she'd been better at dealing with her sister, more attentive, maybe things wouldn't be so bad now.

Seizing the moment, Anya broke from cover, lifting her knees high and running. Unfortunately, she stumbled and fell, hitting the ground hard. She also groaned in pain, and that drew the attention of the three guards stationed there.

"Hey!" someone shouted.

A light flared in the darkness and whipped through the alley to pin Anya against the ground.

"Eeep," Anya squeaked.

Buffy watched as the two of the guards raised their pistols and opened fire.

Willow stepped toward Derek Traynor and held her hands up to Derek's head and spread her fingers. They were in his bedroom now, but Willow was thinking the situation would have been made a lot better if Derek had been wearing more than just a towel. The situation didn't bother Derek at all; he'd stated that ghosts visited him all the time, even had conversations with him in the shower. Willow had told him that had been TMI—Too Much Information.

Donny Williford standing by and looking antsy didn't help much either.

"What are you doing?" Derek demanded, looking up at Willow.

Willow froze, her fingers on Derek's skull. Actually, since she wasn't there in flesh she couldn't really touch him. "I'm trying to tune myself to whatever frequency you're using to see the demon world."

"By a Vulcan mind meld?" Derek laughed.

Willow scowled, but she really felt nervous. "I haven't really done this before."

"It's easier than that." Derek reached up, turning his hands palm up. "Put your hands on mine."

As nervous as she was, Willow put her hands on his, but they passed right through. "Oops."

"Try again," Derek suggested, waiting patiently.

Willow placed her hands on top of Derek's. Although she couldn't touch him, she felt the heat of his body. And that was kind of weird too.

"Can you feel the vibration?" Derek asked. "If you can tune in to auras, you've got to be able to feel what's wrong with mine. The sensation is like a growth, a tumor of some kind."

Willow concentrated on the heat she felt from his palms. That was all she felt, though, just the heat.

"C'mon," Derek said. "Reach for the vibration. You've got to be able to feel the difference, feel the wrongness. If you're any kind of a witch, you can do this." He was serious, but his voice almost taunted her.

"Hey," Donny said, "if you ask me, this guy's just a creep. He's just playing with you."

"No," Derek said. "I want to be rid of this. It's screwing up my power. I can't do my show if I'm constantly tuned in to Demon Central. You've just got to reach a little deeper. If you can talk to ghosts and do astral projection, surely you can—"

In the next instant, the demon world sucked Willow into it. Her senses fled, and she felt as cold as if she'd been dropped into a glacier. But that was only until the desert heat seared into her.

"A 'diversion,' she says," Spike grumbled as he looked out over Herman's Marine Salvage and the six guards he'd counted posted at the front of the building. "You think she put any thought into what kind of diversion she'd be wantin'?"

"No," Bobby Lee Tooker answered.

"Got any ideas?"

"Throw rocks at the building across from the salvage buildin'?"

Spike spied a door on the building beside their target. He eased forward and tried the handle, finding the door unlocked. He drew in a breath, smelling petrol fumes from inside. "Now this could be interestin'."

Pushing on through the door, careful not to make any noise, Spike spotted a thirty-five-foot sport fishing boat on a two-wheeled trailer sitting inside the warehouse. He crossed the room to the boat and smiled happily.

"Know what I see?" Spike asked.

"A boat?" Bobby Lee asked.

"No," Spike said. "A diversion. Know anything about Viking funerals?"

Bobby Lee grinned in the darkness. "You aim to burn this man's boat?"

"Yep. Let me introduce you to the incendiary side of my nature." Spike leaped up into the fishing boat and performed a quick search. There were three five-gallon petrol cans aboard the boat. He unscrewed the tops and started sloshing gasoline all over the boat, saturating the vessel from stem to stern. "Check on that front door."

Bobby Lee went to the bay doors. "They're locked."

"Unlock them." Spike hopped out of the boat and went around to the front. He picked up the front of the trailer easily. The trailer rolled back and forth.

"Done," Bobby Lee said.

"Good," Spike said. "Get the bay door up."

"The guards will hear it."

"So what if they bloody do? We're a flamin' diversion here. Or, we will be in a minute."

Bobby Lee lifted the bay doors, yanking on a chain that hung from a drum assembly. The bay door rose with a screech and rattle of chains as loud as Marley's ghost.

Before Spike could get the boat underway, gunshots crashed through the stillness of the night. He ran then, pushing the boat through the bay door ahead of him, knowing that he was running a little late with his diversion. Still, he didn't intend to fail his mission.

Spike took his Zippo from his pocket, flicked the lighter to life as he turned the corner outside the building and charged for Herman's Marine Salvage. He roared in full battle cry, then heaved the lighter up into the petrol-covered fishing boat.

The petrol went up in a *whumpf!* of twisting flames that wreathed the boat and stood at least twenty feet high.

Spike pushed the boat toward the front entrance, yelling like a madman.

Now this, he told himself, *this is a diversion!*

The only trick was to deliver the burning boat to the target building before the gas tanks blew.

Willow opened her eyes and stared out at the desert before her. From the descriptions of the place that Derek Traynor had given, she knew she'd made the transition into the demon world. The blue sun burned down on her.

The problem was, she had arrived, but she had no way of knowing in what direction Torqualmar's bones lay. Or even if she'd arrived in time. She stood still and turned around, staring off into the distance.

Gradually, she made out a cluster of demons at the top of the mountains to the—the—*What direction is that?* She wondered. She realized she didn't know any of the cardinal points of the compass.

Doesn't matter, Willow told herself. *Go.* And she did, walking quickly at first, then breaking out into an all-out run. Buffy and Giles and the others had started their attack on the demons' stronghold. There was no time to lose. She only hoped that she could get to Xander and the others in time to stop them from giving Dredfahl the last bone.

And she hoped that no one got hurt back in Sunnydale.

Bullets struck sparks from the gravel around Anya. Startled and obviously afraid, she cowered for a moment, wrapping her hands over her head.

Buffy pushed herself off from the building, sprinting for Anya, expecting to feel a bullet slam into her at any time. As the Slayer, she healed fast when she was injured, but dead was dead. Right?

Reaching Anya, the Slayer grabbed her by the arm and yanked her to her feet. "C'mon!" She pulled Anya back toward the warehouse, one hand raised as if that would protect her from a bullet. The loud reports of the pistols sounded even louder in the narrow confines of the alley between the buildings and with the sea as a backdrop.

Then the pistols suddenly went silent.

Safely behind the warehouse again, Buffy peered around the corner and saw the three demons looking quizzically at their pistols. They shook them and turned them over and over as if trying to figure out what had gone wrong.

Okay, Buffy thought, *either they've forgotten how to reload them, or no one ever showed them. Or they've been watching too much television where guns never run out of bullets.*

She turned back to Giles and Anya. "Let's go." She picked up the *tomfa* fighting stick Giles had brought her from the arsenal at the Magic Box. The wooden fighting stick was twenty inches long and had a handle jutting out at a ninety-degree angle only a few inches from one end. The *tomfa* was from the Okinawan *kobujutsu* weapons fighting schools. Buffy had chosen the *tomfa* because the weapon had several non-lethal attacks and defenses.

She raced up the rickety stairs, feeling them quiver and shake beneath her, and yanked the door open. The guards shouted from the alley, calling out warnings.

A guard with lavender eyes stood near the doorway. As Buffy entered he turned and brought his pistol up. She ducked, knowing neither Anya nor Giles were close enough behind her to be in danger.

The pistol spat flame and rolling thunder, and the bullet cut the air over her head. Reacting immediately, Buffy slapped the *tomfa* into the guy's wrist, barely restraining herself in time to keep from breaking bone. The gun flew from his hand and a snap-kick to the forehead put him down for the count.

Even as the guy sprawled on the floor before her, Buffy saw a dozen other guys with lavender eyes bring their weapons to bear.

Then the front door flew open as a burning fishing boat tore through.

Spike! Buffy saw the vampire at the front of the fishing boat, pushing the vessel at a dead run now. Then he stopped, giving the boat a final push toward the cargo van that was parked in the middle of the warehouse floor. The lavender-eyed demons scattered.

Spike stood framed in the warehouse doorway with Bobby Lee only a couple steps behind him. "Buffy!" Spike shouted. "Get down! She's going to blow!"

Buffy stepped back through the door, blocking Giles and Anya as they tried to enter.

"What's wrong?" Giles asked.

Buffy pulled the door closed behind her. "Diversion," she explained.

The explosion inside the warehouse rattled the whole building and deafened Buffy for a moment. The rickety stairs wobbled like a ship caught in a storm.

"Okay," Buffy said, "I think they're diverted now." She opened the door again.

Inside the warehouse, the building looked like it had been made over in hell. Fire clung to all four walls and the floor. The cargo van was wreathed in flames as well. A quick scan revealed no bodies, so although the boat had exploded, no one appeared to have died.

And most of the lavender-eyed possessed guys were genuinely diverted. Spike and Bobby Lee rushed into the warehouse to divert the ones attempting to recover. Spike morphed into his vampire face and battled the guys. He was kept from actually harming them by the chip in his skull, but he could impede their progress.

Satisfied that everything was well in hand, Buffy spotted the stairs leading up to the second floor. Heat washed over her as she sprinted for the stairs. Dawn was up there somewhere.

Most of the blast from the exploding boat had gone upward, blowing out the skylights built into the roof. Flames clung to the wooden rafters, and Buffy knew it was only a matter of time before the building became a firetrap.

Two lavender-eyed possessed gamers stumbled into Buffy's path, taking up positions in front of the stairs and lifting their weapons. Buffy threw herself down, skidding across the smooth, sealed cement floor in a baseball slide, knocking the legs out from under one of her opponents.

"Die!" the other possessed guy said, shoving his pistol into her face.

Buffy swung the *tomfa* by the handle and struck the pistol barrel. The shot ricocheted from the cement floor only inches from her head, tearing a chunk free. The Slayer rolled back on her shoulders, thrust her feet forward, and pushed off with her free hand, landing on her feet. She whirled, spinning the *tomfa* in her hand and gripping the weapon on its longest part. She hooked the short handle behind the guy's ankle and yanked, pulling his foot up over his head as he fell.

The other man fumbled and brought his pistol up. Buffy blocked the pistol with her free hand, then drove the *tomfa* into her opponent's stomach, knocking the wind from him. Before he could recover, she slammed the *tomfa* against his temple, just keeping the blow from being a killing one.

The possessed gamer's eyes rolled up into his head and he relaxed into a boneless heap. A spinning roundhouse kick laid the other possessed guy out, sending his unconscious body skidding several feet away.

Bruised, Buffy thought, *maybe something broken. But not dead. That's got to be good.* She glanced back and saw that Anya and Giles were battling a pair of possessed gamers with swords.

Knowing her friends could handle themselves, Buffy sprinted up the stairs, trying to match the configuration against the layout she had in her mind from her earlier viewing through the IR binoculars.

Chapter Nineteen

At the top of the stairs, Buffy turned right, away from the room where she'd spotted the glowing turquoise patch and toward the room where the bound, struggling figure had been. The second floor was little more than a catwalk that skirted four rooms that had been used as small storage areas or offices.

Buffy tried the door but discovered it was locked. "Dawn!" Buffy yelled.

"Buffy!" Dawn screamed.

"Stay back from the door."

"I am."

Buffy lifted her leg and drove her foot against the door. Wood splintered and the door broke. Two possessed guys rushed her from the far room, the one where the turquoise patch had been.

Gripping the broken door, Buffy yanked it free of the doorframe and whirled around. When she released the door, it flew into the two possessed guys and knocked them backward.

"Buffy!"

Glancing back inside the room, Buffy saw Dawn lying on the floor. She rushed over to her sister and started ripping the hemp cord that bound her.

"When we get done with this," Buffy said, "we've gotta talk."

"I'm in trouble, right?" Dawn asked.

Buffy looked at her sister and felt confused and hurt and relieved and mad all at the same time. It was, she thought in that moment, probably how her mom had felt most of the time. Impulsively, she hugged Dawn. "Maybe a little trouble," Buffy said. "I'm just glad you're all right."

Dawn hugged her back, and Buffy realized there was nothing like the bond that they shared. Her friends meant the world to her, but they weren't dependent on her the same way that Dawn was. She suddenly realized that she couldn't just be a friend or a sister to Dawn; she had to be better than that. Somehow. *And I will. I'll find a way,* she told herself.

"Buffy," Dawn said.

"Just a minute," Buffy said. "I'm kind of enjoying the moment here."

"Demon," Dawn warned.

Buffy spotted the shadow on the wall in front of her and knew it was caused by a guy standing in the doorway, the imprint made even stronger by the flames in the center of the warehouse. She moved, throwing Dawn and herself to one side as bullets ripped through the room's Sheetrock walls.

Still in motion, Buffy took up the *tomfa* she'd lain on the floor and released Dawn. The Slayer pushed herself to her knees and threw the *tomfa* backhanded.

The *tomfa* flew through the air and caught the possessed guy between the eyes as he turned—still firing—

and tried to track his targets. The guy's head snapped back with a dulled thump, and he sagged unconscious to the floor.

"Get out of here," Buffy said, retrieving the *tomfa* from the floor as she stepped over the unconscious man. Below, Bobby Lee and Spike continued to fight the dwindling forces of the possessed gamers. Maybe they were totally loyal to their master, but they lacked a demon's invincibility.

"I'm not leaving you," Dawn argued.

Buffy saw the stubbornness in her sister's eyes. It frustrated her as well as made her feel proud. And loved. Lots of love.

"Okay," Buffy said. "You can watch my back. Make sure nobody sneaks up on me while I go find Dredfahl."

"Dredfahl's here?"

Buffy nodded. "Last room that way." She hurried to the room, feeling the heat of the spreading flames, knowing the building was lost and that if they didn't hurry, it would come down on them. She leaned over the railing. "Spike. Bobby Lee. Giles. Anya."

The four of them looked up at her.

"We can't leave the unconscious gamers here. Anybody who's not up and running from the fire needs help. Drag them outside."

"Heroics," Spike grumbled. "You know, once you start these things—saving people and everything—it just seems there's no end to it." But he grabbed the nearest unconscious gamer and threw him over his shoulder.

When she reached the door, Buffy didn't even bother to check if it was locked. She raised her foot and kicked the door off its hinges.

As the door flew backward it caught two of the guards inside the room, plowing them over and down. Behind the three guards who were left standing, a demon stood in front of a turquoise, ellipse-shaped portal. A pile of bones occupied the floor beside him.

The portal was held in place by amber strands that adhered to—or were anchored into—the walls, floor, and ceiling. The portal pulsed with energy, and misty shapes of demon creatures that looked like gargoyles and buffaloes battled in a desert on the other side.

"Back," Buffy told Dawn as she sprinted into the room toward the possessed gamers. She grabbed the nearest gamer, spun around, lifted the guy from his feet, and threw him into the other two gamers. All of them went down in a tangle. Before those two or the two trapped under the door could recover, Buffy punched them and kicked them into unconsciousness on her way to the demon.

The demon turned to face Buffy. He was thin and small, an animated corpse that looked desiccated, completely unlike a vampire's usual eternal youth and health. His ebony skin was mottled and ashen, so tight on his face that he looked like a skull. Although bald on most of the top of his head, his white hair hung in back to the shoulders of his electric-blue suit.

"So, Slayer," the old demon croaked in a dry voice. "We meet."

"Yeah," Buffy replied. "But it's going to be a short visit. You've taken up most of my night. This is where it ends, though. I've got class in the morning."

"And Bobby Lee Tooker?" Dredfahl asked. The portal pulsed behind him.

"He gets leftovers," Buffy said. "It won't be much of a meal because I'm really annoyed at this point. You took one of my friends and stuck him in some demon dimension, and you kidnapped my little sister. Big mistake. *Big*." Despite the easy patter she used, she remained wary. Being the Slayer meant never making really big mistakes more than once.

"You're too late, Slayer," Dredfahl croaked. He threw his hand forward.

The small, bone-handled knife flew toward Buffy, but with her speed and quickness she was able to see the blade's approach. She swept the *tomfa* out to counter the knife. Even as the fighting stick touched the blade to deflect its path, the knife changed into a ten-foot-long viper with heads at either end.

Surprised, certain that the snake heads were poisonous, Buffy stepped back. She managed to grab one of the snake heads with her free hand, but the other wrapped around her twice like a bola. She dropped the *tomfa,* her arms partially pinned to her sides. The loose snake head struck at her, but she managed to dodge it. Immediately the snake head recoiled and readied itself to strike again while the captured one fought against Buffy.

"If you still live when I return, Slayer," Dredfahl said, "I'll be happy to kill you myself. I've never killed a Slayer before, and have only met a few who have." He gestured to the pile of bones on the floor beside him.

Immediately, the pile of bones rose, connecting like a child's puppet that Buffy had played with when she was a little girl. Push the bottom, and the puppet's strings relaxed and let it fall to pieces, but releasing the bottom made the puppet reform.

The bones reformed into a skeleton—complete with a hollow-eyed skull.

Torqualmar, Buffy realized. The spell wasn't complete. Torqualmar hadn't been reanimated, and Dredfahl hadn't killed him yet. She dodged the snake head again and again, and watched in helpless frustration as Dredfahl and the walking bag of bones entered the portal.

Stardust scattered across the portal as they disappeared.

The snake head struck again. This time Buffy concentrated on it, managing to catch the scaled neck behind the snake head in her teeth. She bit down, crunching through the bone and ripping through the flesh.

Ewww! Gross! Buffy spat but was certain the evil taste of the snake would never be gone. She hadn't bitten through the snake's body, but she had broken its spine, making it impossible to use the snake head. With a quick twist of the hand holding the other snake head, she broke that one as well.

Stepping out from the dead, loose coils of the two-headed snake, Buffy ran toward the portal and tried to leap through. She rebounded off the portal like she was jet-assisted, unable to penetrate the surface. She hit the wall and almost blacked out, then struggled to get up.

If Dredfahl managed to bring Torqualmar back to life in the other dimension and kill him, usurping his power, he would prove even more difficult to kill.

"Robby," Xander said. "This is wrong. I'm telling you this is wrong."

"We're going to win, Xander," Robby said. "When it comes to games, I'm all about winning. You know that." He picked up a boulder, turned it into a fireball, and threw the fiery projectile into the face of the rampaging Kalinth demon charging him.

Xander didn't have much time to talk. He was fighting for his life against the Kalinth demons.

Of course, the Kalinth demons were fighting for their lives against the Dorinog demons and the gamers. The Kalinths were losing. From the time Travis, the scout, had discovered the Kalinth group hiding out in the box canyon—shortly after Xander had arrived in the world—their loss was a foregone conclusion.

Robby had placed his troops with cunning and care. And, to a degree, heartlessness. First the gamers had bombarded the Kalinth with fireballs from the cliffs above the box canyon, as well as closing it off so their quarry couldn't flee.

Then Robby had led the mop-up wave. And the Kalinths had died screaming where they lay.

The whole time, Xander had pursued Robby—who had chosen his place in the thickest of battles—trying to talk sense into him.

"You can't do this," Xander protested, pushing the hands of a dying Kalinth from him.

"It's done," Robby said, driving his stone spear through the chest of another Kalinth. "We've won."

Dust rose in amber fogs around them. Blood patterned the sand.

"Robby!" one of the Dorinog gamers yelled excitedly. "I've got the bone!" He stood at the end of the box canyon near one of the acid pools. The area was littered with Kalinth bodies.

Xander stepped in front of Robby. "You're not listening, Robby."

"Look, Xander," Robby said, his gargoyle face grimacing. "I don't know what your malfunction is, but I know it's gotta be something. Maybe the VR interface Dredfahl gave you is majorly screwing up."

"Dredfahl is a demon," Xander said, exasperated. He'd been telling Robby that for a while now. Not that it had done any good. "These other demons, the ones you call NPCs, they're other demons that haven't been given minds by a gamer. That's why they're so stupid. And that's why Dredfahl sent us here. We're smarter than the demons he had here, and you guys aren't afraid of dying because you think this is a game." Xander had figured that out, piecing together the different parts of the story.

"It *is* a game," Robby said. "It's the greatest game I've ever played. And I'm about to win it as soon as we claim that last bone." His eyes slitted. "Now, you step out of my way, or I'm going to walk right over you."

Xander squared off with Robby. "I don't want to see it come to this, but I'm going make you understand. Even if I have to beat it into you."

Robby squared off as well, but before either of them could make a move, a dozen Dorinog "NPCs" advanced toward the gamer who had yelled about the discovery of the final bone.

"Hey," Robby said. "What the hell are you guys doing?"

"The bone must be given to Dredfahl," one of the Dorinog demons said.

"That isn't for you to do," Robby objected. "Get back away from there."

Without warning, the Dorinog demons struck down the gamer holding the bone and took it. Another gamer stepped forward, protesting. One of the Dorinogs planted a stone spear in the second gamer's chest, piercing his heart.

"Stop!" a voice rang out.

Recognizing the voice, Xander glanced up and saw Willow standing at the top of the box canyon. She didn't wear a demon's form, though. She just looked like Willow.

"Xander," Willow called.

"Here," Xander yelled back, waving because he knew all Dorinogs probably looked alike to Willow. "What are you doing here?"

"I came to tell you that you can't give any more bones to Dredfahl," Willow said. "He's going to use them to raise a demon named Torqualmar."

Xander heard the murmur of conversation race through the ranks of the gamers.

"Man, must be a glitch in the gaming environment," one of the gamers said. "She shouldn't be here looking like that. She looks human."

"Are you kidding? We're getting close to the end of this thing. Maybe there is a human in the game at the end."

Robby stared at Xander. "You weren't freaking out, were you?" Robby asked. "This really is a demon world."

"Yeah," Xander said.

"And they have the bone," Robby said.

"We're going to have to get it back." Xander picked up a boulder and prepared to turn it into a fireball.

"Some of us have been really dying over here," Robby said in a hoarse voice.

"Yeah," Xander said, not even wanting to guess how many of his friends and acquaintances in the gaming and comics community were gone forever.

The Dorinog demons quickly linked arms and began the chant Xander had seen them use once before to call Dredfahl from Sunnydale.

"We've got to stop them," Xander said, and headed for the Dorinogs.

Partly in shock and definitely scared now, suddenly knowing that they weren't invincible after all, the gamers were slow to rally.

"C'mon," Xander said. "If we let these guys take that bone and give it to Dredfahl, do you really think he's just going to let you go back home?"

Before the gamers could do anything, one of the real Dorinogs yelled, "Kill the humans!"

Screaming in bloodlust and frenzy, the Dorinogs charged, ripping through the line of gamers. Xander hurled his fireball into one of the demons, but he knew his group didn't have a chance. There were too many real Dorinogs left and too few gamers.

Without warning, winds whipped up from nowhere. In the next instant, Dorinog demons flew backward, creating breathing space for the overwhelmed gamers.

A shadow passed the ground at Xander's feet. Glancing up, he saw Willow—arms outstretched gracefully—

floating down from the box canyon walls. She pointed and raised her hands, using her witchcraft to hurl the demons away.

"The bone!" Xander yelled, pointing in the direction of the Dorinogs that had captured it.

Landing on the box canyon floor slightly ahead of Xander, Robby, and the other gamers, Willow gestured toward the small knot of Dorinogs guarding the bone. The demons flew in all directions like a bomb had gone off.

The bone—the last piece of Torqualmar's skeleton, Willow had said—hung in the air.

Willow gestured again, and the bone zipped over to her. She caught it in one hand, then turned to Robby. "Xander, look. I got it!"

Before Xander could respond, a shimmering turquoise portal opened behind her. Xander tried to shout a warning, but everything happened too quickly.

Dredfahl stepped from the portal, caught Willow's hand in one of his, then backhanded her with his other hand, knocking her to the ground. Stunned, Willow couldn't do anything as the Dorinogs advanced on the gamers again.

A shambling skeleton stepped through the opening after Dredfahl, then the portal closed shut like an eyelid, leaving a thin dark line floating in the air. Wheeling quickly, Dredfahl placed the bone splinter within the skeleton.

A magick shimmering cloaked the skeleton, and Xander watched in amazement as flesh began to knit itself around the bones, started turning the remnants of the demon whole again. The demon stood seven feet tall, shorter than the Dorinogs and Kalinths, but massively muscled and perfectly symmetrical. He had two long, curved horns, and a square black beard. His ears had two spikes at the top, giving him an instant predatory look. His skin was a webwork of tiny scales—all the color of burnished copper. Despite the mostly human appearance, the demon possessed a lizard's smooth, darting movements, wholly inhuman. He stepped back quickly, raising his hands defensively.

Even more swiftly, Dredfahl gestured, and a sword appeared in his hand. He screamed coarse, inhuman words as he lopped off the demon's head just as its great yellow cat's eyes were opening. Almost with the same sword stroke, Dredfahl cut off his own head. He grabbed his own head by the hair and reached up to place it on the other demon's body. The resurrected demon continued healing, and as it did, it incorporated Dredfahl's head into the total being, while Dredfahl's old-man body slumped to the dry sand.

Xander had to admit that the regeneration was one of the most amazing things he'd ever seen. And he didn't know what he was going to do about it. He started forward, intending to help Willow.

"Now," Dredfahl said in a stronger voice than he'd had before, "you will all come to know true power."

The old-man head perched on top of the healthy demon's body looked obscene, but even as Xander watched, Dredfahl's white hair started to turn black. New hair sprouted, and burnished copper scales crept up his face, filling in the hollowed cheeks.

"After I've finished with you, I'll return to conquer your world," Dredfahl promised. "Then I'll bring my faithful servants through to your world." He reached down for Willow.

Xander raced across the distance, knowing he'd never reach Willow in time, but knowing also that he had to try.

Ringing blues notes suddenly filled the box canyon. The portal opened back up, and Xander watched incredulously as Buffy plunged through into the demon world.

• • •

While Bobby Lee Tooker was working his magick to open the portal, Buffy had seen the last part of the transformation Dredfahl had undergone and had seen the headless corpse place its own head on top of the regenerating demon's body. It was suddenly a new, improved Dredfahl. And she saw him reaching for Willow who was lying stunned at his feet.

Once through the portal, Buffy reversed the *tomfa*, gripped it by the long stick, and hooked the handle over Dredfahl's thick wrist. She pulled hard, bracing herself and using all her strength.

Dredfahl's hand slid away from Willow, then he turned to face Buffy. "Slayer," Dredfahl said, and his voice sounded stronger than ever.

For the first time, Buffy noticed how truly huge the demon was. Fear quaked through her, but it was a fear that she had faced a hundred times before, so she pushed it out of her mind.

"We weren't done," Buffy said. "Kind of rude of you to throw a snake at me and run."

Dredfahl grinned, the flesh filling in around his transplanted head. "You should know better than to try to kill me. I've been killed before. By Bobby Lee Tooker's grandfather. Then I came back and killed the grandfather's son. I'll kill you, too, Slayer."

"No," Buffy said confidently, "you won't. And this time you're not coming back, either." She threw herself forward, driving a roundhouse kick into Dredfahl's side.

The demon grunted in pain but didn't appear to be even close to incapacitated in any way. He threw a big fist at her, slightly off balance.

Probably not used to the new body yet, Buffy thought. *Give him any real time with it and he could be big-time dangerous.* She batted the punch away, then stepped in and drove a snap-kick to Dredfahl's reconstructing face. Blood spurted from his nose.

Growling with rage and pain, Dredfahl backed away from her and raised a hand, gesturing.

Buffy prepared herself, not knowing what to expect after seeing a knife become a two-headed snake. Instead, she only felt a slight jarring, then noticed the shimmering fieldlike heat rising from the desert sand that separated them.

"Get him, Buffy," Willow said.

One of the gargoyles helped Willow to her feet. Buffy could only assume that the gargoyle was Xander's demon self.

"His magick still isn't focused yet," Willow said. "He's weak for the moment, but it's not going to last long."

Buffy ran forward, whirling the *tomfa* in her right hand.

Dredfahl howled again and reached for her.

Moving quickly, Buffy slammed his outstretched fingers with the wooden *tomfa*. Finger bones snapped like pretzels. She hammered at him, scoring repeatedly on his face, watching as the skin broke around his neck, showing where his flesh had joined with Torqualmar's.

One flailing fist the size of a paint can caught her in the face and knocked her back.

Dazed, legs trembling, Buffy forced herself to her feet again.

"You can't beat me, Slayer," Dredfahl stated. "I'm too strong, too powerful. I am one of the eternal evils that has dwelt in the subconscious of man forever."

The fear touched Buffy then. She thought about her mother dying, leaving her there to take care of Dawn without any warning. She thought about her relationship with Dawn, about how things seemed so tense between them. She thought about how unfair it was that she had to try to balance school and slaying and parenting, and she didn't really know if she was good at any of those things some days.

Sensing an advantage, Dredfahl charged. He grabbed Buffy in both hands, bear-hugging her and trying to break her spine.

Incredible pain filled Buffy. She tried to break Dredfahl's grip but couldn't.

"Give up, Slayer," Dredfahl said. "I've beaten you."

"No!" Buffy pushed harder against the demon's arms. She couldn't breathe, couldn't draw a breath into her lungs. Blackness rimmed her vision. Remembering the *tomfa* clutched in her hand, she gripped the handle and drew the weapon back. Popping her hand forward, going by sense as much as by sight, she drove the blunt end of the *tomfa* into the demon's left eye.

The eye ruptured and gushed blood everywhere.

Groaning in pain, Dredfahl released her and stumbled back.

Buffy dropped to the sand and breathed. What would happen to Dawn if Buffy died? Who would take care of Dawn? Slayers die. That was a given. As soon as a Slayer was called, the death march started. How could she, marked for death as she was, be expected to take care of Dawn?

It wasn't fair.

Panting, getting her wind back, Buffy forced herself to her feet. She remembered all those days with her mother. Sometimes they'd gotten along, sometimes they'd fought. Would it have been any different if she'd known her mother was going to die? If they both knew she was going to die?

And Buffy knew that their lives would have been different. They wouldn't have been honest. They would have tiptoed around life, tried to take things carefully, struggled to cheat death.

But death couldn't be cheated. Buffy knew that. As soon as a person was born, a death was owed. A person had the choice of living in the shadow of death or living free.

"I'm going to kill you for that, Slayer," Dredfahl promised. He wiped the blood from his face. His ruined eye was already starting to regenerate. "You're going to die."

"Someday," Buffy agreed calmly. She threw the *tomfa* down. "But I'm not going to live in the shadow of death. You can't make me. I'm going to live free, Dredfahl. And whenever the time comes, I'm going to go out living life to the fullest. No worries. No regrets. I'm going to do what I know how to do, what I have to do, and what I believe in till my last breath. And you're not going to take that away from me."

Howling with inarticulate rage, Dredfahl rushed at her, throwing up sand behind him because he drove his feet so hard. Buffy ran at him too, knowing she was down to an all-or-nothing effort. She watched Dredfahl's hands, reading the sway of his body, knowing her timing had to be perfect, had to be unexpected.

He closed in on her, reaching out with his hands, obviously intending to bear her down to the ground and pin her with his greater weight, bulk, and strength, holding her helpless while he killed her at his leisure.

Buffy leaped through his outstretched hands, turning a forward flip as the demon's arms scissored behind her. On her way through, she managed to grab the sword, curling her fingers around the hilt. She listened to Bobby Lee Tooker's song, caught a brief flash of the blue sunlight against the sword blade, then launched herself into another flip as Dredfahl turned on her. Still in motion, whirling and moving just ahead of the demon's blows, Buffy whipped the sword around, giving everything she had for one frozen moment of vulnerability on Dredfahl's part. If she missed, she knew she would be vulnerable herself.

The sword glittered as the blade sliced air, then continued to slice through Dredfahl's neck, catching just for an instant in the spine before bone shattered. The demon's head left his shoulders, flying through the air and thudding on the dry, alkaline dust.

Off-balance, Buffy sprawled across the sand. Footsteps sounded behind her. She turned and watched as the headless demon's body came for her. Then it seemed to lose all motor control, toppling to the ground only inches from Buffy.

Standing on trembling legs but knowing she had to put up a brave front in front of the demons ringing around Willow, Xander, and the gamers, Buffy grabbed Dredfahl's head, then held the snarling visage of bloody flesh and bone up high.

"Heads," she said. "I win."

For a moment she thought the Dorinog demons might try to fight her. Then, in ones and twos at first, they started drifting away.

Sighing with relief and hurting all over, Buffy tossed Dredfahl's head into the pool only a few feet away. It wasn't until after the head started smoking from the immersion that she remembered about the acid pools Giles had briefed her on.

Tired, almost not believing the threat was over, Buffy stood at the pool's edge and watched as Bobby Lee Tooker stepped through the portal to join her.

The Dorinog demons nearby started snarling and came closer.

Buffy picked up the sword again. Willow waved at them, and an invisible wall slammed into the demons, knocking them over like tenpins.

"The gamers are being pulled back into our world," Willow explained. "So naturally these guys think they can kill and eat anybody they want to."

Still growling, the Dorinog demons retreated from the battlefield.

"What about Xander?" Buffy asked.

"He's back in our world. He's okay."

"That's good." Buffy glanced up at Bobby Lee. "Do you think it's really over this time?"

Bobby Lee nodded. "Yeah." He stared silently at the head in the pool.

"We probably need to go," Buffy said.

"I will. I just need a minute."

Buffy regarded Bobby Lee, certain she knew what was on his mind. "Killing Dredfahl doesn't help, does it?"

Slowly, Bobby Lee shook his head. "My father's still dead."

"I know. I remember when my mom died, I wished someone—some*thing*—had been responsible. At the time it seemed like it would have made more sense and would have given me a target. But in the end, they're still gone, aren't they?"

"Yeah," Bobby Lee said, his voice husky.

"What we do," Buffy said, "is we continue doing what they showed us to do. You know, living life and taking care of the people that we're supposed to take care of." She paused. "That's what they did."

"I know."

Buffy took Bobby Lee's hand, surprising him, but he gripped her hand back. Together, silent but knowing they shared some of the same thoughts, they stayed and watched the flesh peel from the demon's skull and fade away. It didn't take long at all.

Epilogue

"**S**o," Dawn said.

"So," Buffy repeated, taking the linen napkin from the table.

"This is the first time you checked me out of school for lunch," Dawn said.

Buffy smiled at her sister. "Don't get used to it. I don't want to mess up your schoolwork, and we don't have the budget to do this all the time. But I thought maybe today it would be good for us."

They were at one of the small, round tables in the courtyard outside The Vineyard, a little Italian restaurant around the corner from where Joyce Summers had managed her art gallery. Bright lanterns hung from sconces and threw colored light over the grape arbors. Underground pumps kept a miniature brook babbling through the center of the courtyard. The battle with Dredfahl had been two days previous, and Buffy had mostly healed up.

"Thought I'd take a break from being the mommy figure for a while," Buffy said. "Then I'll yell at you for not doing dishes when we get home this afternoon."

"Dishes are done," Dawn said.

"Laundry?" Buffy suggested.

"Washed, dried, hung. Except for yours. Piled in baskets, getting ugly."

"Been kind of busy with the slaying thing the last couple days," Buffy said.

"Bribe me with dessert," Dawn suggested, "and take me back to class late, and maybe your laundry can be done by elves."

"That wouldn't be a responsible parent response, now would it?" Buffy asked.

Dawn's face darkened a little. "You're not Mom."

Sadness touched Buffy. "I know I'm not. That's why I wanted to eat here where Mom used to bring us sometimes. Kind of remind myself that Mom's gone. And that I'm not Mom."

"Mom was Mom," Dawn said.

"Yeah, I know. About the way I've been behaving. I just wanted you to have what I had, you know? Somebody who's always there for you, always telling you the right thing to do."

"You didn't always do the right thing even after Mom told you," Dawn reminded.

"I know, but at least I was told. The opportunity was there." Buffy took a breadstick from the basket in the center of the table and broke a piece off. "I look at you, and I feel bad because you don't have a mom."

"You don't have a mom either," Dawn replied.

"I know. But I'm grown. Almost. And I think maybe that's the problem, too. I don't know what to do with you, and I feel like I should be doing something, but I don't know everything I'm supposed to do."

"You make it sound like I'm a science fair project."

"I just wish things were different," Buffy said. "And that we both had Mom." She paused. "But we don't, and we're going to have to try to work out the changes in our relationship."

"I know."

"I was talking to Bobby Lee," Buffy said.

Dawn looked interested.

Bobby Lee had gone home the day before, and Spike had made noises about going down to New Orleans with him. Buffy still didn't know if Spike had left or was still hanging around Sunnydale. Xander and Anya had regrouped and spent the last couple of days locked in each other's arms. Giles was left holding down the fort at the Magic Box while Anya was gone, but Willow and Tara had both helped out.

Life was kind of returning to normal. Except for the eleven gamer guys, including Donny Williford, who had mysteriously died two days ago. Once Bobby Lee had closed the portal to the demon world, the demons had been banished as well, leaving the corpses of those who had died over there. Xander and the other living gamers had been returned to their bodies. Of course, mysterious deaths were kind of normal for Sunnydale as well, and sooner or later someone would think of a perfectly logical reason for how and why it had happened. Until that time, no one talked about the deaths.

"Bobby Lee told me about his family," Buffy said. "About how close they all are."

"Sounds good," Dawn said.

"He made me think," Buffy went on. "Probably we'd have trouble even if I weren't the Slayer. But I am. And being the Slayer is a big part of my life." She fiddled with her breadstick, hoping she was making the right decision. "I wanted to keep you away from that part because it's so dangerous."

"And I want to help you," Dawn said, "because being the Slayer is so dangerous. I showed you I can help."

"Dawn," Buffy said, "I already knew that. I just figured I kind of owed it to Mom not to get you involved."

"But I *am* involved. Whether I'm there at the Magic Box going through Giles's books, or sitting at home wondering if you're coming home. I'm involved, and it's easier worrying about you with Giles and the others than it is sitting at home worrying all by myself."

"I know," Buffy said. "That's why I've decided that I can use your help."

Dawn smiled in disbelief.

"In a limited capacity regarding researching demony things, of course," Buffy hurried on, "and only if you keep your grades in line and the homework done in a reasonable amount of time." She took a deep breath and felt better. "There, I think I'm done."

Dawn was quiet for a moment. "Thank you."

Buffy nodded. "You're welcome." *Please let me never regret this.*

"There is one thing I've got that you don't have, Buffy," Dawn said.

"What?"

"A big sister," Dawn replied. "Not that that's always a good thing. There's chores that crop up, and that whole sharing thing. But it's nice most of the time."

Touched by the moment, Buffy leaned over and hugged Dawn. "Thank you," Buffy said.

Dawn hugged her back, then they let go of each other and looked around.

"You don't think anybody saw, do you?" Dawn asked.

"No," Buffy replied. "Nobody saw." But the truth was, she didn't care if someone had. "We'll split a dessert, then you're going to have to help me figure out a reason why I'm getting you back to school late."

ABOUT THE AUTHOR

Mel Odom lives in Moore, Oklahoma, and is the author of dozens of books. His hardcover fantasy novel, *The Rover*, has garnered favorable recognition from the *Booklist* Editor's Choice List 2001, the American Library Association, and the New York Public Library.

Everyone's got his demons....

ANGEL™

If it takes an eternity, he will make amends.

Original stories based
on the TV show
Created by Joss Whedon
& David Greenwalt

Available from Simon Pulse
Published by Simon & Schuster

SIMON
PULSE